Norah

Also by Paddy McKinney

Donegal Tears

Norah

Paddy McKinney

Published by
Swordpoint Intercontinental, Ltd.

Originally published as *By The Waters of Elmwood* by Choice Publishing, 2010

Cover photograph, Copyright © 2013 Morpheseum | Dreamstime

ISBN: 0615520162
ISBN 13: 9780615520162

Typeset in Minion Pro
By Swordpoint Intercontinental, Ltd.

Contents

PADDY McKINNEY

Chapter One

The black four by four Jeep that carried the American tourists ambled roughly over the deep-rutted driveway that brought them back to the main road after their tour of inspection had ended.

Turning to his wife, the man at the wheel nodded his head while saying to her, "Yes, I guess this place has got potential all right. It could quite easily be turned into what I think it should be, and what I would like to make of it."

Her faint smile indicated more than just a little skepticism. "My dear Johnny, I am sure it has got all that you say, but like everything else, if only we had the dollars."

Seated behind were her ageing parents, both of whom knew their likable son-in-law to be but an elaborate dreamer. In fact, this was a repeat of what they had experienced three days earlier on the grounds of an old Rectory in Co Leitrim. Drawing to a halt at the end of the long avenue, all four had a final look back at the dismal edifice that stood lifeless amidst the tall, leafless trees. The cawing of the crows was the only sound to disturb the silence and the bare trees were dotted with crows' nests that created a kind of pattern against the half-light of a gray sky.

"Darling, I will sure be back here in the Fall to explore this further, for this is something you and I are going to do, and this time I am dead-serious," proclaimed the eager American to a wife who had grown tired of hearing too much of his fanciful dreaming. The older pair was busying themselves counting the number of crofter-type dwellings evenly dispersed at different locations on the adjoining land. These were Land Commission settlements, each of about fifty acres that had been allotted in the Sixties to various people wishing to make a kind of living for themselves on the land. These holdings were no longer considered viable units under the EU farm directive, hence most of their occupants were but part-time farmers engaged in other pursuits of livelihood.

Even though spring was very much in the air, there seemed to be little sign of life or any kind of daytime activity anywhere along that quiet, fertile valley. As the Jeep moved away slowly, the couple in the back seat was showing an interest that was anything but fanciful. The daughter reached back to touch the cold hand of a frail mother who had tear-filled eyes. Not only was it the second to the last day of her two-week vacation, it was also a momentous day of personal fulfillment for her in getting to meet someone she thought she never would.

"No need getting upset now, Mother. We are almost there and most likely we will all be back here again tomorrow."

Then it was up the road towards Letterkenny, where a special family dinner was on order in the Mount Errigal Hotel, which also happened to be the venue for the Daniel O'Donnell concert that was also on the agenda. This simple scene was the culmination of an epic tale that began in a different era, also at springtime, as the six hundred-acre Elmwood Estate was moving into a phase of renewal under new ownership. The new owner was a retired British Army Officer called Major West, who had a very definite plan, not only for the large extent of this rich meadowland, but also for a sizable extent of the adjoining river as well.

The old-fashioned peacefulness, so long associated with this place, as well as the entire district of Portneill, was now about to perish into oblivion. This change came about through the death of the Major's old aunt, Miss Roberta Walker. She was the last of three spinster sister ladies who had been highly thought of in the neighborhood and, indeed, throughout the entire Roughan Valley as well. They had run the enterprise along traditional lines for many years, under the management of a local workman called Hughie Maguire. Three other workmen, along with a servant maid-cum-cook, made up the entire workforce of Elmwood Farm. It was a pleasant place to be and all of them counted their blessings many times. In their comfort, it never occurred to any of them that the entire unit was badly under-achieving and could not go on much longer.

It was a subject that aroused considerable interest in the locality. The Major and his wife, Florence, had arrived. At first, it was thought they were childless, but later it emerged they had a son in his early twenties who was supposedly attending law school in London. Even though he was the son of the only married member of the old Walker ladies, the Major's visits to Elmwood had been very few indeed. As such, the Major was not familiar to his new neighbors: most of them had never seen him before. He looked to be a man in his late fifties, straight and regimented, with a seemingly condescending manner. It would be hard to see him as just a local farmer.

Regardless, he got off to a good start with the locals by holding what they called a large house-warming party. The workers spread word that all the people of the area were invited.

The lady of the house, along with Madge Crawford, the experienced housemaid, was taking it upon herself to organize the party, which promised to be an elaborate affair. The Major had retained Madge, along with two of the workmen from the old regime, but not Maguire, whom it appeared, had outlived his usefulness. The old Fordson tractor, along with the four horses, was going to be replaced by a more modern tractor. Changes were also taking place in the kitchen, as well as all the other domestic arrangements pertaining to the big house. The aging Madge was given the responsibility of finding a suitable young woman to be her assistant as housemaid and cook. It was obvious the new lady of the house had listened to the glowing reports about Miss Crawford and her culinary excellence.

Madge had a few names in mind, but one appealed to her more than any of the others. She was Norah Mullen, a very attractive young maid in her early twenties who worked in the home of a prominent businessman and farmer who lived close to the area. Madge was related to Norah's father and had learned from him that the girl was not happy in her present employment, where she had served for the previous five years. The woman of the house seemed to be in poor health and was always difficult to get along with, while the husband was the ultimate in dourness. However, it was one of their two grown-up sons that posed the greatest problem for modest Norah. He was totally besotted by her appealing beauty and the mystery of latent sexuality that she exuded so unwittingly. She had long auburn hair that gave off a glowing sheen in the evening sunshine. Her hazel brown eyes were of the sort that stunned the observer into sensual meltdown. It was natural that this easily aroused young fellow began to pursue her aggressively. To his annoyance, Norah remained non-compliant and let him know that she was not for having any of it. This situation was making life rather troublesome for a young girl that wanted nothing more than to do her chores and earn an honest pound, so Madge Crawford's intervention was timely indeed.

"She will be needed for the party and will perhaps enjoy it as well," said Madge to Mrs. West. The event was now less than two weeks away and the theme of every discussion, where two or more locals had gathered. Norah was warmly welcomed to the home of Major and Mrs. West. She would be provided with a single room in the big house for the times when she would be needed for late night or early morning duty. Another advantage to her new position was the fact that she would be answerable only to the Madge, whom she knew and liked a lot. It would take her a while to settle into the routine of formality and protocol, which was part and parcel of life with the aristocracy.

Her father's sister Kate and her husband Jack, who lived in a small Northern town not far from Belfast, had brought up Norah. They were a childless couple that gladly took custody of the little six-year old at the time of her mother's untimely death. She had mixed feelings about her relationship with this couple. Aunt Kate was kind but firmly restrictive, while the man was cold and rudely insensitive, the sort of man a child could learn to fear. He worked in the farmyard of a nearby Monastery, as a laborer for a popular community of monks that ran a school there. So, when the time came, Norah quickly made her way back to the father she had such happy memories of, as a little child.

That was when Aunt Kate passed away unexpectedly after developing a fatal brain disorder less than two months before. It was yet another traumatic event in the life of one now in the process of growing out of her childhood. So now, the sixteen-year old swiftly made up her mind as to where she wanted to be.

The ten years spent with her foster parents did not permit her a lot of social integration, apart from attending the local primary school. As part of her daily routine Aunt Kate would send her to the farmyard after school with a beaker of hot tea and a portion of home-baked bread for Jack, the man of the house. This was something she had been doing for as long as she could remember and it was never a happy errand. That was until she reached the age of fourteen and began working full-time in the kitchen of the village restaurant. For a couple or more reasons, Norah was glad to be sixteen and returning to the place of her birth, where she would make her way in the field of domestic service. Soon she began to re-integrate with the culture and customs of the locality and by the time she took up duty in the big house, was very much a local girl who had many friends.

Spring was a good time to be starting in her new job: the weather was improving and the days were lengthening. The place was a hive of activity, both inside and out; every one was on the move from early morning until quitting time at six o'clock. A team of builders and carpenters began erecting new farm buildings as well as refurbishing the old ones. Most of these workers were local, except for a few who came from more distant parts and were accommodated in a small house attached to the farmyard. A local woman who lived nearby was given the job of looking after this house and its occupants. She was also expected to help the two maids of the big house when the occasion should arise. It was certainly a lively place to be and the work was seen as a blessing for the people. In addition to all that was going on there, Elmwood house was also draw-ing a considerable number of overseas visitors and guests, on an almost weekly basis. These were not guests of the paying type. It was the simple fact that the Wests had an oversupply of high-class friends. To the or-dinary people of Portneill, this was an unreal way of life and to none more so than Madge Crawford and her assistant Norah. It was a cultural awakening for both of them.

The party was, indeed, a grand affair but to a large extent segregated. All of the special guests dined with the host couple in the main dining room, while the staff, along with the neighbors, feasted at will from a variety of savory fare that was provided in abundance on the tables of a large refectory-type room, down in the basement. No one complained, however, as the *craic* was mighty throughout and continued well into the early hours of the morning. In fairness to the Major and his wife, they did, for a time, join the merry group and chatted with the locals, who thanked them for their generosity. It would have been obvious to them that here was a simple fun loving people who were capable of intelligent expression and making their own enjoyment. There was music, song and dance as well as yarns from Vincent Wilkie that were hilariously funny, with one fat lady saying his jokes caused her to wet her drawers. Madge and Norah were still busy with the dishes and the general tidying up after dinner, even though the other woman had been brought in to help out for the occasion. Both she and Madge made a brief appearance at the real party that was going on down below. Norah would be staying for the night and could join in the fun along with friends and neighbors.

Passion, too, made its way into the proceedings as the merrymakers drank and danced to soft music. An occasional pair would steal away down the yard and into the hay-barn, not all of them with the right part-ner. This would inevitably be followed by scruples and feelings of guilt with rueful penitents heading down the road to confessions the follow-ing Saturday; Fr. McKenna would be hearing all about the Major's party. Billy Mullen would also hear the story of the party from daughter Norah. He was one of the few that declined his invitation, having had a certain mission to the river that evening instead. He was a sturdily built man of around fifty years and worked as a lorry driver for a local agricultural produce merchant. In addition to his work, he shared a fishing boat with another man for the purpose of salmon fishing on the River Camus. This father and daughter relationship again became very close and loving in the best possible way. They both had a lot of catching up to do at first, but over the years Norah learned to trust her dad as a close friend and confidant, a man with whom she could feel safe. It was that, more than anything else, which made her decide not to reside full-time in the big house.

In their sharing, Norah would relate much about her life as a lonely child, sometimes worried and often afraid. She now had an attentive listener in a father who cared deeply about his dear and only daughter. Some disturbing events she gave a little mention of, about what happened to her during the early years of her time with Aunt Kate. These were secrets she had buried deep in her consciousness; they never, had nor ever would be shared with anybody else. For Billy, these revelations were far beyond his comprehension, yet they disturbed him like nothing had ever done before. But things were much better now that she was here at home and seemingly happy in her new position.

Norah's attractiveness and brightness, along with her modesty, made her a very popular figure indeed, especially amongst the many young men who were employed at Elmwood House. She was the subject of most of their idle chatter. It was a good time to be young, in the early to mid-fifties, when Ireland was beginning to move away from its shady, restrictive past. Apart from the refreshing airs of spring with the advent of growth and new life, there were more widespread signs that hope was beginning to assert itself amongst the people.

Chapter Two

Elmwood estate was transforming at a rapid pace; there were few remaining signs of what it was like during the reign of the old Miss Walkers. It was the Major himself who was taking control of operations and was becoming a tough taskmaster, indeed. His methods were not being rated all that highly amongst the local men, especially those self-acclaimed experts like the recently deposed Hughie Maguire, who scorned the Major for being a textbook farmer, a man with lofty ideas but without practical knowledge or common sense. His learning, they said, would be both costly and swift. They reckoned it would not be all that long before he gives in and sets about seeking the services of a proper man who knows how it should be done. This was going to be a mixed farming enterprise with half of the estate going under the plow for a variety of crops. A man called Christy Flood was being commissioned to purchase a quantity of heavy store cattle to graze on the rich grassland over the summer months. Christy was considered one of the best judges of cattle in the country and traveled with the Major around most of Donegal as well as parts of the West of Ireland in pursuit of suitable stock. For the Boss, this was an exciting couple of weeks and a time of great learning for him in his new adventure. It was, however, a short-lived adventure that came to an end when they reached their target of three hundred and fifty Aberdeen Angus bullocks. As a single unit, this place was beginning to operate on a scale that was hitherto unimaginable.

Christy continued to pay the occasional visit to Elmwood throughout that summer; this was to monitor the progress of the livestock and to advise on matters pertaining to the herd. He seemed to make a point of arriving at the place around lunchtime and usually had something to eat with the two housemaids in the workers' end of the house. Although this bachelor man was well into his fifties, he seemed to be paying much more attention to Norah Mullen than to her senior workmate. Madge was not in the least put out by this. In fact, she thought it quite amusing and jested about it to the other workers. This, in turn, left poor Norah open to a barrage of trite comment, which she took good-heartedly, knowing that no offense was intended. But the last thing she needed was the attention of either a middle-aged man or any other potential suitor. It had not escaped the notice of the others that this attractive beauty never engaged seriously with any man around the place. Why, they wondered, was she so aloof to all of them? Was she so aware of her own good looks that none of them was considered worthy of her?

That conjecture could hardly be true, considering Norah's social adventures never exceeded the Sunday night dance in the old parish hall. This was one outing that she thoroughly enjoyed and always looked forward to. That was until the night Christy arrived on the scene, wearing a brown-striped suit and shoes that were shining red from oxblood polish; he certainly looked like a man on a mission. He was quickest off the mark to the start of the music and had her on the floor before the others had time to think. Indeed most of the local lads were lacking in sympathy towards Norah, for after all, she was not all that warming towards any of them who tried to know her better. Christy's footwork was not the best, but experience had taught him to move in a way that did not make him look overly clumsy. Norah was glad to see the others take to the floor and shield both her and her partner from overexposure. He talked to her a lot while they moved round the dance floor; he wore a high-collared white shirt and a toothy smile as he guided her through the crowd. Some of his younger rivals commented that he looked like a donkey peering over a whitewashed wall, sniffing the hormonal air. She heard all about his home and family, about his business, as well as the wee Ford Van that took him around the country to fair days and markets. One such session would have been enough for any young girl out for a night's craic with her friends, but not for bold Christy, who was determined to have her to the total exclusion of all others. Her refusal to be taken home by him in the old van was not taken to be a total rebuff. He understood she was with her friends and would probably prefer to walk home with them. It now looked like Norah had not seen the last of this persistent suitor.

The following Sunday night was a reenactment of what went on the week before; Christy was back and applying even more subtle tactics.

"How would you like to go with me to a Drama Festival in Ballyshannon? My niece is taking part in a play that is being performed there next Tuesday evening."

Norah listened as he continued to relate all about his niece and her being a leading member of a drama group that had earned quite a reputation regarding the quality of its productions. Christy, now the cultured man, would surely impress the lady in a way that was far beyond the reach of this common type riffraff.

14

"Things will not be all that busy in the big house on Tuesday evening. I'm sure this is the sort of thing you will thoroughly enjoy and we can have a bite to eat on the way as well. You see, my niece, Betty, is a very fine girl, just like yourself. I think you would both get on like a house on fire."

The flames of the proverbial "house on fire," notwithstanding, there was little hope of Christy succeeding in his efforts to inflame the passion of his wary listener. She was not the sort who felt she had to immediately quell this kind of courting at the outset and, for, that reason may have been guilty of giving the wrong impression.

Needless to say, Norah found a way out of the situation; she would not be going to Ballyshannon on this occasion. It was hardly her idea of an evening's outing to be traveling such a long journey with Christy Flood, accompanied by the smell of two collie dogs that were always in the back of the famous van. She also made up her mind, along with two of her friends, to give up on the Sunday night at the old parish hall. Instead, they took themselves further down the valley to the little Coolaghy Hall. They found this change to be refreshingly new and pleasant; they were meeting and mixing with people who were young, lively and interesting. The musicians were perched high upon a specially erected platform at the gable end of the tiny hall. This was to economize on floor space by allowing the dancers to use the area directly underneath. The roof was uninsulated corrugated iron and the sound of heavy rain and hailstones added tone to the rhythm to the music. But the real music was in the hearts and minds of the many young people who came there for enjoyment and romance. Norah was winning the attention of a young lad who introduced himself as Benny Ryan from just down the road. Both of them seemed comfortable in each other's company and were dancing partners for most of the night. What passed between them was by and large small talk, like where they lived and what they did. Benny was a footballer and proud of his talent. The affairs of the wider world had not yet impinged upon either of them. Norah was twenty-two while he was just eighteen.

It was a happy Norah who traveled home with her friends fairly late that Sunday night. She talked about how she had enjoyed herself and did not mind being almost the sole partner to young Benny, whom she confessed to liking a lot. He was a handsome, clean and chatty type of fellow who asked for nothing more than to be her dancing partner. Before getting back home, the three girls met up with a few late travelers coming home from the old parish hall. Each group told about how their evening had been, about how all of them had enjoyed themselves and of course who went home with whom. The story of Coolaghy was related in the best possible light, while things at the old local were much as before, with a disappointed-looking Christy Flood being seen to leave before it was over.

While all of this was a source of entertainment for them who could stay detached from it, poor Norah was not so amused. This sordid development was causing her much unease. She could no longer be at ease in the company of the man who always addressed her as "Norah Girl" on the occasions when he would call to chat with both her and Madge in the big house. But it remained a happy place to be; the work schedule was constant but well organized and by no means laborious. There were many weekend dinner parties that required meticulous preparation and execution. Madge would have been, to a lesser extent, involved in this sort of thing during the better days of the Miss Walkers, but these were tame affairs compared to what was happening now.

For Norah, this was all so challenging and exciting; she could see it as a source of great enlightenment and a chance to meet a variety of different kinds of the human species who were made up from a rare mixture of individuals. Some were cold and distant individuals, while others showed the more benign quality of warmth and friendship. Nor were all of them of the same race and color. So all and all there was diversity about her life, which enabled her to cope with the uninvited attention of an older man.

Of the ones who were considered as distant, the person who stood out more than the others was a man called David, who by his manner, seemed to be a very important guest. His lengthy engagements with the Major certainly made it appear that way. Except for the occasional snide remark to the lady servants, he paid scant attention to the employees of the Estate. He was the sort who could pass them by without as much as a courteous glance, as if he had been observing something or other that was stationary in front of him. There was something about this individual that induced a feeling of uneasiness in the women, perhaps more so with Norah, who thought he looked a bit familiar and suggested that he, too, might be from the Walker gene pool. He looked to be a fair bit younger than the Major and, in spite of his perceived shortcomings, was considered by the ladies to be fairly handsome. At the same time, he did not look all that strange or exotic. From hearing him talk with other guests at the dinner table, they figured his accent was not quite so foreign or indeed all that strange.

But it was a refined tongue, and hard to tell whether it was Irish or English. This man was only an occasional visitor to Elmwood House; he always arrived unannounced and his departures seemed to be of a similar pattern, being seen actively about the place for an evening and gone without a trace the next morning. It was known that, on the mornings of his leaving, he always walked down the railway track to catch the first train from Portneill Station at a very early hour. But it was his disdainful manner that was causing him to be noticed more than the others. He was very much a man of set routines, even though his visits were of short duration. The women observed him to be both fastidious in his eating habits and fanatical about personal fitness. He could be seen jogging along the riverbank as early as six in the mornings and perhaps again in the evenings. No one other than the Wests knew the nature of the business that brought this man quite often to Elmwood and why he always carrying a fancy leather briefcase. One of the farm workers speculated that he and the Major played the stock market in a big way and that David was the one with knowledge and expertise in this particular field. But this information was coming from a doubtful source, from a man that always seemed to be more in the know than any of his work mates. He even claimed of having the trust and confidence of none other than Mrs. West herself, hence it was only natural that he should be privy to some of the goings on at Elmwood House.

There was no doubting the fact that the lady of the house was beginning to play a much bigger part in the affairs of the estate. She was very much an outdoor woman who liked nothing better than driving through the big fields in the old two-seater Land Rover that was dark green with a canvas roof over the back portion. Every morning, she could be seen out there counting the cattle that were grazing the lush pasture. She talked about the pleasure of watching them thrive and seeing the glossy sheen coming over their hides as they cast off their winter coats. It was a routine she obviously enjoyed, out in the open observing the green of the countryside and savoring the scent of white clover that lured the honeybee to the morning dew.

To the workmen, she was chatty and friendly. She seemed happy to be with them, whether it was out in the fields or in the farmyard. Her love of animals was much apparent from the outset; under her supervision the entire herd would be brought to the yard in mid-Summer for routine dosing and inspection. This was always a big day on the Estate and Christy Flood would be very much part of it. Even the Major himself was allowed only a minor role behind her and Christy in this special operation. As a procedure, it was long and tiresome, with the stronger men having to restrain each animal for the feeding of the dose. It was the lady herself who meticulously measured each portion into the bottle and Christy told the others what to do. There was quite a stirring noise around the place on such days from the lowing of cattle to the raised voices of the busy workmen. Indeed, the language was anything but civil, even in the presence of the lady. But she was taking it all in good heart and seemingly not in the least averse to any of it. Indeed, they would soon discover that she was capable of engaging the best of them in these kinds of exchanges. But the Major who could never condescend to the common level would never respond to these demeaning comments.

In these circumstances, as is only to be expected, a form of rivalry began to invade the setting with all of the workers seeking the affirmation of Mrs. West. She was, by no means, an attractive lady but had the ability to exude a degree of warmth that was both pleasant and sexually enticing. For that reason most of the men—especially the older ones—were competing against each other for the approval of the one they all called the Missus, but the younger fellows simply referred to her as the Old Doll. It was hard to tell her exact age, but Madge Crawford figured her to be of an age similar to the Major, perhaps sixty or over. But she was fit and active in every way and certainly looked the part when attired in overalls and Wellington boots. Her personality was, without doubt, a positive asset to the entire operation of Elmwood Estate, as no one else could have extracted from a workforce the same degree of performance. As a method, it was by far superior to the one of dour regimentation that was being employed by the Major. It would have been nigh impossible for this man to detach from military practice and the disciplinary code therein. As his woman often joked to the men, "He is set in his ways, poor man."

All in all, this place became the great focal point of the neighborhood; seldom did a week pass without at least one occurrence to stir the curiosity of the local people and the workers were all proud of their involvement with it. It was a successful year for all concerned; the staff had found security and farm output was all that the Wests could have desired it to be. Much of this had to be attributed to an excellent workforce who were thorough and devoted to the execution of their duties. But a special appreciation had to be afforded the purveyor of quality livestock and that man was none other than Christy Flood. This, in turn, brought Christy closer to the inner circles of the higher order; he was highly regarded within the household.

But none of this was bringing him any closer to Norah Mullen. She had not gotten over the humiliation of him arriving at the Sunday night dance in her new-found Coolaghy Hall. Yes, it was about her third time there and her having a fun time with lively friends. More and more, she was enjoying the attention of young Benny Ryan. In a small rural community, the guarding of such secrets are by no means easy. Her wanderings down the Coolaghy way soon came to the attention of Christy. He had scant regard for the likes of young Ryan and quickly made his views known to Norah, telling her she was worthy of much better. It never occurred to this man that he was an imposition that was making her life very unpleasant; there was no place left for her to go.

Chapter Three

By the following year, most of the new buildings, as well as the refurbishment of the old ones, had been completed and were in use. Soon after the crops had been sown, a new and major works operation got under way. It was the laying of a concrete slip way into the river. While a few skilled men were undoubtedly needed for this kind of work, there was still a useful role for the farm workers as well. Again, there was much speculation as to why this was being done and the curiosity extended beyond those involved and out to the wider community, especially those who fished for salmon on the river. All that could be extracted from Mrs. West was that they were going to buy a boat and that the Major was examining certain rights pertaining both to the river and the estate that abutted it for over one and a half miles. It was a stretch of river known locally as the best for salmon fishing and the locals valued it very much for the same reason. But it was also known as the area of deep holes and there were at least two of these close to the riverbank; a man had been drowned in one of them a few years earlier.

It was during this operation that the first signs of unrest began to surface in the relationship between the Boss and his workers. Perhaps this uneasiness had more to do with the secrecy surrounding the entire operation than to the working conditions that were, by no means, bad. The main protagonist happened to be the friend and fishing partner of Billy Mullen. He was called Laurence Keatley, known widely to be a thick man who could be easily riled. His aggressive line of questioning was not being well received by the Major who abruptly told him to get on with his work.

"Mr. Keatley, the only thing that should be concerning you right now is the preserving of your employment. What I intend doing with these lands and this stretch of the river is no one's concern but mine and mine alone."

Apart from wishing to admonish an imposing subordinate, part of the Major's act was for the benefit of his mysterious friend, David, who happened to be present at the time.

It was a Saturday morning and work would cease at lunchtime. They had received their wages the evening before, so a few of them, including Mr. Keatley, had celebrated rather late in the Poacher's Inn. Now, what he had just been told, was close enough to confirming what he had suspected and feared; West was laying claim to this stretch of water that had been so valuable to him and his fellow fishermen-cum-poachers for so long. Not feeling all that good from the morning-after effect, he was in no mood to hearing the Major's follow-up comment to David: "These men are a curious lot. They want to know everything you know."

With his head bent low attending the pick he was working with, Keatley muttered, in typical crudeness, the words, "Go and shit yirsell."

The unsavory utterance was partly audible to the ear of the Major who demanded he repeat the comment in a manner that was more discernible. With heated blood, anger began to surge within Keatley and raising, the heavy pick high above his head, shouted with a strong Ulster Scots tongue:

"A towl ya tay go and shit, and you are plenty full o that ya big heeded hoor, ya. For three pins, a would throw ya intay wan o them deep holes where ya can rot to feed the conger eels or some other hungry reptile that likes tay feed fay shit, but they would hay tay be dam'd hungry tay tackle a sour cunt like you."

The other workers were stunned into silence; only the faint sound that came from the implements they were working with could be heard. When Vincent Wilkie, with his characteristic smirk, emitted an amusing kind of cackle, it did induce laughter into most of the others. Not in his wildest dreams could the Major have imagined such a reaction from a common laborer with the status of a serf. This was a severe blow to his pride and status. He had been ravaged in a way that perplexed him and it had taken place in the presence of his refined friend. It was far removed from his glorious days as an army officer, when all he had to do was give the command and the subordinates stood to attention. Now, in the real world of labor relations, he was seeing for the first time that things were vastly different. But he was quick to compose himself; past experiences had taught him how to do so with good effect.

Moving closer towards his adversary, he called upon David to follow behind. He was able to translate enough to know it represented a kind of threat.

"Keatley," he said, "I am afraid there is only one way of dealing with the likes of you. My friend here, along with these other workers, have been witnesses to what you have just said. It is a serious and violent threat against me and it can only be dealt with by the law."

In concurrence with the Major, the contemptible David made a gesture of support. In attempting to do so, his voice was being heard by the workmen for the first time. It was a firm self-assured utterance that seemed to come easy to him.

"Gentlemen, while I am not a trained lawyer I do, nevertheless, know what it is that constitutes a breach of the peace. Yes, this is most certainly a serious threat against my very good friend, the Major, and I stand full-square behind him."

Thinking it better to be hanged as a sheep than a lamb, Keatley was again quickly off the mark.

"Dee whativer ya lick ya narrow-arsed hoor, but if ya tack wan step nearer tay me, a will lay your lip like a sallows tail."

For those who were witness to all of what was taking place, it was a tense drama that was free and amusing so there was little work being done. Seeing this, the Major called upon the aggressor to leave the premises peacefully before he would call the Guards. That was the termination of employment for Laurence Keatley who got one final warning not to ever set foot on the lands of Elmwood Estate or to ever be seen on the waters belonging it. While issuing the warning, the Major and his friend stepped back a safe distance to allow Keatley to get out of the pit and make his final exit. Again the retort was immediate.

"Every bit o that river will be fished bay me and may gid neighbors. Mack nay mistake aboot that and if any hoor tries to stap me, a will sink that pick in his belly. Aye, intay the fuckin' sheft."

Then, as a parting shot delivered in the only way he knew, said, "My advice tay you and that shithawk alang way ya is dinny iver git in my way, for there is naythin' rang way either o' you two that a billhook woodney cure."

By the time the fracas ended, it was time to lay down tools for the weekend break. It was the end to a week that had concluded with a mighty explosion. Except for one quiet and nervous wee man called Dickie Boyle, most of the workers took it all in good heart. It was something they would be able to talk about in the days ahead and no doubt there were many ears ready to take it all in. Like most good stories, it would gather momentum as it passed along the way and by the time its course was run, might have gained substantially in added detail. Laurence Keatley was never a man to blow his own trumpet, but he grew considerably in the eyes of some who applauded his valor. But, wee Dickie who happened not to be a fisherman, was contentedly cozy in his lot and found it hard to understand why any one would want to rock the boat. Others felt the same way and expressed a view that the Major was a valuable asset to the community, giving it what was most needed, work for the people. But it was by no means an issue that divided the people. There was right on both sides. Yes, the work was badly needed but not at the heavy cost of losing the right to do what was precious to many: fish the local river.

On the Monday that followed the big Friday, the men were back at work on the Slipway project and the Major came to address the gathering.

"Gentlemen I am very pleased to see all of you back at work minus Mr. Keatley. The incident the other evening was most unfortunate and has increased my determination to carry on with my plans. I know that some of you men are involved in net fishing on this river and it is my wish you will be able to continue doing so. But at the same time, I do have plans for my own stretch of the water, which I am not prepared to discuss with anyone. It has to be remembered that I am the Boss around this place."

Vincent Wilkie took a deep pull from his half-spent cigarette and looked towards the speaker and then replied with a less convoluted form of the rare dialect.

"That all seems fair enough, Major. As lang as these folks can keep deein the same as they hay always been deein, you will naw be gittin' a lot o' bother fay the people aboot here."

Then it was Nervous Dickie's turn. He, too, looked to the Major and with a slight tremor in his tongue, uttered the conciliatory note:

"Sir, we should all be thankful tay yourself for the work so the best thing tay dee right now is tay get started and never say another bad word."

"Aye," chuckled Vincent, "and better again, never say 'Keatley.'"

That reference to Keatley became a local adage and would be quoted by Wilkie many times after. But with the reassurance coming from the boss, all of them got back to work on the West slipway. A promise is a pledge of honor and that was all that these simple, honest people were asking for. How true and honorable were these words of promise only time would tell, but they were just enough to re-enthuse a team of workers that were needed to serve an end.

As the days and weeks slipped by, the work progressed without any further disturbances. But there was a temporary halt put to operations for a while, as there came a late order for fifty tons of Kerr Pink potatoes. It had been one of those years when demand for spuds was slow, hence a valuable order such as this to be met at all costs. It was a hurried operation with an occasional argument about method. These were not, by any means, serious disputes and were usually settled with the verbal wit of Vincent Wilkie who might shout "Niver say Keatley." The Boss did not spend a lot of time at this particular operation; for him it was not the most interesting of tasks. But his good wife kept an eye on things; she was always suitably attired for the occasion and the men were happy enough to have her company.

By then, she had gotten quite familiar with all of the men, as well as their work routine. The workers, in turn, had also begun talking to her in a way that had familiarity about it just as they would converse with each other. She enjoyed the everyday banter that was a common feature of the all male gathering and Vincent Wilkie was the one to provide the craic. His quick-witted comments gave her a laugh and she could give as well as take. She enquired about Mr. Keatley and how it has been for him since leaving the estate. It was never a bother for her to converse laughingly with the workers about the famous fracas between Keatley and her husband. Like the rest of them, she was happy to be able to joke about this in the knowledge that the incident was well and truly in the past and that no law proceedings were to be taken.

During one of his idle days, Keatley was standing by the roadside near to his cottage home when a well-dressed young man pulled up beside him. He was a Department of Agriculture official and perhaps thought himself to be the Minister. Lowering the car window and, speaking in an unfamiliar tongue he asked, "Do you know a man around here called Major West?"
Bold Keatley pushed his head in through the window.

"I know him too well; the worst hoor that iver pisshed agin a wall."

That is how Wilkie told the story to Mrs. West, who wondered how true it was, but laughed heartily at the fun of it nonetheless.

Chapter Four

Now in her second year of employment, Norah Mullen was an established and highly regarded member of the West household. Her work, dress and appearance, was earning for her the acclaim not only of her employers but of their guests as well. She was happier now than ever before and particularly so to learn that young Benny Ryan had just joined the farm workforce and had, along with two others, taken up residence in the workers' quarters down in the yard. He had been taken on sometime after the departure of Howard Keatley. The pair would often be seen chatting together when the opportunity presented itself for them to do so. This no doubt caused some consternation amongst the other young workers there. What, they wondered, were the qualities this young whippersnapper possessed and him not yet out of his teens? But Mrs. West reasoned, with due respect to the rest of them, that Benny was a handsome young fellow with modesty and a willingness to work.

Yet it was a different picture of the young man that was being painted by her friend Christy Flood. He seldom missed an opportunity to smite his seemingly popular rival; he would point out to Norah how much the boy was lacking in ambition and responsibility.

"When I was that fellow's age I had eight or nine springing heifers grazing on rented land and made good money from them, too. Don't be wasting your time, girl, on a waster like that."

Norah's reply was always one of shyness and spoke the truth when saying that her talking to Benny was out of friendship and nothing else. Little she knew, poor girl, that her timid words were ones of encouragement to a persistent man who had not given up the chase. But Norah and Benny's liking for each other was not going to perish because of an imposition so ridiculous and bizarre. So perhaps, in time, their fondness could be allowed to grow and flourish.

It nearly happened for them one June evening after work when Major and Mrs. West had just gone on one of their occasional visits to England and would be away for two or more weeks. Norah was alone in the kitchen; the demand on her and Madge was not all that pressing with the owners being away. For that reason Madge took off early, as many home chores needed her attention. Perhaps Benny became aware of this and availed of the opportunity to be alone with Norah for a cozy chat. By the time he reached the back door, his courage began to ebb; but as he attempted to retreat, she called his name from the kitchen window.

"Benny, would you mind helping me to check the doors and lock this place up? I am not able to turn the heavy key of the mortise lock for the back door. Everyone is away and I don't like being here on my own."

He was a willing helper and gladly complied with her request, but before he locked the door, she offered to make him a cup of tea.

Sitting down on a wooden seat that looked like a park bench beside the Aga cooker, he smiled fondly and asked her to sit with him.

"Do you take sugar in your tea?" Norah asked as she carried the two mugs and moved some tasty homemade scones towards him.

"Yes, I do," replied Benny, "but I know it will be sweet enough with you smiling over it."

Although it was mainly small talk they engaged in at first, the sharing of feelings was special and pleasing for both of them, nonetheless.

"Norah, do you not miss the fun down at old Coolaghy Hall on Sunday nights? I know that I miss you and it's not the same since you stopped coming."

"Thank you, Benny. It is very nice of you to say that and yes, I do miss it, but you know that man Christy is creating a problem for me and I don't know what I am going to do about him. The last thing I want to do is be offensive or rude to anyone, but this man is annoying me all the time. As you know, he is very highly thought of around this place. Hardly a week ever passes without him calling here to the house."

In spite of her deep embarrassment about this imposition, Norah knew there was no point in her hiding from it, as far as Benny was concerned. With tears of obvious distress, she sat down beside him and put the Delft mug to her lips. Their conversation lasted long after they had finished their tea. Benny implored upon her not to give up on going out and to enjoy what fun there is on offer, especially the fun of long summer evenings that were now beckoning.

"Norah, there are many places we could go together, if only you would be my girl. Surely that would solve your problem."

By the time these endearing words were spoken, his left arm was around her tender neck, with nervous fingers resting on her breast.

As he attempted to draw her closer to him a spasm of tautness came quickly over her entire body and she let off a faint scream.

"No" she said, "get away and please don't come near me again."

For the young man, this was quite disturbing. Certainly not the kind of reaction he expected from the one he was so anxious to befriend. Even though his experience in this field was somewhat limited, he was not totally immature or green and on past occasions has had the pleasure of fondling and kissing some of the prettiest around Coolaghy. Norah immediately departed the scene and ran towards the living quarters, then up to her room. Feeling the villain and somewhat confused, Benny left and went back to his own living quarters. A while after he remembered that he was supposed to have locked the back door, but was reluctant to venture back there until he was certain she had gone home. Much later he did make his way back to the kitchen door to discover it had already been locked from inside; the big house was empty for the night.

Walking alone up the narrow road that would take Norah to her home, she was pensive and hearing the sounds of a quaint countryside: the call of the corncrake, a barking dog, men's voices coming from the river. She felt some embarrassment about what had taken place between her and the boy she liked.

It was something she would not be sharing with Billy on this occasion; she did not want him to be reproaching Benny Ryan whom she still liked and knew that his intentions were not of wrongness towards her. Benny too was embarrassed and worried about meeting her again, at the same time he felt reassured that it was a secret between the two of them and was most likely to remain so. But his thinking was more than a little perplexed. Was his manner and personality so defective as to make her recoil from his attempt at closeness? Whatever their thoughts, both of them remained in the service of Elmwood Estate and made a conscious effort to keep out of each others way.

That was not so easy for either of them because many times over the days that followed they came face to face but fortunately, always in the company of others. It was hard for either of them to put memories of the unhappy encounter out of their thoughts; it was going to take time and other diversions to halt its intrusion into their daily thinking.

Alas, they did not have long to wait before that diversion intruded heavily upon them. This came in the form of a serious burglary into the big house just two days before the Major and Mrs. West was due back. It was Madge and Norah that were first on the scene and realized that a number of valuable items had been taken. Norah ran to the yard to raise the alarm and seek the advice of the men that were preparing to leave for the furthermost field on the estate. Instead of going to the hay field, all of them ran up the yard towards the back door of the house, but before any of them got that far Vincent Wilkie shouted for none of them to enter. It was a wise suggestion indeed as was his advice to call the Guards.

"I don't think it would be a good idea for any of us boys to go in there before the boys in blue tacks a look at the place."

Madge agreed and made the call to the Guards barracks.

She was only able to give a rough account of what had been taken to the Garda Sergeant who was quickly on the scene. She accompanied him around all of the rooms where they could see definite signs that the intruders had been in most of them. Poor Norah remained in the kitchen in a very upset state; she worried about the return of the man and woman of the house. There was a lot of Garda activity around the place from that morning and well into the days after the Wests had returned. They did not apportion blame to any member of the staff and commended them for calling on the assistance of the police. It was a near accurate assessment of what had been stolen they were able to give the investigating officer. The sum of money taken was not all that much but the items of jewelry were quite valuable and personal to Mrs. West. But most disturbing of all was the precious William Turner painting brought by the Major from England to hang in the main hallway, as his prize possession. For him this was a tremendous loss, one that he would find hard to bear.

The investigation that followed was yielding little benefit, for the Guards it was simply baffling, a cleverly executed operation by people that had been watching the big house and knew that its owners were away. They even managed to trick the two guard dogs that were enclosed in a pen at the side of the house. These fierce animals had access to the house during the night through an opening to the washroom. According to the Sergeant, one of the criminals fed or distracted the dogs while the others entered through the side window and then managed to shut the washroom door. Having achieved that they were then free to move through the entire house at will. This conjecture was supported by the two members of the Garda technical unit brought to the scene for the taking of fingerprints and to search for other clues.

Not surprisingly, the Major was anything but a bundle of laughs in the days that followed the break-in. Work continued in the fields and the scent of new mown hay filled the air around the place. But the wonder of summer freshness held little charm for a man in such a dejected mood. The workers were relieved to see so much Garda activity continuing around the place; at least it kept this man far away from them most of the time. All of the workmen and women had to be interviewed individually by two of the Guards and their statements put on file. Norah, being the last to leave the premises each evening, had a more detailed account to give and, as a consequence, would have to endure more than her share of this torturous ordeal. It was during one of these times she let it slip that Benny Ryan was once in the kitchen with her. She explained how the heavy key for the back door lock was, on occasions, difficult for her to turn and that on seeing Benny, she called on him to assist.

Little she knew that this disclosure would set in train a series of in-depth probings that would have consequences for both her and the innocent young man. The investigating Garda passed on this piece of information to the Wests, but it was not an issue to be bothered all that much about. They were well aware of the stiff lock on the back door and accepted her story without question. It was when they related the story to their trusted friend Christy that another slant began to be concocted.

"I would not trust that young fellow all that much. It would not surprise me a lot to hear that he had something to do with this, but for goodness sake don't repeat what I say."

Through further questioning, Norah conceded that Benny Ryan had left the house on the night in question without locking the door and in answer to the 'why?' of this she broke down and said:

"It was because he grabbed and tried to kiss me I left the kitchen and went to my room."

This disclosure was made in the presence of the Major and his wife; the woman was sympathetic towards her junior housemaid and took her into the living room for comforting. She assured the disturbed young woman that what she was doing was being very helpful to the police and that there was no reason for her to be alarmed. Out in the kitchen the Major and the two officers of the law were discussing Benny Ryan and what kind of guy he might happen to be. So in order to ascertain this, they would need to undertake a more intense questioning of him immediately.

Benny was willingly compliant and answered each of their questions with clarity and honesty. Although he did not have the benefit of knowing what Norah had revealed to the Guards he did concur in relation to the back door key. Where he did blunder the most was in telling the lie about him locking the door for Norah and then coming out the front door with her. Erroneously, he thought that this kind of account would benefit her as much as it would him. But instead, it had the effect of putting him more under the spotlight. Much more questioning he would have to endure. This meant he was eventually going to change his story and tell exactly what took place that night with Norah. Now a bit disconcerted at being caught out in a lie, he offered an apology and assured that Norah's account was indeed the correct one. But he did strongly protest that what they were talking about happened exactly one week before the night of the robbery. With a quiver of emotion that was more of the child than man he said,

"Think what you like but what happened between the two of us in the kitchen had nothing whatever to do with the break-in and I think it very unfair that I am being blamed for this."

"Young man," snapped the Belsen-style officer, "what we are about here is establishing the truth in the interest of fairness. What has happened to these fine people was anything but fair, so don't talk to me about what is fair or unfair. In view of the fact that you have told deliberate lies, I now think it best that you come with me to the station."

Having never been to such a place before, Benny was nervous and afraid of the unknown. At the same time certain of his innocence; he grew in confidence that no harm would come to him. Left alone in a dismal room for a period that seemed like hours before his interview recommenced, it helped him to know that his civil parents still knew nothing about what was going on as it would have been seriously distressful for both of them. He thought about himself and how all this came about. Was it his infatuation with the beautiful Norah that brought this terrible curse upon him?

After a grueling session with the Guards, Benny was released without charge. There was no evidence by way of forensics to suggest he had anything to do with the crime. He was told to go home or to his place of work and to always be available for further questioning, if the need should ever arise. That was a Friday evening and it was almost quitting time when he arrived back at the yard of Elmwood Estate. His work mates were seriously concerned about their young friend of whose innocence they had little doubt; they would speak to anyone on his behalf. But nobody ever got the chance to plead for the one that was being wrongly accused; he was given his wages and callously told to be off the premises for good. There was little he could do to ease his plight. He was wrongly under suspicion, but them that suspected were careful not to accuse.

Norah was extremely worried and confused over what was happening to the one who had been her friend. She went to Mrs. West to speak on his behalf saying he was good and decent in every way. Through tears of heartbreak the poor girl sobbed,

"I feel so much to blame for what this has brought upon him; I now feel a terrible guilt and pity for him; Mrs. West, please do something for him if you can."

Florence, the lady, listened with empathy to what her rueful servant was saying but wondered how reliable was her judgment of this young man's character.

"Yes, I will speak to the Major but it may not do a lot of good. You see, with his background it is most unlikely that he could be persuaded by anyone to change his mind. Norah, I can see how upset you are about all of this and I am too, but stop blaming yourself or worrying about the future. Your job is safe. We both like you very much."

As they talked, Benny Ryan was walking out the long avenue to take the road for home. He had just lost the job that he liked and needed. These were times long before the days of organized labor; there was nowhere to go to seek justice; no court or tribunal to hear his story. With sunken spirits he was heading back to the loving support of parents and family where he would be believed without question. Yet there was one redeeming feature in the fact that he was widely recognized to be an excellent footballer. His performances on the playing pitch with Roughan Celtic were being noticed further afield and Derry City was taking an interest. The possibility of him being offered work in the city had been mentioned, that is if he should be found good enough for senior level. Now, with doubt hanging over his reputation, there was a major obstacle being placed in the way of his sporting future. These thoughts were weighing heavily upon him as he trod that weary road that would bring him back to Coolaghey.

His quiet, caring parents and only sister, who was older, were surprised but glad to see him. They were able to sense that all was not well. News about the break-in had already gotten to them a few days earlier and little they thought it would soon impinge upon them. He told the disturbing story in detail to their attentive listening, the story of Norah Mullen and his involvement with her was related without a hint of blame being attributed to her. They heard how he felt about not being believed or trusted and what it was like to be taken away to the Barracks. Now all he wanted was for the real culprits to be caught and him to be told that everything is all right again.

"Why do I have to suffer this?" he asked his hurting parents. It was a terrible and downcast state he found himself to be in and with motherly arms around him, child Benny shed his tears.

Chapter Five

It was in the early hours of a Sunday morning that the real battle began on the lands and waters of Elmwood Estate. Nothing violent or extraordinary occurred that morning, but the first shot was fired just the same. Two local fishermen were going their usual route down the right-of-way lane through the Estate towards the river when they found that two of the gates were securely locked with a heavy chain and padlock. There was a large sign attached to the first gate that read "TRESPASSERS WILL BE PROSECUTED" and it bore the Major's name. The two men climbed over the gates and proceeded on their journey to where their boat was tied at the waters edge. Then they were confronted with yet another sign nailed to a baton stake and again bearing the Major's name. On further examination they found two other such signs, one at either end of Estate land. They warned that the waters between were private and that fishing of any kind was prohibited.

"This can not be allowed," shouts big Henry Doran to his smaller friend Eddy McGinn. With that, he proceeded to dismantle the three offensive signs and tossed them into the river. As the uprooted signs began their floating journey to the sea, Henry and Eddie untied their boat and cast their nets. It was a reasonably successful shot they had in terms of catch and no one came to bother them. They fished the area until the sun rose high enough to give a golden glint on the calm waters about them. But their thoughts were far from calm as they bagged the few summer salmon and hoisted them over their shoulders for home. With a nervous anger in his tone, Henry looked to his uneasy mate,

"Will hay tay be deein somethin' aboot this and will hay tay be deein it bravin' quick. We canny let an interloper like that tack the bite out o' wir mooth."

The rest of that Sunday was spent spreading the word around the district that a meeting was being held in the Poachers' Inn that evening at eight o'clock.

This was one gathering guaranteed to bring out the best and perhaps the worst in these simple, honest people. As expected the meeting was loud, irate and protracted. The small lounge was barely able to hold the numbers that came from every corner of the parish. Fr McKenna sent his regrets at not being able to attend but pledged his full support nonetheless. In view of the nature and language of what were being exchanged during the proceedings, it was felt that the good man was better somewhere else. But there was a bachelor man there called Willy McGivern, known locally as Hat McGivern. He was considered a man who thought rather highly of himself and claimed to be an ardent reader with a liking for the works of Charles Dickens. He would be more than ready to take the priest's place on the chair. It was his common sense approach that prevented a course of action being adopted that would have put the Portneill fishermen into serious conflict with the law. That, he said, was not the way to go about their challenge and fortunately there were enough like-minded people present to carry his proposal through, albeit in the face of considerable dissension.

An action committee was set up with a brief to take a three-man deputation to Major West, first to inform him about the setting up of the committee and its desire to have the matter resolved peacefully, then to inform him that legal advice was being sought with a view to establishing the rights of the local fishermen. Along with McGivern two of the more articulate members were chosen to execute the task. It was to happen on Monday evening. The three-man delegation got together after the meeting for the purpose of preparing a best case; they were taking their responsibilities seriously indeed. Not knowing what to expect by way of reception from their host, they were understandably apprehensive. But unknown to any of them, their task had been made practically impossible by the actions of two enraged and uncompromising men.

Later, in the dark of that same Sunday Night, Big Henry and Laurence Keatley, armed with a crowbar and lump hammer smashed the locks that had been put on the two gates of the right-of-way. In view of what had happened, there was no way that the deputation would get past the threshold of the Major's front door. They were told to be off the premises immediately and that the matter was now in the hands of the Guards. Even though they protested and disclaimed any knowledge relating to the act of vandalism, their attempts at reasoning were very much in vain. The ensuing Garda investigation yielded nothing beyond the likely suspects. "Likely" was as far as they could deduce, as this close-knit community closed ranks and gave nothing away to incriminate one of their own. It was a stance of solidarity but it was doing nothing to help the cause of the fishermen that had a stiff battle on their hands. The legal route now seemed the only option.

The committee initiated a door-to-door collection that would create a fund to pay the legal costs of a court battle that now seemed inevitable. Word about this would very soon get to the Major and the organizers were counting on it sending him a clear message of their determination. To their great relief the response was magnificent; the generosity of the people far exceeded their expectations. Hopefully this too would send the right message to the landed protagonist. Now with considerable funds at their disposal, the same three delegates employed Packie Gordon with his old Hackney to take them to the office of O'Donnell and Co. Solicitors, in far away West Donegal. They had been advised that Pauric O'Donnell, the younger partner of the firm was one of the best around for their type of case. He was a sharp and witty adversary with the power of oratory that could silence the toughest.

His advice was very much in keeping with their own thinking: "Stay within the law and play for public sympathy. I presume this guy is endeavoring to invoke some outdated or assumed right associated with the Estate in bygone days. Most likely, he is simply trying this one out in the hope that nobody will challenge him. What I intend doing initially is send him a letter stating our intentions to assert the rights of the local fishermen and then to inform the Fisheries Board of their responsibility in relation to licensed fishermen."

As the three were leaving, he accompanied them to the door and said he would gladly attend one of their meetings to explain the situation and hopefully bring some positive news.

The biggest obstacle to any kind of campaign has to be the unruly element within its own ranks and here was no exception. It was not a comfortable time for the workers on Elmwood Estate; some of them were either part-time fishermen or in some way connected to it. There was a definite conflict of interest and loyalty at play for most of them and Norah Mullen was certainly one of them. She was hoping for some kind of resolution that would bring a speedy end to these days of unrest and anger. Her father, Billy, very quickly aligned himself with his fellow fishermen and she feared he might lean more on the side of the militant sector. This was an added worry for her, along with the lingering guilt she still felt about what had happened to her one-time friend, Benny Ryan. She liked her work as she did the people that employed her, but fretted the possibility of losing favor through her father's actions.

In spite of the positive report brought back by the three delegates, along with their call for calm, there were definite signs that others were not so ready to fall into line. They felt that the process was going to be long and tedious and that the season would probably be over by the time their rights had been re-established. For that reason a splinter group began to assert itself with a membership that was anything but benign. In spite of appeals from the moderate wing they were not prepared to wait beyond a couple of days after the Solicitor's letter had been delivered.

"Confirmation of this can easily be obtained by making a simple phone call to the Solicitor's office, so now, McGivern, it is up to you to let us know how long we are supposed to wait."

The speaker was young Tony McKeague, better known as Rusty, and with a reputation for aggressiveness, he and a few of his mates seemed always to have a readiness for the fight.

Even though they were both on the same side in relation to the dispute with the Major, Rusty and Keatley were bitter enemies; they fought one serious battle at the river the previous year. It was in the cool of the evening with the contentious Rusty being most ready for action and seemingly the fitter of the two; but to his surprise and ignominy the older man got the upper hand. This kind of public affront enraged the bellicose McKeague and soon brought forth the more ugly side of his nature. In a flush of bitter anger, he beckoned two of his henchmen to his assistance and his call was promptly answered. Had it not been for the intervention of his friend, Billy Mullen, poor Keatley would have came off the sorry loser. Rather than face Mullen, Rusty and his paltry props backed off only to be verbally ravaged by Keatley for many a day after. It was a battle lost but not forgotten as far as the vanquished and his friends were concerned.

The stretch of water concerned was known locally to contain two of the best shots in the river for net fishing, but according to the workers it was now to be reserved for angling and water sport only. Of the Wests' circle of friends, many of them—not least, the pompous David—were known to be keen anglers but what the hell did they mean by water sport? Not long would they have to wait for the finding out, for as a diversion away from his unpopular stance, the Major announced the holding of a Grand Water Carnival for the following Sunday afternoon. It was billed as a Gala event consisting mainly of speedboat racing and aquatics; it even included a rowing boat race, which was seen as a ploy to induce local interest.

Posters were circulated and displayed throughout the area and far beyond; notices were carried in the weekend newspapers; it was even announced at Church Services. Every effort would have to be made to ensure a large attendance and that the event itself would be a resounding success. Had it not been for the heightened bitterness already engendered within the community, these expectations could have been realized. This kind of thing had the potential to be a fantastic family and community event; it was the kind of thing the people needed. The attendance was indeed good, in spite of the fact that many of the locals stayed away, but to their credit no acts of sabotage were carried out by them or by anyone else on their behalf. It was the warmest and sunniest of summer evenings with all the spectators, men, women and children assembled on both sides of the river, there simply to enjoy the fun of it. What an impressive display it turned out to be with a collection of powerful speedboats as well as luxury yachts that were there only on display and it transpired that one of these belonged to the Major himself. David's voice carried clear and deliberate over the loud speaker as he called the competitors to the starting point and announced the winners at the end of each race.

A young enthusiast named Gillespie seemed far ahead of all the others competitors. With skill and craftsmanship, he took the major honors at his ease. For some, it was a bit of a disappointment that none of the locals bothered to enter for the rowing boat race. But in the circumstances it was hardly to be expected that they would. After all, they knew exactly why the event was being held at this particular time. In many ways it added to their anxiety about the future of their way of life and it certainly told the workers why the slipway had been built. It now seemed certain that the Major's intentions were resolute and it was going to take a lot to blow him off course. At the same time there were more than a few around that were getting themselves ready to do just that.

On Monday, a letter arrived by post to Hat McGivern that his legal mentor, Pauric O'Donnell, was coming to address the fishermen on Wednesday evening at eight o'clock. Word got around fast and all concerned people were expected to be there. Again it was a well-attended gathering consisting of two factions, each in pursuit of a similar objective but with different ideas about how to achieve it. O'Donnell, in colorful language, outlined the scenario from a legal perspective and was positive about the eventual outcome. He spoke at length about how some of the landed gentry still hanker privilege that is based on nothing more than historical precedent. For that reason he was confident that the protagonist would eventually come to see the reality as well as the legality of the situation. But as yet he has had no response from either West or the Fisheries Board. Finishing off, he urged them to be patient a little longer and not to fall foul of the law.

Meanwhile, the Major and his wife were reliving the success of what was a great carnival day. They had little doubt that its success had secured its future as a regular event. The both agreed that there was a slight problem with the fishermen and that letter from the Solicitor could make it more problematic. Mrs. West, through her greater involvement with the workmen, did have a better feel for their concerns. While she did like the idea of what her husband was planning for this stretch of the river, she felt that it should not be at the expense of their popularity in the community.

"Why can this not be achieved without all the bitterness it seems to be engendering? Surely it is not beyond a man of your caliber to find a way round this. If you could agree some kind of compromise with these people, it would certainly be much more comfortable for all of us."

With due regard for his wife's opinion, the self-righteous Major just shook his stubborn head and said his honor was at stake. "There is plenty of that river left for all of these people and they should be grateful for it. Whatever about this Mr. O'Donnell, I can assure you that I have every confidence in my own legal advisors. If you care to go back far enough, you will find that the fishing rights of the entire river were vested in the Walker Estate."

Realizing the futility of her pursuing a line of reasoning, the woman took herself off to something more worthwhile.

Early next morning David was walking down the railway to catch the first train on the start of his journey away from the big house. As he walked along with briefcase in hand, he could hear the sound of oars hitting the water. Stepping across and on to the riverbank, he could see two men in a boat with a fishing net on board. One of them was easy to recognize as the aggressive Laurence Keatley. His call to them was loud and threatening:

"You lot are on private property. What you are doing is illegal and I order you to get off the waters of this estate."

"Shut your effin' mouth you narrow-arsed hoor or I will go up there and drive that leather bag down your thaoat."

Knowing he was at a safe distance, David replied, "I will be calling the Major this very evening. This time the law is going to be applied to you Mr. Keatley, as well as that other cowardly rat hiding there behind you." To the man in question this was like the proverbial red rag. Billy Mullen was not the type to hide from anyone; he was well known to be a man that could hold his own with the best around. However, he lacked the immediacy of his friend Keatley.

At the same time, he did compose himself enough to stand up on the boat to announce his name and say, "I will see you another day and I will let you know the kind of coward I really am."

Both men related their story to an attentive audience that night in the Poachers' Inn. Hat McGivern was also present and agreed that the men were justified in exercising their right to fish the forbidden waters. But he was adamant that no one should engage in the type of behavior that took place that Sunday morning a couple of weeks earlier. Men from both sides of the argument spoke their piece without serious disagreement. In their absence, the Major and his cohorts were lashed without mercy. The resentment against all of them was indeed palpable. It was a genuine resentment brought about by deep hurt and now nourished by strong beverage. But in the midst of their common purpose there still lay within a few of their ranks a festering sore that refused to heal. At the same time the main protagonists managed to stay well clear of each other. This was not an official meeting, but by the size of the attendance and matters discussed, it could very well have been called a business type gathering.

Some of the workers on Elmwood Estate were not from the immediate district; they had little or no association with the fishing industry. Of the few remaining locals, Vincent Wilkie, was the least interested in the river. He had given it up some years back after his young brother lost his life in one of the famous deep holes. Now the main man on the Estate, he was a first class tractor operator that the Major and his wife thought very highly of. Mrs. West could not imagine life around the place without Vincent's wit and funny comments. He too was fond of the affable lady and, to some degree, her husband as well. He was more than happy to be employed by them. For that reason he took no part in the contentious discussion that was going on in the Inn that night. Instead, he just played his natural role of telling yarns and keeping the others amused, which was his way of contending with this dilemma of divided loyalty. He was such a character that nobody expected him to be anything other than what he was.

It was the early hours of the morning before some of them got back to their homes; Rusty and friends were later than most of the others. On their way home they entered Mulrine's farmyard; there they found a sledgehammer and iron bar; they were obviously on a mission of serious intent. It was not until the next morning that the seriousness of what had taken place became known. Again, all the locks had been smashed violently. Not only that but the gates and stone pillars were badly damaged as well. This was a most serious development and certainly one that would not help the cause of the aggrieved fishermen, but much worse was yet to be revealed. Yes, it was the Major's precious new yacht that had been berthed at the side of the slipway and lay half-submerged with a large hole in its side. The damage was extensive and deliberate, caused by a heavy instrument being applied with force.

That was the assessment of the Garda team that was instigating an immediate criminal investigation. Aware of their failure at making any headway in solving the case of the house burglary, they were over-anxious about apprehending these, the most recent criminals. What followed was a Garda visit to the homes of every member of the action committee. They also took a statement from the proprietor of the Poachers' Inn who gave the names of all the previous night's patrons. But it was the Major's own statement that seemed the most significant in the opinion of the investigating team. His friend David had called him from England the night before and related to him the story about what had taken place when he was going to catch his train that morning. This had the effect of implicating the names of Keatley and Mullen in suspicion of what was a most serious criminal act.

The two were taken into custody and duly questioned individually by an imposing officer whose manner was stern and slightly aggressive; their fingerprints were also taken. During the intense questioning it emerged that another crime had been committed against the Wests. It was the opening of a gate that separated a field of heavy bullocks from two adjoining cornfields. The ensuing damage to the crop was serious and costly; both men called it a low and contemptible act that they were ashamed of. During the interviews another Guard sat taking notes and asked the occasional question to clarify a statement. Both men were resolute in their denial of any kind of involvement in these acts for which they were being accused. Nor had they any knowledge as to who else might be capable of doing such a deed. Billy was neither afraid nor ashamed of his stance in relation to the dispute with Major West.

"Yes, I have fished the area concerned and will continue to do so for as long as I am able. I have nothing at all against these people. In fact, they employ my daughter, Norah, and treat her more than well."

Then it was the turn of the interrogator to ask, "Is it not true that very recently you and your friend Keatley had angry exchanges with one of the Major's guests? I happen to know that both of you made violent threats against this man."

"Sir, this particular guest, or whatever you care to call him, should know better than to refer to me in the manner he did. So I had little hesitation in telling him exactly that and what is more Guard, you can tell him that as well. I will not allow a contemptible man like that call me a coward without giving him the opportunity to prove it and I fully intend to do so, but there is one thing you can be sure about, and that is I would never be guilty of a deliberate criminal act."

The next question was directed at Keatley: "Mr. Keatley, would you care to tell us about the circumstances of you leaving the employment of Major West? Did both of you part on good terms?"

"Good terms! How in the hell could anybody be in good terms way a hoor like that? He needs a crack ower the heed way a half-worn spade, but a niver touched him or anything belang tay him. Whativer happened tay his oul boat had nathin tay dee way me."

No sooner had he finished than a twinge of guilt stirred within him. He had helped big Henry to break the locks that first Sunday morning. For that reason he was relieved to see that stage of the questioning come to an end. They were for taking a break and the two suspects were being held in separate rooms; there was obviously more to be gone through. But these two were seasoned and tough, not the kind to be easily intimidated. Mullen was by far the more articulate; unlike his friend he thought each question through before giving his reply that was sure to be a measured one.

When they were finally released, the instructions given were in many ways similar to what had been given to Benny Ryan.

"Stay around, behave yourselves and be prepared for further questioning."

Out on the street both men breathed a sigh of relief and were feeling in need of a decent drink. They made their way to Harte's Corner Bar. There they got to talk about their situation and share the details of what each of them had been asked and said. What they gathered from each others account seemed reassuring, that both of them had performed well under some duress. Now they were able to savor their bottles of stout with a degree of confidence that their innocence was established beyond doubt, so they thought. But when they got to think about the deed itself, their minds went back to the night it happened and the question of who might have carried it out. It was a crime committed by dissolutes and cast a blight over a community of decent people. The anger in them intensified as they pondered the villainous hooligan behind the abominable crime while seeing two innocent men take the rap.

From the evidence so far they were fairly certain that more than one person was involved in carrying out the vicious act, but as in all such cases there is usually only one ringleader. Now it was going to be their mission to see that the guilty ones were sought out. They were as anxious as the Guards were in having these thuggish ruffians brought to account. For Rusty McKeague this was sweet revenge against the two that once subdued and humiliated him. He was prepared to sit this one out for as long as it took to bring disgrace and shame upon his foes. This he continued to do with steadfast endurance While out of fear, his friends kept quiet. To anyone with a thread of decency this sickly stance could only be described as the ultimate in treacherous depravity. But right well Keatley and Mullen knew the precariousness of their own position; they were under suspicion and would have to proceed within the boundaries of the law. Apart from Keatley's violent temper, both of these men had an impeccable record as far as the law was concerned and few would have questioned that assessment of them.

Chapter Six

It was an intriguing time for a community of simple hard working people; the old Walker Estate was unbelievably alive to a new culture. Seldom, if ever, did any occurrence in the area merit the attention of the law enforcers. Now they seemed a part of everyday life with no less than two major investigations on their hands. They were certainly impacting heavily on the resources of the local Garda Station; it was not the kind of work this three-man outfit was accustomed to. A far cry surely from walking a country road in the hope of catching someone cycling in the dark without a light or perhaps a dog owner without a license. For this new dispensation two younger and more accomplished members were temporarily assigned to the case in the hope of adding impetus to it. After all, Major West would not be favorably disposed towards a police force that failed him on two occasions.

Others too were judging them harshly over the fact that in both of these cases it was innocent people that were being harassed. Of all the concerned people, Norah Mullen was by far the most distressed. She was finding it quite impossible to forget what had happened to Benny Ryan and often wondered how he was. He had not been seen or heard of since that Friday evening she watched him depart the Estate carrying a little sack that held his few simple belongings. Now the fret was revisiting her with more intensity than ever, as the father she loved seemed to be in deep trouble. Although she could not be certain of this, it did appear that the Major and his wife were attempting to avoid her as much as possible. This in turn was filling her troubled little head with negative thoughts, like, perhaps they were in the process of planning the termination of her employment.

All of these worries and fears they discussed at length back in their cottage home in the evenings after work. It was a time of great uncertainty for both of them, yet they counted their blessings at being there to comfort and encourage one another. That was the one thing that sustained them as they continued to do their work with honesty and conviction; they could not allow anything get in the way of them doing what they had to. In troubled times, there is nothing to beat the support of friends and neighbors and that was the one thing that both of them had in abundance. Billy was highly popular amongst his work colleagues and even more so in the estimation of his employers. As a neighbor he was simply the best, always willingly at hand to help them that were in need. Likewise, they too looked out for him and his lovely daughter.

He was a relieved man that Saturday evening as she told him excitedly about receiving her wages plus a slight increase from Mrs. West. There was not a hint of any displeasure coming from the good lady as she commended Norah for the quality of her work. This was indeed a welcome development and a sign that things were not as gloomy as they appeared to be. Welcome though it was, it did not have the effect on Billy that he might see the Wests in a more favorable light. In spite of his abhorrence of the scoundrels responsible for a foul and dirty deed, he still viewed the Grand Old Major as the primary source of his present predicament.

"My dear Norah, the last thing I want to do is make life down there hard for you, but I am not going to sit around doing nothing while that man tramples on our rights. Nor am I going to go down for something I did not do. Keatley and myself will find the guilty ones surely, even should we die in the effort."

"Daddy, I know fine well that you would never do anything like that but please be careful because I could not stand to see anything happen to you. Would it not be better for the two of us if you could stay quietly out of all this for the time being? At least I would be much happier?"

Then, with a look that showed the depth of his caring, he told her not to worry.

"My dear daughter, this will all pass and soon be forgotten. That you can be sure of, just as I will be here to protect you."

These exchanges ended with Norah putting one arm tightly around his neck and hugging him warmly.

Just as she moved to make the tea for supper, a sharp knock hit against the door. Billy looked out the window and saw what he immediately recognized to be the old Morris Ten that his employer Mr. Duffy used for transport. It was the boss himself there to convey a message that Jack, the husband of his late sister Kate, had died in a Belfast Hospital and would be buried the day after tomorrow. A sister of the deceased had phoned the message to his office shortly after the workers had left the yard. Listening to what was being said from the scullery, Norah could feel a strange emotion come over her. It was not a feeling of deep sorrow or sense of loss. The news invoked in her feelings of another kind about the one that had been her foster parent but seldom a gentle guardian.

His manner towards her, as well as his comments, was anything but civil especially at the time she was growing into womanhood. But with the passage of time, she had managed to block out almost all the unpleasantries associated with her earlier life. Although there had been a few school friends she still thought about from time to time, never once did she considered going back there, even for a visit.

Composing herself to meet the good man that brought them the news, she came out to the kitchen and offered him thanks. The years she spent in the service of the rich had taught her the protocol of courtesy and civility; she invited him to join them for a cup of tea. Assuming that one or both of them would be wanting to travel to the funeral and knowing that Billy was a capable driver, he offered him the use of the Morris Ten.

Norah broke the silence that followed the man's departure.

"Daddy, sure there is not any need for me to go there, nor do I feel that I want to go."

"Whatever you want to do is fine by me but I thought perhaps you might like to come along for the outing. Now that we have a fine car for the day we could go to other places and find other things to do after the burial. After all, you don't have to decide right now; we have all day tomorrow to think about it; you might feel different when you do and I would be so glad to have you with me."

That was how they agreed to leave it for the night. It was a little past bedtime and they both had work to go to in the morning. In the privacy of her room, Norah knelt down by her bedside to say her night prayers and with true sincerity she prayed that Jack would enjoy eternal rest along with aunt Kate.

What, she wondered, do they mean by eternal rest; or what kind of interaction takes place between them that are enjoying it and how do the weak contend with the strong and powerful? Or is this promise of equality such, that these questions do not fit into the equation? These kinds of questions kept intruding on her consciousness as she tried to get to sleep. With a background such as hers, it was hard to envisage an existence without pain or the interplay of power and submissiveness.

They had a brief chat in the morning over breakfast and Norah agreed to think about going to the funeral. Back at work, Madge Crawford listened attentively to the story about the death of a man she did not know beyond hearing about him. With Norah's reticence about her childhood, the good woman would not have known the sensitivity surrounding her reluctance to go back there, even with her daddy. But Madge was firmly of the belief that she should accompany her father on the journey and that he would be in need of her presence for the occasion.

"Why would you not like to go with your father on a nice car run this fine summer weather? Come along to we have a talk to her Ladyship about you getting the day off."

Mrs. West was most compliant and agreed that even in the circumstances it would be a pleasant outing for a girl that is well deserving of it. These words of affirmation gave Norah a good feeling about herself and quickly dispelled any lingering doubts she had about accompanying her dad to the interment of Uncle Jack next morning.

"It is a beautiful morning to be traveling and I am pleased that you are coming with me. Have a listen to the sweet music that is coming from the birds out in the back garden. They are surely telling us to enjoy this day that will be ours together."

They took to the road at an early hour, passing a couple of neighboring farmyards as their owners were bringing in the cows for morning milking. No doubt the neatly dressed duo in the well-polished Morris Ten stirred a questioning thought in some of these thrifty heads as to where they might be going? Billy drove at a steady pace that was comfortable and conducive to easy conversation.

"Daddy, I never thought the day would come when I would be going back to the place I was so glad to get away from that morning the day after Aunt Kate was buried. Jack had gone off to his usual early morning start and going out the door he shouted me to get up for work. As I listened to the footsteps going out the path towards the road I knew that this was the end for me. So instead of going to work I wasted little time in gathering my few belongings and getting the first bus to Strabane. That short note I left on the kitchen table contained the last words I ever communicated with the man, God rest His Soul. In it I stated clearly my intention never to return there; now here I am going to pray and say farewell to him; hopefully in a spirit that holds no bitterness."

It was in a spirit of sharing and attentive listening that their journey progressed through many towns and open countryside. There was the occasional place or sight to attract their attention as they traveled onwards savoring the newness of it all. Much earlier than anticipated they were nearing their destination and Norah was beginning to see places that looked like she had seen before. Even with the passage of time there was no escaping the familiarity of the old road that led to what was once her home and the Monastery further on. Norah protested strongly when her father suggested they might go to the house and travel with the funeral cortege to the church.

"I am sorry Daddy, but I would rather you did not ask me go there today; is it not enough that we go to the funeral service and burial at the church? That will not be for another hour so let us go into the village for a cup of tea and you need to relax a bit after the long drive."

Billy was a sensitive man. He understood why his daughter felt the way she did and he was not going to do anything that would make it uncomfortable or stressful for her. He was more than agreeable to do what she asked of him; she obviously had her reasons and he was not going to question them. It was a half hour of blessed relaxation that the two spent in a cozy little café where nobody knew them, not even Norah who had worked there a number of years ago. There was nothing at all recognizable or familiar about the place. The interior décor, as well as the staff, had undergone considerable change perhaps under new ownership. It was not in a mood of nostalgia that she was observing this but more in sense that things, as well as people, must keep changing.

As family, they thought it best to be seated in a pew that was not too far away from the holy altar. They were there before the remains arrived in church. In black vestments and praying aloud, the priest walked before the pallbearers from the entrance door right up to the railing that separated the sanctuary from the main body of the church. As the coffin was being placed on the resting trestles, Norah took a brief glance towards the back of the church that was practically empty. What, she wondered, was this saying about her late uncle and his standing within the community? So different from the day her aunt Kate was laid to rest. With true sincerity, she prayed along with the rest of the congregation that the two be now reunited in their heavenly and eternal home. She listened attentively to a homily-cum-eulogy that was delivered with taste and sensitivity. As per usual, it extolled the best side of the late lamented departed.

In spite of the small number present, it was a dignified requiem and the solemn few walked respectfully from the church to the final resting place. It was not a tearful affair; no signs of heartbreaking grief at the grave side for the one that was being delivered back to Mother Earth. Billy and daughter got to meet and talk with their bereaved relatives after the final act of interment had been accomplished. Norah had met Jack's brother Paddy and his wife many times during her stay there and always found them to be politely friendly. So too was that sister who took the trouble to phone Billy's work place two evenings before and they thanked her for her thoughtfulness. All of these people were interested to know how it was for the little girl they had not seen or heard of for all those years. They were most complimentary about her appearance and how she had matured into such a beautiful girl. This kind of compliment may have encumbered upon the modesty of the one at the receiving end but it was the sort that her dad Billy was quick to concur with.

They were duly invited to one of the homes that were a good distance further on, but, by saying that the car had to be returned early in the afternoon, they gracefully declined the offer. The excuse given by Billy was far from the truth; the car was at their disposal for the entire day but he understood Norah's loathing about over-engaging with these relations. It was a bright sunny day and they wanted to make the best of it by touring some of the Antrim Glens and coastline. So at noontime the pair from Donegal said their good-byes before taking leave of friends that thanked them for coming so far to be with them. Having performed their family duty, a sense of relief was very much on both of them and not one word passed between them about either the funeral or the people.

For Norah, the mood was like she had just passed a major test or relieved from some kind of overpowering fret or anxiety; she was free now; they were both free and the feeling was good. In a more heightened state, she did agree that they take a drive down the narrow road past the small house where she had spent the best part of her childhood. It looked dilapidated in comparison to what she had known it to be; the door and walls had not seen paint for many a long day. The viewing was done from within the car as neither of the two had any inclination to do a closer inspection. There was evidence to show that some kind of people activity had taken place there over the previous two days; the wake had obviously attracted a number of friends and neighbors.

"I have little feeling for this place; it was my home for a time and some of the memories are not all bad but then there are others I would rather forget. He never spoke a nice or gentle word to me in all the time I was with him and Aunt Kate and how often I cried to myself for you to come and take me home. It was not your fault, of that I am certain, but at such a young age, how was I to know what you or they were thinking? I was always needing you but you were not there."

Billy was not the sort that would succumb easily to emotion but here the setting was more conducive to the softer cord. At first he tried to hide it by lowering the car window and looking across the flat countryside and towards the secluded monastery a little beyond. Yet he knew she needed to hear what he had to say as he took the hand of his hurting child. In this he found that tears come more easily than he thought and Norah saw what she had never seen before.

"What has happened to both of us cannot be undone and if it had been in my power, I would not have let it happen in the first place. I say both of us because you must know that I have suffered too, not as much as you have my good daughter but I did pine for you many a day and night after Kate took you away. It appeared to be a solution at the time and there was little else I could do but agree to let you go. Sorry Norah, now I wish there was some way I could make the pain of it go away. Sorry for not being there when you needed me, my poor wee girl."

Resting her head against his shoulder and spilling tears on to the upper sleeve of his clean white shirt, she told her daddy for the first time that she loved him. Even with the existence of deep fondness between them this was definitely a major crossing of the line. They had both gone that extra mile down the road that would lead to their mutual healing and found it was not all that hard to do.

Billy's suggestion that they go to the monastery for a look around and perhaps say a prayer in the church was met with stubborn resistance.

"It was enough for me to go down this road to take a look at the old house that was so much part of my child life but I am certainly not for going anywhere near that place over there. What is left of this day I want to make as pleasant and enjoyable as possible. For me, there are too many ghosts about that place and that is where I am going to leave them."

Without uttering another word, he turned the car and was heading back up the road that would take them to places new and far away from regressive thinking. There was nothing left there to hold their interest; they were glad to be leaving it behind them for good. It was highly unlikely that either of them would ever be back in that part of the world again.

Still it was a journey that destiny seemed to have planned for them and one with a purpose that had not yet revealed itself to either of them. In spite of her initial reluctance, Norah found benefit in being brought close to a past that was still unresolved and never fully faced up to. But the sense of freedom was fresh and invigorating to her spirit. She could feel it empower her like never before. She could see more clearly all that was good in her life and was gaining in strength to embrace a new world, one that was free and unshackled. It was still early in the day and what was left of it was theirs to enjoy. Now, good humor and laughter carried them merrily along the open road.

As their day progressed so too did their feelings of gladness and with lightheartedness about them, it passed all too quickly. They both became aware of this as they caught sight of the purple heather and orange whin blossoms that exuded color and beauty under the evening sunshine on Croghan Hill. Yes, they were nearing home with a feeling of well-being and a more heightened awareness of who they were. Norah prepared a light supper which both of them shared in quiet peace as they recounted the pleasures of their day together. That was before the events that were causing annoyance for them and some of their neighbors began to intrude once more into their thoughts.

"I will not be going to the river tonight; Keatley can manage the boat on his own if he wants to. I am a bit sick of it all right now. It's certainly not the same for me since this damned business began. This is a most ugly situation and I am caught right in the middle of it and through no fault of my own. But don't you be worrying dear for I am not one to go down without a fight. In any case, I will see him tomorrow about what we should do about clearing our names."

This ugly reality marked the ending of what was a lovely day for Billy Mullen and his daughter, Norah. It was the reality of what they had to face together.

Chapter Seven

It was still a looming reality that hung like a dark cloud over Billy and his friend Keatley and neither of them could hide away from it. They both knew that this was the sort of thing the spiteful Rusty McKeague was well capable of and had more than likely executed it in such a cunning way as for someone else to take the blame. Now he could see it as a particularly clever stunt, to let Mullen and Keatley take the rap and coerce his accomplices into silence. As long as they remained the prime suspects the real culprits would never be brought to account for their willful actions. For that reason the dispute with the Major was temporarily being relegated to one of less importance in the thinking of the anxious-minded pair. Now their mission was to find a lawful route of getting to the truth and they knew there were people out there who could help them. Billy warned his friend against losing the cool, and not to forget the law, that was also endeavoring to establish the truth, was watching them closely.

Nothing much came to light in the days that followed; both men were on the lookout in the hope of seeing or hearing something that might lead them in the right direction. Seeing that their approach was not yielding any benefit by way of results, Billy decided that they make a more direct yet discrete contact with some people. These did not include any of the ones he knew to be associated with Rusty McKeague; that would only be done when all else had failed. Most all of those approached were people who knew both men to be the kind that was honest and upright in every way, certainly not the sort to do such a despicable thing.

One such man was Hat McGivern who was with them in the Poachers' Inn on the night in question and would have remained there long after they had gone home. McGivern was most reassuring to both men and told them that in the eyes of most people, their innocence was beyond question. He was absolutely certain that the investigating Garda with the help of the local Sergeant and the two older members of the force would soon come to realize that fact. In considering himself to be highly thought of amongst the more important elements of society, he was pretty sure that the law enforcers would be calling on him for character references. At the same time he was not so keen on giving much away in relation to who he thought might have committed the actual deed. Nor was he all that ready to talk about the other late night boozers or what might have been their take.

"Yes, your man Rusty was still there when I left. He and his mates, young Harrigan and Doran, were drinking together but I was not anywhere near them throughout the night. I don't have to tell you that they are not the type I would be likely to engage in conversation, nor was I able to overhear what they were talking about."

Billy thought it most unusual that the bellicose Rusty could remain unobtrusive while in the inebriated state and him with a head full of malice. He was not the type to restrain his aggression or effectively hide it from others so there had to be a question about the merits of McGivern's account. While not going so far as to call him a liar, Keatley reminded Hat that the same Rusty, who doesn't speak to either him or his friend, was beginning to be heard even before he and Billy left the Inn.

"You must be stone fuckin' deaf if you were in the place and didn't hear that watery-mouthed hoor blowing off steam. Come on Mullen for we are only wasting our time here."

A slightly startled McGivern looked at the two as they made to turn away; for a change he seemed lost for words.

"W-well, I mean, well you see, I was along with wee Eddie McGinn and we talked a lot. Rusty was making a kind of noise all right but to tell you the truth I didn't pay much heed to what he was saying. As you both know he can be a bit on the uncanny side when he has a drop of drink in him. He must have left soon after Eddie and me because we were able to hear their voices on the road behind us, but we kept well ahead and out of hearing distance. It would have been the drink that was deein' the tackin' for him at that stage."

"Drink be damned," says Keatley. "There is a devil as big as a bull calf inside the hoor and the same can be said about any bollacks that tries to cover up for him. But don't worry. His day is coming fast and I will be there to see that it does. Tell him that fay me the next time you see him."

Not the sort of man that wanted to be involved in any form of neighborly discord, McGivern was more anxious to talk about his legal crusade with Pauric O'Donnell.

"Being the link man between the Solicitor and the fishermen, I have to keep a dignified distance away from personal quarrels. You must understand that my way of dealing with these issues differs considerably from the ways of the ordinary man and I think it is going to pay off in the end. Pauric has written to me to say that the Fisheries Board has contacted him and they enclosed a copy of the letter that was sent to the Major, outlining the rights of the licensed fishermen."

This was nothing more than routine procedure in cases where the law is being employed in the process of defending rights and well Billy Mullen knew it. But right then the dispute between the Major and the Fishermen was not a priority for him or his friend. They would let Mc-Givern do his own thing; he could bum his load and feel important but their time had to be about a graver matter.

"So again, we have to take it that you could not hear or see what our friend Rusty was up to on the way home that night either, but perhaps wee Eddie might have a sharper ear."

There was a hint of sarcasm in Billy's tone as he and Keatley departed from Hat's company, leaving him standing there with Pauric O'Donnell's letter still in his hand. As they walked away from his premises he called after them something about arranging another important meeting in the Poachers' Inn. Important was the word as far as McGivern was concerned, but his crafty canniness was impairing his willingness to align with the common man. As for him being of use to his beleaguered neighbors, only time would tell.

Eddy McGinn sat himself down on the armchair beside the fireplace of his small laborers cottage. He touched the cigarette that was in his mouth with a lighted paper; an agreeable respite after the bare evening tea that was only affordable to a council road worker. Except for one son that was serving his time as a motor mechanic, his other son and two daughters were still of school-going age. He was considered a decent upright kind of fellow who believed in the principles of honesty and fairness. Perhaps these were the kind of attributes that attracted the likes of non-working Mr. McGivern towards him. For the very same reason, it was he along with big Harry that struck the first blow against the Major's attempts to block the right of way.

It was Mrs. McGinn who greeted the two men at the door. Eddie called for them to come in and be seated. There was neighborliness between them.

"I hear that you men have been having a hard time these last few days and I am sorry that it has come to this. We all have a fair idea who was responsible for the damage done to the Major's property and it was certainly not Billy Mullen or Laurence Keatley. I have no doubt but the truth will eventually come out but I am very surprised that the Sergeant and the two older Guards have not intervened on your behalf. Unfortunately, I am not in a position to prove exactly who the villain was but I do know from listening to and observing your man McKeague that he had nothing good on his mind that night."

"Did he mention any of our names?" asked Billy, who was beginning to see that they had a friend on their side.

"None by name but he certainly cursed and ridiculed the lot of us for being a useless and cowardly bunch. For that reason McGivern and me moved away to the top end of the bar to be out of his view but as I don't have to tell you Rusty and his mates could still be heard. Yes, I would have to agree with Hat that it was quite impossible for us to make out what they were talking about coming up the road. It was very late and we kept a good distance ahead of them. I have a strong feeling though that they went into Mulrine's yard, for it was just about there we stopped hearing their voices. It must be said that we are dealing with a dangerous and vicious young hooligan in Rusty McKeague and those two guys that run around with him are not much better. I am surprised to see a son of big Harry's or indeed young Harrigan hanging around with a scamp like that."

"Eddie, dinny be all that surprised," says Keatley. These are the same two boys that were standing ready tay help McKeague agin me that night at the river ower a year ago. If it hadnay been for may freen here, I would surely hay gotten a bad beating up fay the three of them. It's ganny be hard for me to keep my hands fay any o them if I iver git the chance."

This was not the kind of talk that Billy wanted to hear coming from his raised friend although Eddie McGinn did not have to be told anything about this thick man or his woeful temper. Yet, Billy knew better than most how to handle Keatley and never loathe about calling him to order.

"Listen Keatley, if you don't watch it we are both going to be in big trouble with the law and that would definitely be into Rusty's barrow. Remember, I only agreed to go along with you on the understanding that you would behave yourself. So don't mess it up before we even get started. I think we could be on to something here. What would have taken them boys into Mulrine's yard on their way home from the pub? They certainly didn't go in there to say their prayers. Come on Laurence, I think we should take a walk down there and maybe have a talk with Hughie Harvey, the yardman. He would surely know if anything has been taken."

Expressing their gratitude to Eddie, they hoped he did not mind them using his name whenever it was right for them to go to the Guards.

Hughie was creating a steamy stench from dunging out a calf shed that had been vacated for the summer. It was tiresome work and he welcomed the short respite. Leaning on the shaft of the implement he was using, Hughie filled his pipe and engaged the snooping sleuths. He was able to tell them that a light sledgehammer had been stolen from the tool shed.

"It and a steel bar that was once the axel shaft of the old Barn Mill must have been taken very recently for it was only in the past few days that I have noticed them missing. I advised the old man and his sister to report the theft to the Guards but I don't know if they ever did."

Billy Mullen thanked the hardworking Hughie for the information supplied and went on to say he and his friend were being wrongfully accused of a criminal act. They needed to get to the truth of what had exactly taken place as well as who was responsible for the damage done to the Major's property. Keatley was well behaved and remained almost silent throughout the interview but agreed that the information received was most valuable indeed. He was just about to go into the tool shed when Billy called him to stop, saying it would be advisable not to go in there as the Guards might be wanting to take fingerprints.

Now in possession of some useful information, Billy suggested that they both go immediately to the Garda Station and if possible, speak to Sergeant Brennan. As yet they were not ready to name the one who was their prime suspect but wee Eddie McGinn was prepared to say who came up the road behind him and McGivern on the night in question. The barrack was a more amicable place for both of them on this occasion and they themselves felt more assured. Ushering the two into his office, Brennan was polite and friendly. He carefully recorded what they had to say. Yes, the story about Mulrine's yard was relevant indeed, even though the matter had not been reported to the station. He said it would have to be investigated forthwith. He undertook to go out there as soon as he could find one of the young officers to accompany him. For Mullen and Keatley it seemed that things were now beginning to move in the right direction and it was their own crusade that brought this about.

The two lawmen did not spend all that long with the Mulrines and their workman but they did lock the door of the tool shed securely and took the key with them. This procedure was simply to preserve whatever forensic evidence might be extractable inside. The Sergeant apologized for whatever inconvenience this might cause but assured that it would only be until the technical people came from Letterkenny. This examination, they knew, would not take place until next morning as the evening was wearing late. In any case they had other business to do before they left the area and that was to talk to the one man that Billy said could help. Eddie McGinn was willingly compliant and had no compunction about giving whatever information he thought might benefit two decent men. Not only did he tell the Guards all he had seen and heard on the night but that his neighbor and friend Willie McGivern was with him throughout. In fairness to McGivern, he too was forthcoming but nothing like he was to the two that tried to question him earlier in the day. What he told the Guards very much concurred with what Eddie had already told them. He also advised them not to be harboring any negative thoughts about Mullen and Keatley.

Things got moving at a very early hour next morning. The Sergeant and a strange young man wearing civilian clothes and carrying a box kit, came to Mulrine's yard as Hughie was about to commence the morning routine. The young officer with his kit then entered the tool shed and closed the door from inside, while the Sergeant stood on guard at the entrance gate. It took less than one hour for the procedure to be completed but the two men continued to deliberate inside the shed door for a time before finally departing the scene. None of this, however, took place unbeknownst to the local people; they had already been talking about the Garda presence the evening before.

Except for the working staff at Elmwood Estate, no one knew about the events that began there at exactly the same time as Mulrine's shed was being examined. It was Vincent Wilkie that noticed two uniformed members of the force standing at the river's edge, near to the new slipway. Although reluctant at first, he then decided it best to go over and see what was happening; Dickie Boyle was not far behind him. Neither of the officers appeared to be much bothered about the two intruders. They seemed more interested in what was happening in the water, for it was a most interesting sight to behold. There, standing up to the waist in the cool water, was a huge man wearing nothing but a pair of shorts and a snorkel mask on his face. The man seemed to be enjoying himself as he bade good morning to the new arrivals and then brandished the sledgehammer for all to see.

Dickey nudged Vincent with an elbow that showed the strain of nervousness and pointed to the old mill axel, which lay at the feet of one of the Garda officers.

"Tell me Vincent, what do you think will all this mean? Will it put an end to all this trouble once and for all? I hope to God it does just that."

"Dinny be botherin' yersel' Dickie. Sure it's only a bit o' craic for boys like us. Niver say Keatley."

Just as they were speaking, the Sergeant along with his technician drove on to the slipway. The two in uniform walked over to them carrying the steel axle, while the man in the water began to wade towards them. Now out of the water, he donned a pair of overalls and along with the items retrieved, the five officers began walking towards the big house while Vincent and Dickie went back to begin their day.

This was an important development and one they all hoped might bring a satisfactory result for the benefit of the two wrongfully accused. The meeting with the Major took place behind closed doors, in what was called his office room; it lasted well over thirty minutes. He was briefed on all of the most recent developments. The two items taken from the river had been stolen from Mr. Mulrine's shed, most likely on the night the offense was committed. The technical officer had already been to the house in relation to the break-in that was still under investigation and a continuing concern for the Major. As for this investigation, he was not so sure that the print traces he had found would be conclusive enough to secure a conviction. At the same time, Sergeant Brennan assured the Major that all of this represented progress but as it stood, he was not at liberty to say anything beyond that.

Norah Mullen and Madge Crawford watched the departure of the lawmen from the kitchen window; they were at pains to know what, if anything, was happening. All that had taken place the evening before had been brought to Norah by her father Billy, so she had a fair idea why this was taking place. Like Dickie Boyle, she prayed that it would bring this continuing curse to a speedy end and she asked Madge to do the same. The forensic tests were taken to Letterkenny for a more thorough examination and analysis, while Rusty

McKeague and his mates were taken to the station for questioning.

Rusty was well aware of what had been taking place but unsure as to how much they had on him. He was steadfast in denial and appeared a difficult nut to crack, yet he did seem a little nervous. Perhaps this had something to do with his concern about how the other two were holding up somewhere else in the building. The fact that all of them had been fingerprinted was also beginning to shake his confidence a little. It looked like his interrogation was going to be lengthy and intense. He began to sense that he was dealing with people who were not in a hurry.

"Mr. McKeague, it appears the evidence is very much against you right now and we are pretty certain that the forensic evidence will confirm that view. In the meantime you will have to remain in custody until the results come through or until you are prepared to admit your guilt."

With that, the interrogator left the room and closed the door. In the silence that followed, Rusty could hear the click of the lock that imprisoned him.

The intensity of the questioning was proving too much for the young accomplices. They were allowed to stay together for some of the time but not for the actual interrogation. Doran was tougher than Harrigan and was the one that provided most of the answers. He was the better of the two at composing his thoughts. But the problem for all three was that none of them knew what the other had said or indeed admitted. McKeague was left alone for a very long period and darkness was beginning to shadow the light of the small window.

The Guard who was observing him through the secret peephole could clearly see his agitated state; he gave a violent punch to the desk table while cursing the Guards and Major West. The holding room of a Guards Barrack is not the most inviting of places and Rusty was beginning to sense the loneliness of his predicament. To add to his misery he received a very brief visit from one of the Guards; it was to inform him that the forensic technician was not likely to be coming until morning. Whether or not the story was true, only the authority knew the answer, but its impact on the prisoner was profound.

It was wearing close to midnight and an eerie silence had descended upon the place; brave Rusty was still alone with his thoughts. Now in a situation where he could no longer rely on his aggression, he had ample time to consider his options or if indeed he had any. The night that lay ahead of him was going to be long and tedious with little hope that the morning would bring relief. With these disturbing thoughts beginning to plague his mind, he swore a woeful mouthful and knocked loudly on the door. The signal was answered with due promptness and the Guards knew what it meant. With sheets of foolscap paper in his hand, the officer sat down at the table with Rusty McKeague.

It was not until big Harry Doran and Packie Gordon arrived to sign a bail bond that the three were finally released from custody. Both men were highly regarded by everyone including the local Garda, but poor Harry felt a deep embarrassment nonetheless. A mighty man diminished through the foolery of a heedless son whose action had tarnished the entire family. None of them, he assured, had been brought up in an environment that subscribed to conduct of this sort. This was something that Sergeant Brennan did not have to be told and he was kindly sympathetic to the man's plight.

"However, the procedure of the law most be allowed take its course; we will now be preparing a case against the three of them for the next sitting of the District Court. I am certain that the judge will take a serious view of the offense, particularly against the ringleader. From what your son and young Harrigan have told us, it was McKeague that actually committed the act and they did nothing more than accompany him. I am not at liberty to disclose what is in McKeague's statement but needless to say it does implicate the other two as well. That lad of yours, at twenty-one years of age, should know better than to be hanging around with a hooligan like that. As for the other poor fellow, well, he did not experience the benefit of having a father-like figure in his growing up. His poor mother, along with her own mother, had to manage by themselves. Mind you, they are the best of people, but that boy has been spoiled by both of them."

At a very late hour, the three accused along with big Harry got into Packie Gordon's old hackney in a subdued state. The only thing they were certain about was of having to face Judge Evans at Lifford District Court. News about Rusty McKeague and the boys being out on bail pending trial was spreading fast next morning and throughout the day. A much-relieved Laurence Keatley was foremost in delivering the news and most people were glad for him.

Norah Mullen was not the type to rejoice at the downfall of other people, especially when it happened to be young neighbors that she knew quite well. At the same time, she could not but be happy to see her father looking so relieved and free from the attention of the law. She gave the good news to her friend Madge first thing in the morning, knowing that she in turn would pass it on to Mrs. West and then it would soon reach the Major. But they had already received the news from the Sergeant who had called out to them earlier in the morning. They were pleased to learn the truth and it renewed their faith in the civil authority; they obviously knew nothing about the pair of amateur detectives that set the process in motion. Mrs. West was as pleased as Madge was about the latest development, but her gladness was mainly about Norah's relief from the anxiety that all this had been causing her.

It was indeed a big relief for the junior housemaid, but she had not forgotten about Benny Ryan and her complicity in his downfall. She had not heard much about him since that evening he walked away from the Estate looking worried and dejected. Vincent Wilkie talked to her of hearing about him working on a building site near Derry. His gravitating towards the city was something she could understand; often he had told her about his footballing ambitions with the Brandywell side. Norah's prayerful hope was that he should succeed and that good fortune and happiness would be his in abundance. She thought about the terrible burden of suspicion that was surely weighing heavily on his mind wherever he went or whatever he did. These somber thoughts were undoubtedly impeding her ability to be totally happy about the exoneration of the dear dad she so loved. This new development was indeed significant for all concerned with this ugly and bitter dispute. It taught the militant mob the value of keeping their protest within the confines of the law and it brought the old Major to see he was dealing mainly with law-abiding people. Yet he remained stubbornly resolute about keeping the fishermen off, what he continued to call, his stretch of the river.

But the Rusty McKeague story was now the main talking point both on and off the Estate and would remain so until after the verdict of the court had been read. Much speculation was abroad as to what kind of sentence might or should be imposed on the three defendants. Whatever about the accomplices, there was little sympathy for the author of the crime and he was swiftly coming to a realization of that. Mrs. West was also hearing the same sentiments being expressed by the workers with whom she continued to spend most of her working day. She understood that a few of them were men that liked to take an odd turn at the river in their spare time. For that reason she was not all behind her husband in what he was attempting to do to their way of life and knowing that his blind defiance was damaging their standing in the community. They, in turn, knew her to be a reasonable woman with a sense of humor; one who liked the idea of being a friendly neighbor that could stop for a chat along the road.

The court case was brief and formal. After the charges were read out, the Garda spokesman read the statement and handed it to the clerk for verification.

Through their solicitor, the defendants were pleading guilty. He also asked that clemency be considered on behalf of the two younger offenders. Sergeant Brennan indicated that he too was in favor of this request being favorably considered. The judge was then free to deliberate and pass sentence. His speak was stern and resolute. His court would not be used to minimize the seriousness of such a vile act. Doran and Harrigan were both given probation; they would have to be on best behavior for the next twelve months; failing to comply with the order would mean them coming back before him for sentencing.

"As for you Mr. McKeague, it appears that you were the one that planned and executed the act. Such malice, I have to say, is despicable and cannot be tolerated by any court of law. I think the only effective way of dealing with the likes of you is to send you to prison; so I hereby impose a custodial sentence of twelve months for you to serve in Sligo Jail."

These words, along with the passing of sentence, was observed by Major West, whose presence the judge acknowledged by way of stating his regret about the loss sustained through criminal damage. Billy Mullen and Keatley were also present and watched an uneasy-looking Rusty being led away between two uniformed guards. For them the case was finally over and Sergeant Brennan was man enough to apologize to both of them on behalf of *An Garda Siochána.* As the Major was leaving the court, he passed close to where Mullen and Keatley were standing, but with a fixed gaze that was slightly downwards towards the floor in front of him. He did not acknowledge their presence. In the circumstances it was probably better that way, for if he had attempted to speak to them, his courtesy would have been lost on Laurence Keatley. From past experience he had learned to know that this man would verbally ravish him without mercy, so perhaps it was best to make a quiet and unobtrusive exit. This particular case had the effect of taking the heat out of the main dispute between the fishermen and the Major, hence a period of relative calm ensued. But it was not an issue that could be put to rest all that easy. It would surely re-emerge and once again engage the attention of both sides, but it now looked as if the legal route was the only practical way.

Chapter Eight

Summer work progressed on the Estate, with the lady of the house playing an increasing role along with the workmen. She seemed to have acquired a method of supervision that was not invasive and the men responded favorably to it. In order to achieve this, she began to know more and more about these men as well as the colloquialism that was unique to the area. Apart from her more refined tongue, she could willingly engaged with them in local gossip and seemed more comfortable there than in the midst of the formality and grandeur that she was part of and had a dutiful role to play in. The entire workforce recognized the quality of her method and often complimented her on how good she was at what she did. Their spokesperson was usually Vincent Wilkie, a man who could say what he felt without it being perceived as an offense to others.

"Men, you make me feel good. No greater compliment can one receive than to be told you are good at what you do and now I will have to try even harder to be worthy of your approval. There is nothing I like better than to be out here with you lot and I have no doubt that we are doing a good job too; so perhaps you do find me a better personnel manager than himself."

"Personnel Manager"–that was surely a new kind of job description; one that was foreign to them that she was addressing. Wilkie looked towards her with a characteristic smirk. He thought for a while but not too long:

"Missus, that sounds bloody good. Aye, personnel manager, sure you would hay tay be better nor him. That man o' yours would know as much aboot that as a pig would know aboot a white shirt."

Her laughter was loud and prolonged. It affected the others and they all joined in.

"I had better not tell him that one. He does have a sense of humor, though you may find it hard to believe, but I don't think I would be able to get a laugh out of him with that one. Mind you, he is not in the mood for laughs these days with all the trouble of the past few weeks, not to mention his precious William Turner."

"Is there nothing new on that Missus?" The speaker was Dickie Boyle and it was his earnest hope that the valuable painting would be found and brought back to where it belongs. Mrs. West concurred with the sentiment but did not appear anxious to pursue the subject any further. Yet she was not loathe to talk about the court case, as well as the people that were involved in it, both them that were innocent and the three that were guilty. She took no pleasure out of the fact that a young man was in prison and that two others were out on probation. Though she did not have a lot in common with them, she nevertheless had a strong desire to be in friendship with the local people. Many times she tried in vain to coax her husband towards a more reasoned approach. While her tact and skill was good with the workmen, it certainly had a thicker barrier to penetrate in dealing with the Major. But she was a persistent lady that was unlikely to give up on a crusade that she believed to be for the best. It was the recent court case that re-enthused and nudged her towards embarking upon a more assertive approach.

On the other side, McGivern was in the throws of trying to get his meeting organized. He liked the semblance of authority that sitting on the chair seemed to confer upon him. He now had the added benefit of being in possession of a few papers in the form of letters from Solicitor Pauric O'Donnell as well as some draft copies of correspondence between the legal teams and the Fisheries Board. In the interest of the cause, he urged that all fishermen as well as would-be fishermen come together in a spirit of benign solidarity and let this proposed meeting be the starting point. This was the message he took round the neighborhood for the three days prior to the Sunday evening meeting; again in the Poachers' Inn. He was now in a more confident frame of mind. The unruly element had been dealt with and others had learned a valuable lesson. The manner in which he had redeemed himself in relation to the exoneration of Mullen and Keatley as well as the apprehension of the guilty party added to his conceit. Surely this was an added boost to his standing in the community.

The community was indeed responsive. That Sunday evening saw a gathering the likes of which had not been seen before in the popular watering hole. Everyone with even a half-interest in the river made a point of being there, the exception being Rusty McKeague and the two that were spared his fate. McGivern opened the proceedings with a lengthy and uncoordinated address; it was repetitive, boring and unnecessary. But knowing how it would surely make him feel good, who would be the one to deprive him of his moment? By their standards it was a successful meeting; many of the participants spoke their piece with few, if any, dissenting voices. The Chairman's advice was that whatever action is to be taken should at all times be in accordance with what is lawful. This had the backing of the bulk of those present and quite a number gave voice to that belief; no longer were they going to be criminalized through the actions of the irresponsible.

One of the letters from the solicitor, and read to the meeting by McGivern, suggested a possible option was for one of the group to take a test case against the Fisheries Board for failing to protect his rights as a licensed fisherman. It was a suggestion that generated considerable interest and it raised many questions that were beyond the comprehension of the top table. But the one who was, after all, their legal mentor must have thought the idea had enough merit to be worthy of consideration. So for that reason, a unanimous decision was taken to seek further advice, even if it meant another lengthy jaunt to the west of the county. Another suggestion from the floor was about an approach that had already been tried; it was that another attempt be made at talking to West, perhaps along with someone from the Board to act as mediator. This too got some hearing, but a strong minority was totally against the idea on the grounds that the man was unapproachable. Then the chair moved to remind everyone what they were about; it was to find a way out of this, within the law, but if possible, without involving the law. He would again be prepared to go on a delegation if there was even a remote chance that it would do some good. There was little optimism that this would yield anything by way of finding a resolution to the contentious issue. At the same time, the man who made the suggestion along with a couple of others had heard something about Mrs. Wests displeasure at the Major's unyielding stance; so a tentative approach was surely worth a try.

Whichever course of action was going to be followed, Hat McGivern was confident of his involvement in both of them. His wisdom and judgment was going to be needed, be it either with the solicitor or in leading a delegation to Elmwood House. In the interest of convenience and good neighborliness, the latter option was to be tried first. A delegation of not more than two people along with a representative from the Board, he felt, was the most appropriate way of seriously engaging the Major. Again he stated his willingness to be the most important half of that delegation but asked for help in deciding who would be best to accompany him. But in truth he had but one name in mind and it was not any of them that were present on the day. So before any names were put to him, he lifted his hat from where it rested on the table beside him and moved it to a new position; he had something to say.

"How would you men feel if I asked Dr Clarke to come with me to face the Major and the guy from the Board, After all, he is the local doctor and highly respected by everyone. It is also a fact that he likes to spend some of his spare time with the fishing rod on the river further up stream."

Keatley nudged Billy Mullen with his elbow and with some muffled words that were audible to a few:

"Yir a wonderful man McGivern, a wonderful fuckin' man. Pity ya wornay as quick at helpin' me and Mullen yon evenin."

"Shhhh," says Mullen, "Sure he did help us in the end. Let him do whatever pleases him, but don't worry, for fuck all is going to come out of this anyway."

By the time the meeting concluded, most of the participants were called to the bar where the real business of the meeting got under way. In this relaxed setting, even the most reticent participant can eventually find the inspired word that allows him to think that his was the word of wisdom. But in allowing for all of that, here was a gathering of people that now wanted to do what was right and with a determination to exercise control over potential troublemakers. There was nothing more than a few words spoken about Rusty McKeague; the general feeling was that he had gotten what he deserved. As for the other two, there was a more compassionate view being taken. Nobody wanted to see them being victimized for their lack of judgment. This was a genuine feeling being expressed by good-hearted and caring people, not because the big man who felt let down by an errant son happened to be there. Harry was quiet and understandably so; there was no one in the gathering that lacked sympathy or understanding for his embarrassing predicament.

McGivern left shortly after the formal meeting had ended and those that remained had a fair idea where he was heading. He could relate to Dr Clarke in a way that the others, most definitely, could not. Laurence Keatley looked out the window as the hatted man was throwing his leg over the high bike to head in the direction of more enlightened company.

"Throw it high ya owl bollocks, for that owl bike is the only thing that lang leg was ever threw ower."

It was the middle of the week before the Fisheries Board representative contacted McGivern to say he had set up a meeting with the Major for the Friday night. Beyond saying that West had reluctantly consented to hearing what the popular doctor had to say, he was not in a position to predict how successful the encounter might be. Hat had little option but to accept that he was not being rated quite as highly by either of the parties as the man he had chosen to be his ally. Whether he cared to believe it or not, there be in existence a kind of deferential tolerance between the strata of society, where rank and class had a part to play. For that reason, their chances of gaining entry to the Big House would have increased considerably.

"Dr Clarke, you are most welcome to Elmwood. Just go straight through with your friend to the drawing room where the Major and the other man are waiting for you."

Now in her formal role, Mrs. West performed the greeting ceremony. Her speak was polite and she looked very much the lady of class and refinement. Her adaptability was what made her the woman for all seasons; she possessed a skill that enabled her to turn all situations into good account. The two visitors thanked her and remarked what a fine place she had. Their footsteps echoed off the hardwood floor along a darkish hallway that was long and with a high, cornice ceiling. She acknowledged the compliments with a gracious smile, again more focused towards the doctor, whose approval was obviously the more gratifying for her.

"Yes, I like it a lot. This is a most beautiful countryside to be living in and more than anything, I love the land. Hopefully when we get things more settled, I will be better able to involve myself with the wider community and its affairs."

Before taking their seats with the Major and the Board member, McGivern knew he had to be quick off the mark, least he be sidelined to the margins amidst the exchanges of clever diplomacy.

"Major West, I was just saying to your good wife and the doctor here what a fine place you have and what a fine place you have turned it into. Indeed, I am glad to see it happen, for you know, my people and the Walkers were always very friendly towards each other. They were the greatest of people. They were, what you would call, the nobility, and I am more than glad to see one of their own in possession of Elmwood."

He was off to what he judged to be a good start. Although it had little to do with the business they had come to talk about, he nevertheless felt he had staked his claim to being seen and heard. But alas, his goodness was lost in the summer air. The jolly old Major responded by addressing the doctor with a word of welcome and an introduction to Mr. Orr from the Fisheries Board.

The discourtesy towards McGivern seemed to have an unsettling affect on Dr Clarke, although he did not allow it to hinder his reasoning.

He stated his pleasure at being about the business of the fishermen of Portneill and that Mr. McGivern, along with himself, had a genuine interest in seeing this long tradition on the River Camus being respected and preserved.

"I have lived amongst these people for more years than I care to remember; it is here in their midst I have spent my entire working life as a doctor and indeed have assisted at the births of a large proportion of them. Through my dealings and interaction with them over the years, I do feel better qualified than most to give an accurate assessment of their quality and character. The people of Portneill are not just a collectivity of families and individuals, they are very much a community with a spirit and pride in themselves. I know these people because this is my community and I am proud to be a small part of it. Their honesty and integrity I can vouch for. They are an industrious, hard-working people that pay their way and support each other. I know that in recent times certain acts have been committed against the Major and his property and these are acts that the people are deeply ashamed of. But all that is now in the past and I offer our apologies to you. As far as we, the people, are concerned, such conduct will never again be allowed to happen. These are sentiments I felt needed to be expressed at the outset and before we enter into the business that has brought us here this evening."

Apart from the esteem of his position, Dr Clarke was an effective communicator and his words could not but have an effect on his listeners. The Major responded by thanking him for the sentiments so elegantly expressed and accepted the assurance that they did represent the majority of the people.

"It is a relief for me to be told that, and I certainly do appreciate it with gratitude, but I also know that you men are not here simply to convey that benign message and nothing else. Rightly Doctor, you did allude to the business that has brought you here, but I am afraid it is not something I can discuss comfortably with anybody right now. While I have no desire to be at odds with the local people, it has to be understood that what we are dealing with here is the ownership of rights. No doubt you people are aware that the fishing rights to the Camus River have a historical association with the Walker Estate but I am only interested in the portion of it that is contiguous to my land. We have definite plans for that stretch of water and it certainly does not include net fishing or access to the river through the Estate. I cannot see how this would in any way damage or obstruct what you have referred to as the long tradition; these people will still have the rest of the river to fish as always."

These rather lengthy statements were tending to leave McGivern somewhat out in the cold and now it seemed that the Doctor was holding back, perhaps to allow some of the others the opportunity to speak. Just as Hat was opening his mouth to take in an inspirational breath to aid his composure, Mr. Orr said 'Gentlemen,' and got in before him. Orr began by saying how impossible it would be for him as an official of the Board to mediate in a dispute of this kind.

"The reason for this, I need not tell you, is a legal one and it may seem that I am taking sides. You see, we are the legal custodians of the entire river and as such, have the right to issue licenses for the purpose of legal net fishing. So, as far as the law is concerned, any person that holds a license and acts within the law, does have a right to fish the entire river. However, the Board and I would very much like for you, Major, and the fishermen to strive towards an arrangement that could be worked and honored by both sides. It should not be beyond the capacity of responsible, intelligent people to find a way out of this unhappy affair. A dispute of this sort puts the Board in a very awkward position because we value more than anything else, our good relationship with the landowners of this valley. At the same time, we have a statutory obligation to uphold the rights of our lawfully licensed fishermen, so it is surely in all our interests that we work towards an amicable settlement."

Whether McGivern's contribution was wisely informed or not, he was, nevertheless, determined not to be allowing the heavyweights rule the entire proceedings. For him, it was better to say the wrong thing than be sidelined completely. He felt that amicability would be hard to arrive at because, as he saw it, one of the two sides would eventually have to give in. His words may not have been well chosen, but in the circumstances, how far wrong was his assessment of the situation? They had all listened to the stated positions of three different interest groups and they appeared to contain little common ground. The doctor then mentioned a kind of compromise that might be worth considering, but it would be at a grave inconvenience to the fishermen.

"What if these men were to forfeit the use of the right-of-way through the Estate in turn for the right to fish all of the river uninhibited. This, I know, would be very awkward for the people down this way but there are other routs of access that they might consider using."

Mr. Orr was neutral on this one and would have favored it as a means to a settlement, but McGivern took on an uneasy look, like he had been sitting on a nail or trying to suppress wind. Right well he knew the kind of reception that awaited him if this was going to be the best deal he and his learned friend could get out of West. But this was not going to be a problem for Hat; the Major ruled it out as inconceivable and certainly not in keeping with his plans for the river.

Seeing the futility of the exercise, the visitors began to shift focus towards a more general kind of talk and found the going much easier. In the more relaxed setting, the conversation drifted to matters of less importance and far removed from the troubled waters of the Camus River.

The Doctor's attention was very much on what looked like a full set of valuable golf clubs that occupied a corner of the room opposite where he sat. Apart from the occasional spot of angling there was nothing for him to equal being out on the links or fairway. He walked across the room to have a closer look at the items that were standing inside a rigid leather golf bag.

"I see you use only the best and you obviously haven't been using them for some time. They are a handy set, I must say."

This diversion of focus was an obvious relief for the Major as he was keen not to be at odds with the popular doctor, or indeed, the members of the Fisheries Board. The fact that Orr was also a member of the golfing fraternity made for an interim period of cozy cordiality. More and more, McGivern could see that he was not in the kind of company that had anything to offer him by way of shared interest. It was not going to be one of his best outings and he ruefully knew it. For the other three, the time was passing at a faster rate and now they were more than half at ease with each other. Mr. Orr played at Portrush and was a long time member of that club, While the links at Buncrana was where the doctor spent much of his leisure time.

"Not since I left the Dales have I had the opportunity to play the game as much as I would like to, so I am not surprised you notice these irons are under used. One of the things I like about going back there for the occasional weekend is the opportunity to play a round of golf. Here I am too busy; at least that is how it has been for me since I came to the estate but now I am about to change all that and hopefully seek membership of a convenient club."

"That can be easy and quick to arrange if you want me to."

The speaker was Mr. Orr who was quick to see that possible advantages might accrue towards him if he were to augment the prestige of his club by securing the membership of Major West. Royal Portrush was a name that did appeal to the Major but he was not a man to jump at the first choice on offer. He was grateful for the offer but it was something he would have to think about first. This was partly because he found Dr

Clarke to be a man he could relate to. While they could not come anywhere near to agreeing a way round the other business, there seemed, nevertheless, to be an agreeableness about the mood between them. A more tangible sign of this development emerged when West opened the drinks cabinet and took out a bottle of Scotch whisky along with a few crystal glasses. This was a true gesture of friendship and it lifted the gloom off McGivern's face, at least for a while.

None of this seemed good for the business that was now suspended. It was looking increasingly like this mission had failed. McGivern listened in exasperation as the other three talked swings and putts, in the rough and bunker shots. Little they knew of his troubled thoughts. He cursed his judgment that was ill advised and the foolish pride that led him in the wrong direction. Was the doctor really a prudent choice? The night was wearing late and nothing good had been achieved. Here they were talking sweet nonsense and forming friendships that were unlikely to serve the interests of the common man. But friendship is a potent force that has often softened stiff resolve; perhaps this truth was now beginning to inform a more enlightened mind. Still, Hat endured while savoring this very exclusive tipple. He knew that this would have to do him for the night; there was no way he could face the crowd in the Poachers' Inn, with nothing at all to bring on offer.

At the end of it all, he sighed with relief. This was not one of his best performances and he learned a thing or two about his place in the social order. Few words were spoken in the Doctor's car as the two made their way home, each with his own assessment of how it was. Dr Clarke was more upbeat as he said good night to the dull demeaned, but his lighter mood must surely have been for another reason. "I am not going to give up on that man just yet; I think he might be worth pursuing a bit further; I could always try another approach so leave it with me for a while longer."

"Thank you Doctor all the same but it seems to me we will be taking the legal route after all. I'm afraid its going to take a lot more than your silly ball game to bring that man to his senses. I will have to call another meeting."

But another meeting was what poor McGivern feared the most; he had wasted time on what appeared to be a foolish mission and the others would delight in telling him so. In his dilemma of knowing what to do, it occurred to him that he was still empowered with the right to consult with their legal mentor. This time he was going alone, except for his driver, Packie Gordon.

Packie could be his other man and the verifier of his report. He was also custodian of the fighting fund that the local people had subscribed to so generously, so he had immediate access to the hackney fare.

With dogged determination, he instructed O'Donnell to instigate court action immediately. As far as he was concerned, the kid gloves were well and truly off. This show of tenacity was for Gordon's benefit as much as anything else. This was the message he wanted him to take back and promulgate. Yes, McGivern is ready for the fight. But this was not the kind of fight that Pauric O'Donnell had in mind. In his professional opinion it was the Fisheries Board that should be taking Major West to task.

"So it is up to you to force them into some kind of action. That is why I advised that one of your members take a case against the Board for failing to protect his legal right. I must also warn that any form of court proceedings is going to take a considerable length of time and would not likely be heard before the end of the current fishing season. So my advice is to go back to your people and tell them about this possible course of action. Then you can decide on who is best to front the case."

The fighting spirit quelled once more, McGivern returned with work to do. Should he call a meeting or approach a friend? Less problematic would be the latter option. It was Billy Mullen he had in mind and Packie Gordon agreed with him. He would wait a while before facing the crowd to tell them about what was now likely to happen and he knew that Mullen would be most acceptable. This he could tell them was the only option and it had the authority of Pauric O'Donnell, so it was simply a case of wait and see.

Chapter Nine

It was nearing harvest time and the weather was giving cause for concern. Mrs. West and her men, with the help of Christy Flood, were busy in the cattle pens. The yard was a hive of activity that morning; they were selecting the heaviest and fattest of the bullocks to be transported by rail to an abattoir up the country. This was work that had to be done before commencement of the long and tedious task of saving the harvest. There was a stifling heat that tended to make the operation all the more difficult. Apart from that, the mood was civil, as Christy Flood judged each beast.

"Too thin, too bare of the flanks, hardly heavy enough. All of them will come in time. Sure there are plenty here to pick from."

Christy was in the height of good humor. The good lady had informed him the evening before that he was to oversee the slaughter, which would take place in the abattoir very early the next morning. He would be traveling on the same train that carried this massive load of prime beef cattle, and the Major himself was for taking the car later in the evening. This was the first time for Christy to accompany the Major on such a mission, as it was something the Missus always liked to do herself. But on this occasion she had to be on home duties to prepare for yet another house party; there were a number of guests from across the water due to descend upon the place on Friday evening. There was another unspoken reason for Christy's inclusion; neither she or the Major were entirely happy with the weighing and grading procedure for the last consignment of cattle they had brought there. She was most disappointed not to be traveling on this occasion; it was an errand she always looked forward to and it included an overnight stay in a Hotel not far from the abattoir. But her loss was Christy's gain and he certainly showed his delight. It was he that would be lapping up the grandeur along with the Major, who would have to foot the bill.

Later, his joy took him in the direction of the kitchen where the two ladies, Madge and Norah, were preparing food for the midday meal. He took a seat in the back pantry knowing that the good ladies would serve him an appetizing snack. This was his first visit there in a while.

To Norah's great relief he had progressed to having more frequent access to the main residence. He had obviously earned the confidence of the Wests and it was in their interest to afford him a status far beyond what is given to a mere worker. For them, he was invaluable as a judge of livestock. He knew the exact value, as well as the potential, of every animal he purchased for them, so for that he was receiving an added reward. His talk with the housemaids was relaxed and jovial, yet it was obvious he wanted to chat to Norah alone. He got a brief opportunity for this when Madge left the kitchen to attend to other duties in the main dining room and Norah was left to clear the table where he had just eaten.

"Norah Girl, I will be living high tonight with no one less than the boss himself. Pity it wasn't you instead of him."

He then went on to tell her everything about where he was going, why he was going and where he would be staying; one of the best Hotels in the country, the very one that the Major and his Missus have always stayed in, not just an ordinary old boarding house.

"Yes, and I will try and get something nice to bring back to you, something special from me to you."

This was to Norah a reminder that the bold Christy had not given up on his ambitions towards her, and it only took the bit of heightened spirit to spur him into action. Although deeply enraged, she let it pass without comment. At the same time, she tried hard to conjure an expression of disdain towards his suggestive behavior. It was Madge's returning that brought welcome relief. Christy thanked them with a smile of simple pleasure. They watched as he crossed towards the yard with a slithering stroll, the happiest man in leather boots. He was cleanly dressed and carried a sack that held his welly boots and overalls; he was ready for the task ahead. At the railway station, he supervised what was a major operation; the entire workforce loaded the cattle on to many wagons, each containing an allotted number of animals for transport within the law. Mrs. West wished him luck.

"It'll naw be his fault if he isney lucky up in that place tonight. If there is a chancy wan aboot, Flood'll mack her aff."

This was Vincent Wilkie's assessment of how good Christy's excursion was going to be. There was jovial good humor among the party as they made their way back from the station along with Mrs. West, who was enjoying the craic, particularly what had been revealed about her valued stock agent. It was steamy news for her, and Wilkie was making it even hotter. She laughed convulsively as he talked about poor Christy's hunger and better still about his personal endowment. Some would say it was no place for a lady but this one was different; she was well fit for the best of it and even more.

It was a lengthy train journey but the summer brightness made it pleasant and relaxing; the sights of a strange countryside captured his interest. He counted the cattle in every field and from time to time had thought about Norah Mullen. At the other end, his work commenced as he watched the men from the abattoir unload the wagons, which was for them, but a daily routine. He walked with them the short distance from the train station to the holding pens at the back of the slaughtering floor. There was an air of authority in the way he checked to ensure that each and every beast was accounted for. He asked them what time the kill would commence. On account of the distance he had traveled, his would be taken for the early morning shift; he would need to be on the line by seven-thirty.

It was clean up time on the factory floor, and Christy watched the entire operation as men with water hose toiled to remove the residue of that day's bloody scene.

Workingmen and women too were leaving the place at the end of day; the sight of a stranger was nothing new and some of them smiled 'Good evening, sir'. "A fine lump of a woman she is in all; might see her later on; ah but sure then himself will be there as well". With an early start and the boss on hand his lustful thinking was put to rest. The Major praised him for a job well done as they shared a table, having a bite to eat. The hotel was small but big on quality. To the simple man it was far from real. It was an easeful night for both of them: a quiet drink while talking shop. Christy, with his country ways, would like to have engaged the company of some ordinary-looking folk that were standing at the counter, but this was not the ways of an over-regimented gentleman. However, an early night would leave him in better shape for keeping an eye on the weighing scales next morning. He was entrusted with a job to do and was not going to be foxed by some town trickster whose game might well be roguery.

Well on time, he took his stand and the Major too stayed for an hour or more but by mid-morning tea break, he had had enough. Seeing how Christy was so well in control, he deserved to be left to get on with it on his own.

"Christy, I will be leaving you for a while; I want to take a drive into Dublin Town, because it happens to be a place I have never been to; I should be back with you by mid-afternoon. I can see that you are doing a very thorough job in there; I value your knowledge and judgment and I leave with the assurance that my business is in the hands of a man I can trust."

"That you can be sure of, Major. None of those boys could pull the wool over my eyes; go and do whatever you have to; we will probably be finished when you get back; them cattle are killing out well mind you."

Then, with a more modest kind of look plus a wee hint of coyness, he asked for a favor with a twenty-pound note in his hand.

Sir, would you mind going into a middling decent kind of jewelers shop and get me a nice piece that you would think a suitable gift for a young woman."

The Major's somber manner suited Christy on this occasion; he treated the request with casual dignity and asked was he prepared to spend that amount. Through his wife, he had heard all about Christy's besotted infatuation, but such goings on could never stir his curiosity. He would do his best for this trustworthy man and asked for further guidance as to what he had in mind.

The killing was over at three o'clock. Christy collected his documents and walked back to the hotel. He knew the results were very good and all credit due to him. Having consumed both food and drink, he began to wonder why the Major had not come back and it now well past the hour of four. This was not a worry for him as he sat in comfort with people around to give him chat, even the woman behind the bar. They knew his tongue was Donegal and he had the mark of a cattleman with a healthy appetite for bottled Guinness.

After six, and with a luring aroma coming from the direction of the dining room, a slight uneasiness began to take hold of him. "What's keeping that man so bloody long?" For the sake of his bladder he gave up on the Guinness, not wanting to be too much of an imposition on the Major during the long drive home. Then, taking a soft seat away from the bar counter, he took the bundle of weight dockets out of his pocket and began to re-examine what he already knew. Close on seven, the boss appeared and looked like a man who had just purchased the Central Bank.

"Christy, I have been delayed longer than I intended; a lot has happened since I left you this morning; come for dinner and I will tell you more."

As they sat down at the dinner table, Christy handed him the abattoir dockets, which showed he had had a profitable day. Without giving them as much as a fleeting glance, he pushed them carelessly into his pocket and commenced to tell a most amazing story. He began by saying how good fortune must have had a hand to play in Christy asking him to do that shopping errand.

"Not knowing my way around the strange city, I had to park on the way in, somewhere along the place called the Quay's, then proceeded on foot in the direction of the city centre. I wanted to see Nelson's Column on the main street as well as the National Gallery and perhaps Trinity College, if time permitted. Taking in the city sights while walking along at an easy pace, I observed a variety of trading establishments all along the busy street. One of these shops bore a sign that said Jewelry and Haberdashery. To me, this looked like the kind of place one could pick up a bargain, so I decided to go in and have a look. The man and woman inside looked like they were the owners of the business that carried a massive and varied amount of items both new and secondhand. They were a friendly couple and the woman came to my assistance as I moved towards the jewelry counter to do the business on your behalf."

"The choice was a little gold watch that was neat and dainty. It was brand new, as I knew it had to be for the purpose intended. I judged it to be of the highest quality so I think your lady friend will like it. Being a man with an eye for a bargain and with an interest in looking at things old and rare, I asked to be shown the older stuff. Two metal trays were set on top of the counter in front of me. The woman assistant said that one of the trays contained items that were of high value while the other also contained good stuff, but of a lesser value. Even with my trained military background, I was ill prepared for the shock that awaited me as I began to examine the lot that was supposedly of higher value. There, before my very eyes, were two items of jewelry that I had little trouble in recognizing. One was a heavy gold chain with pendant attached and the other a large cameo brooch in a pure gold surround. I was absolutely certain that these belonged to my good wife and had been taken by the burglars that night of the break-in."

"Composing my thoughts before reacting to the shock discovery, I continued going through each of the trays and examined almost every piece. This allowed me time to think about what the next move should be and how best to go about it, without giving the game away. My thinking served me very well and devised a strategy that was really clever. I chose the two items that were selling at a price somewhat below their intrinsic value, then paid a deposit to have them set aside to be collected later in the day. Taking temporary leave of the proprietorial attendants, I quickly made my way to O'Connell Street, where I got directions to the nearest Garda Station. An efficient young officer took a thorough statement from me in an atmosphere that was friendly and comfortable, then contact was made with the local Garda for verification of my story."

The story authenticated, little time was lost before the Garda car was on its way to the jeweler's shop, where the man and woman were taken in for questioning. From there on, I knew little of what was happening beyond being told that the guards were following a definite line. Apart from the anxiety of being held for all these hours as well as not knowing what was happening, I felt rather relaxed in the company of the guards and being treated to tea and biscuits. At the same time, I was greatly relieved to be taken into the interview room for an update on developments and more so to be told that they had located the source of the stolen items. The investigation led them to a country house a few miles outside the city of Derry where the police authorities found other valuable items, including a William Turner painting."

It was a lengthy story and Christy listened attentively without interrupting the speaker. To him it seemed a very long time since the Major parted company with him at the abattoir, yet an amazing amount of investigating work had taken place in what was really a short space of time. Although they were guilty of being the recipients of stolen goods, the shop owners were most co-operative with the Garda investigation. On a few occasions they had purchased goods from this man with a Donegal accent and driving a northern registered vehicle. He always assured them that the stuff was bona fide and brought by himself and his Derry friend from a Glasgow supplier. Armed with this information, the local Garda, in co-operating with their northern counterparts, were quickly on the trail of a clever criminal gang. It was a short yet fruitful investigation, one that should be hailed a triumph for two co-operating police forces and it was born out of Christy Flood's romantic dream.

Yet, Christy seemed not fully able to savor the delights of his fervent friend; not far from his mind were thoughts of young Ryan in whose downfall he had played a part. From what the Major had told him, the authorities on both sides of the border were pretty certain that the actual robbery was carried out by a gang from well outside the area. Now it bothered him to think that he allowed jealousy to drive him to the point of shameful vindictiveness. But this was something he would have to live with; there was no way he could make amends without an admission that would deeply offend his own dignity. For that reason, these would remain solitary thoughts. He could never bring himself to sharing them with anyone, least of all the man who trusted him.

So, that considered, it was best to be rid of all forms of negative thinking and a more positive mind-set told him that his appraisal of the young fellow was a secret between the Wests and himself. Now with the Major in such exuberant mood, they could eat and drink to the success of an eventful day. He had informed Mrs. West by telephone from the Garda Station; she was understandably overjoyed and looked forward to the return of her precious adornments. This news gave her an added reason to look forward to the weekend party and to share with her friends the delights of good fortune. There was slight disappointment when the Major arrived back at Elmwood without bringing the items with him; it seemed they had to remain in Garda custody until after the matter was finally resolved through the court of law. But this was not a major issue for either the Major or his wife; the important thing was that their valuables had been recovered and would soon be back where they belonged.

By their standards, the party was a huge success. Madge and Norah observed all the usual faces, including the aloof David who arrived with the briefcase on Thursday evening. There was however one noticeable addition to the guest list in the persons of Dr and Mrs. Clarke, but not a sign of Hat McGivern or Orr from the Fisheries Board. Norah had not seen Christy Flood since his return from the abattoir business nor had she heard anything about the nice gift that awaited her. In relating the story about the chance discovery in a Dublin jewelry shop the Major was careful not to disclose any information about his reason for being there. He was that kind of man who did not discuss the affairs of others, so Norah's surprise was not going to be spoiled by idle talk.

Right then she had a lot more to think about after hearing the news that the house burglars had been apprehended and that court proceedings were to follow. But her deepest concern was for Benny, the young man she never ceased to think about. The sooner he gets to hear about this the better, she thought. All through the party she talked to Madge whenever both of them got the chance. She did not attempt to hide her emotion, saying how deeply it hurt to see her friend being wrongly accused. There was the added pain of her feeling partly responsible for him coming under suspicion in the first place. Madge was the most comforting of listeners. She assured that everything was now going to be all right and that she would see to it that the good news got to his mother first thing in the morning, perhaps even before Benny goes to work.

Madge and the other two helper ladies would be going home as soon as the after-party clean up had been completed. As on such occasions, Norah would be staying overnight. For her, it would be an extra early start next morning to prepare the kitchen and dining room for breakfast. There was a spirited atmosphere that seemed to permeate the entire proceedings of the party; for the women the dullness of past events was not near so prevalent. This had to be for one reason and one reason only; the Major had recovered his precious landscape and the Missus was happy too. They both engaged themselves more noticeably with Dr and Mrs. Clarke. All of their visiting friends, including the adroit David, were introduced to them. Mrs. Clarke then obliged the company with her rendition of 'The Hills of Donegal' to the accompaniment of David on the piano. But the most amazing thing of all happened after the three working ladies had left; Norah was brought in by Mrs. West to join the company.

It was not really her scene, nothing to compare with a night of fun and dance with her friends in the local hall. At the same time it was different; for this short while she was a guest rather than a servant and that was a new experience for her. Apart from Mrs. West and one elegant-looking young lady with an English accent, there was little greeting afforded the newest guest. This particularly nice lady complimented Norah and the others on the quality of their house manner. After singing her second song and recognizing the local girl, Mrs. Clarke came over to Norah for a neighborly chat. She was known by everyone as a good-natured woman and her refined singing voice was most pleasant to listen to. Norah would take the occasional glance in the direction of the pianist; in this situation he appeared more affable and friendly. But this side of David was only affordable to his own class of people that made up the main body of this gathering. Yet she continued to harbor a strange curiousness about this man more than all of the other visitors that had ever frequented Elmwood House.

It was not until the evening after, that Norah finally got back to the comfort of her own home; there she could relax and tell Billy about all the latest happenings. She told him everything about the party and the people who were at it. In the present climate he thought it best not to be thinking about settling the score with David even though his displeasure from their last encounter had not subsided. Nor would he bother to tell Keatley that this man was back and presumably available for the reprimand that he would only be too willing to administer. But wise to the consequences of thoughtless action, he judged it best that this contemptible man be left alone for the time being. Billy Mullen was glad for his daughter's sake that the matters of the famous break-in had finally been put to rest and that justice would free the innocent from blame.

Chapter Ten

The innocent was Benny Ryan, the son of modest parents that wept with relief at the news Madge Crawford's messenger had brought them earlier in the day. But joy for these good folks was short-lived indeed, as the fate of irony played on them the strangest trick. It was into the afternoon before Mrs. Ryan found someone to take her to the site where Benny worked. He was standing on a ladder painting an undercoat onto an upstairs window when she arrived to surprise him with the welcome news. The reaction of an energetic young man to such news is predictably one of unrestrained elation but unfortunately for Benny he overstepped the mark and seemed to forget where he was standing. It was a lengthy fall and on to coarse rubble on the ground beneath; he cried and groaned lamentably from the severity of the pain as he lay beside his frightened mother. Soon many others were on the scene to lend assistance, but it was obvious that the young man had sustained serious injuries. The tender hands of his loving mother, who prayed for God to spare her lovely boy, were caressing his head and trembling body.

There seemed a glimmer of hope in the doctor's appraisal in so far as he could see no signs of serious damage to the head, but the left leg was in pretty bad shape. Throughout all of this and the ambulance journey to the hospital, Mrs. Ryan kept talking and praying to Benny, who appeared to have lost consciousness. She thought for a moment about the good news she brought him and in view of what had happened, was it such good news after all? But faith led her towards more positive thinking, to thoughts that told her that she had a good son and that God was not for taking him from her. She slipped her fingers inside his shirt below the collar, and found the miraculous medal that she had pinned there, after ironing it for him at the weekend. Coincidental to this act, she watched his blue eyes open and look at her; he said, 'Mammy, what happened?' then drifted off again.

By the time his father and sister got to the hospital there were more hopeful signs that Benny's life was not in total danger. He had regained consciousness and was heavily sedated; he received the sacrament of the sick from a caring and friendly priest. The family was told that the injuries to his leg and body were serious and that an effort would be made to put the pieces of shattered bone together as soon as he was judged well enough for the operating theatre. That was unlikely to happen before the next morning and the rule was that only one member of the family would be permitted to stay overnight with the patient. While all three of them wanted to be the one, it was mother who won the argument. A sobbing sister, Kathleen, and her dad had to leave but would be back to see their dear Benny again in the morning.

With the aid of sedation, he slept most of the night while his tired mother sat beside him on an easy chair, sometimes resting her head on the edge of his pillow. At seven o'clock, she was taken to a waiting room where she was treated to tea and toasted bread. That and a touch of freshening up made her feel a lot better. She got back just in time to be told that her son had been taken to theatre and would probably be there for at least two hours. This she accepted as encouraging news; there is nothing so reassuring as to know that something is being done and she thanked God for that small mercy. As a typical Irish mother, Mrs. Ryan relied heavily on the power of prayer and soon made her way to the nearest church where the first of the Sunday masses would be at eight. After hearing mass, she would have the church to herself to light candles and pray many rosaries. With a worried and sleepless night behind her, she allowed herself the comfort of sitting in front of the altar rather than the genuflection of mortification. There, in the solace of silence, she found the comfort of being in the Divine presence, and it told her Benny would be spared.

It was an experience she wanted to hold on to and she found it hard to disturb herself by walking away from a presence that so enraptured her. But in her spiritual journey, more than two hours had elapsed and the second mass was about to begin. She was astonished to discover this, and became anxious to get back to see her ailing son. Still in the slumber of anesthesia, she kissed his forehead and sat down beside him with his hand in hers; he was back in the same bed where they had spent the vigil night. The waiting was not all that long before he opened his slumbery eyes, that looked up towards the ceiling and then to the hand that mother held. His voice was low and muffled; again he asked what had happened and why he was in such a place. In the gentlest of whispers, she told him the story about her bringing him the good news and then the fall that hurt his body.

"Benny, it is only a hurt that will soon get better; your leg is broken and has been fixed again by the doctor; they tell me that at your age the healing will be fast; you will be as good as ever in no time. So don't worry son, you will soon be back home with us and we will help you get back to where you were before. Time will make you better, just like it has given you back your good name."

He responded by tightening his grip on her hand. Like the gentle mother, she could see that his only interest right then was to rest his aching body. The talking could wait until another time. Instead, she could talk to her husband and daughter, both of whom had an uneasy night and were now on their way to see how Benny was. Both of them placed a soothing hand on his warm head but Kathleen's tears could not hold back and fell on the cheek that she had kissed. As the day wore on, confidence grew and fuelled in them a brighter outlook. The two women headed downtown for what they called a quick look around. Dad, on his own, was left with Benny. John Ryan was a homely man whose voice was seldom heard. He was a council road worker who spent his leisure time at home. Never a man to show emotion, yet family upsets disturbed him deeply. Rather he'd got hurt than see it happen to any of them. He walked away to allow the nurses tend the needs of the patient and could feel the hurt each time Benny moaned, as they tried to move him in the bed.

These four were the sum total of the Ryan household and were the epitome of what the family was all about; out of love and faithfulness their support for each other was unconditional. Now, here they were together in a fretful strange surrounding doing what they had to do, in faith that God would see them through. They were also a neighborly people that liked to ease a neighbor's grief and always ready with a helping hand. For that reason, no one but Christy Flood ever passed cruel judgment on young Ryan, but that was done out of jealousy rather than malice, and told to no one but Major and Mrs. West. Still, it was that word of cruel judgment that caused the young man to be sacked from his position on Elmwood Estate. The consequences of any action can at times be far reaching and nowhere is this truer than in the case of Benny Ryan. A triangular relationship encompassing Norah, Benny and Christy, the burglary followed by the sacking of Benny and his subsequent move to a building site; this was the unfortunate progression that has brought us to this hospital bed.

Norah was given the news on her way out of church after Sunday mass; the word was slow at reaching the home area on account of the Ryan's being away most of the time. This news was fiercely disturbing for her; she had agonized about this young man ever since that evening he left the Estate and him under grave suspicion. While it had been a relief to be told that his name was cleared of wrongdoing, it was nothing more than an affirmation of what she knew already. But with his character restored, it bewildered her beyond comprehension to think that he is now prevented from relishing the joys of what it means. Her father too was available to hear about the freak accident that occupied their thoughts and talks on the way back from mass and right through Sunday dinner. Their fondest wish was that he would make a full recovery and Norah prayed that the happiest of his days were all in front of him.

By Monday morning and the start of another working week, word was abroad that Benny was seriously injured but definitely out of danger; his stay in hospital would be prolonged. Mrs. Ryan returned to homemaking. John and daughter went back to work. They would all make do with evening visits from there on. On the Estate, it also got a hearing from the men in the harvest fields. They were now in the throws of the busy season and the weather was showing signs of promise. Vincent drove the tractor that towed the binder round the field of heavy-eared corn, while the Missus herself acquired a liking for the binder seat. She was well able to manage the operating levers.

"If things were right, that young fellow should be here stooking corn on this glorious harvest day, instead of lying down in that hospital bed."

This comment from a more serious Vincent Wilkie was intended for Mrs. Wests' ears more than they were for his fellow workers. He went on to say how all of them knew Ryan to be a decent young chap and wondered how anybody could think otherwise of him. It was not a comfortable subject for the affable lady to break into, but to ignore it she knew was not an option for her and could be taken as an offense to common decency. At the same time, she was not answerable to the people they employed or obligated to give reasons for the actions of her husband. In a more subdued tone of voice, she concurred with Vincent's assessment and said that she too found Benny to be a fine young man.

"It upsets us greatly to hear about what has taken place and I only wish we were able to undo what has happened to him. I know mistakes have been made, but unfortunately what has happened cannot be reversed. People do tend to over-react in the wake of bad things happening to them; we were deeply disturbed when our home was broken into; the Major and his precious Turner Painting I would rather forget. The fact that he was in the house that evening with Norah the maid and subsequently told lies about it to the Guards, had the unfortunate effect of putting him under suspicion. It also appears that he has a strong attraction towards Norah and over-imposed himself on her friendship. You see, the Major takes the view that Benny had no right to be in the house under any circumstances that evening. Others too have expressed the same opinion, including our friend Christy Flood."

On that she stopped abruptly, stung perhaps by a realization that she had said more than she should and in the wrong place. She quickly got back to extolling the boy's virtues, saying how sorry she was about how he had been treated. But alas, it was all in vain; the proverbial horse had well and truly bolted.

"Ah a might hay known the horny hoor had a say in it too. It bothered him a lot to see wee Norah and the young fellow getting on so weel. He wasnay is quick at condemning his own boy, when he helped Rusty McKeague tay wreck the place and smash the new boat as weel."

Realizing she had just committed one serious faux pas in dropping Christy's name, this nonetheless had to be a revelation for Mrs. West as she stood amid a bout of laughter from the other harvesters. In effect, it relieved her of the need to comment any further on the contentious issue of Benny Ryan. It was more in demand than request that she asked Wilkie to clarify what he had just said. What and about whom was he talking? The boy in question was none other than young Harrigan, who along with Harry Doran's son, was now out on probation for a crime of willful intent against the Estate and its owner.

Dumbfounded was how the poor woman described her reaction to Wilkie's disclosure, yet it was nothing more than the revisiting of local gossip that was rife in the area some nineteen or twenty years earlier. The circumstance of Chris Harrigan's conception and birth was widely known throughout the parish at that time. Christy kept a lower than usual profile for that period, but remained in the area throughout. He still had his business to see about. Did he pay her the 'ten bob a week?' Well, that was the secret never to be revealed. There was much speculation abroad, but sly Christy kept them guessing while the Harrigans held the silence of modesty? This diversion away from the tragic plight of Benny Ryan captivated the mind of Mrs. West into speculative curiosity; she had a morbid desire to hear more.

"I could imagine him quite a handsome guy in those days, as you would probably have known, Vincent."

"Aye, and him hung like a randy jackass on the prowl, always way a hungry look in his eye if there happens to be a bit of skirt aboot, ah but sure never say Keatley."

"Quite a man by all accounts then," she replied, through laughter of amazement.

Leaving the men to get on with their work after their snack of bread and cold bottled tea, she walked towards the Land Rover for a jar of drinking water.

"That'll gay her something tay think and talk aboot for a while," laughed Wilkie to the others as they each commenced 'four sheaves per stook.'"

Then, it was all work and no chat as, to the noisy rhythm of the harvest machine, the two lapped the circuit of the cornfield countless times.

Christy's checked past did not in any way reduce his standing in the Elmwood household. The Major paid slight attention to such inconsequentials.

As for herself, she thought him an interesting subject. Regarding his negative assessment of the unfortunate Benny Ryan, she could understand his foolish attraction to Norah Mullen and his failure to see her lack of interest. But what they had done was their own callous doing and they would have to accept it without apportioning blame to the man they needed and trusted.

Another discomforting affect of what had happened was the way it appeared to be affecting Norah. Madge Crawford was able to tell them of the girl's anxiety about Benny and how she partly blames herself for his misfortune. With growing concern, they were able to see increasing signs of this as the busy days of harvest edged them into another week; what, they wondered, can be done?

Four weeks had elapsed and Benny was now out on a wheelchair and able to propel himself around the hospital wards and corridor with the plaster cast leg bolt outright in front of him. Apart from the customary itching, he was not overly afflicted by pain and discomfort, so there was every chance of him getting home in a week or so. His recovery was assured. Physically, it was just a matter of time; but what kind of recovery, he was now beginning to wonder? These were questions now beginning to bother him and ones that the specialists were not yet ready to answer. Nor was he, in truth, ready to ask. The comforting words of reassurance that were spoken in kindness by the nursing staff as well as family and friends, were not enough to ease his fret.

"By Christmas time you will be taking us dancing to your Coolaghy Hall and you with feet like Fred Astaire," said the pretty young nurse that manicured his finger and toenails.

Heartfelt comments they certainly were; helpful gestures from caring people. There was a definite safeness in being there, but Benny's fears were his own and real. To himself alone, he asked in vain: was this the end of his sporting career? Afraid to ask because of what he might be told, for now, it was easier to bear the stress of uncertainty in the bosom of easeful respite. A footballing career that had every sign of promise and achievement, now facing the prospect of termination, was not a scenario he was yet ready to contemplate. Though yet unsaid, the orthopedic specialist had already concluded that participation in forms of sport involving speed and physical agility would be most unlikely for Benny Ryan. The disappointing news was first given to his parents, who ruefully passed it on to well-wishing friends and neighbors. It was but a bearable disappointment for the board of Derry City Football Club. While in trial, Benny showed great potential, they had still not reached a stage where his talent was relied upon totally.

Whatever about the business institution at the Brandywell Park, the Ryan family, as well as those friends and neighbors, were deeply upset at the news. They felt the pain of his loss almost as much as they knew it was going to hit poor Benny. His cherished dream was the one thing that sustained him throughout that stressful period of living under the shadow of blame. Now he was going to need help in coming to terms with the living reality that all of this had come to a sad end but that he still had a valuable life to live. That was the hopeful message coming from good people that rallied to the support of a distraught family in a way that made them consider how fortunate they really were after all. This was a more positive kind of thinking. A kind they would have to adopt and sustain for the sake of moving on to new and brighter days. As a step in that direction, they began to count their blessings; first and foremost Benny was alive and making progress that would hopefully see him home within the week. But equally good was the restoration of his good name; he will again be able to look everyone straight in the eye with not a hint of judgment being cast upon him.

Packie Gordon brought Mrs. Ryan to collect her son and his few belongings at the hospital just two days after being told the unsavory truth by the man whose excellence had saved his leg. Although still at a low, the couple of days allowed him time to come to terms with the situation and get to a state of half acceptance. He was being gently nudged in this direction by the medical staff that was endeavoring to induce in him a more hopeful outlook with the possibility of him nurturing and developing talents of a different kind, as he was undoubtedly a gifted young man. Packie and one of the nurses helped him into the passenger seat where he would have more legroom on the journey home. She was an attractive-looking girl and in her duty of seeing the patient off the premises, he thanked her in a way that showed the liking he had for her. A happy mother added her goodbye and asked that her gratitude be conveyed to all who had cared for her darling son.

The drive home was light-hearted and chatty. Care was taken to avoid the emotive subject of Benny's future. Packie would be well able to converse on other matters. With the passage of almost eight weeks, the country scene would have altered considerably from what it was like that morning he left for work. The harvest sheaves were gathered in which told them that the world was safe. Autumn shades give added beauty to a rich expanse that had laid a generous bounty and now reclining in the epilogue of fulfillment. These facts of nature were more real to him that day than ever before and amidst the chat, he wondered why. Why, indeed, could he see such things like they were new? Was it because of his lengthy confinement or perhaps the dawning of a new sense of value? Nearer to home and the old familiar sights of a land that Benny knew, and it too attending the routine of tradition. "Them young scoundrels!" shouts Packie the driver as a large Kerr Pink smashed against the windscreen in front of them as Mrs. Ryan let a scream of fright. It came from a group of young people that were gathering potatoes in Mulrine's field. It was a dangerous act, but Benny laughed, because it was the kind of thing he had done himself not so many years before. Then, within a mile from home, came the sobering reminder of what was lost and gone forever, as he looked across at Cross Roads Park with its posts and nets still intact after the Summer Cup. A wave of anguish then beset him and he felt the need to scream and shout, "Why has this been done to me?" But the need gave way to sane composure, and Benny looked the other way.

The days ahead were not going to be easy ones; there would be many recurrences of the tormented mind losing control but work towards cure had already begun and many friends had a role to play. Mrs. West was not a friend but perhaps in time she could well become one, even in a less engaging way. She certainly had the benevolent touch. The Major had gone alone to the river to try out the refurbished speedboat. He was toying with the idea of holding an Autumn water carnival, as it was now well past the fishing season and feelings were cooling somewhat. Hat McGivern was still waiting to hear from the Solicitor about a possible date for the proposed court hearing, where Billy Mullen would challenge the Fisheries Board. It was shortly after teatime and Norah was still in the kitchen with Madge. They were both preparing to leave for home when the good lady called them into the living room. Norah followed Madge in, accepting the small glass of sherry that made them feel like visiting guests though it also begged the question, 'What is all this about?'

Madge knew fine well it was about dear Norah, still being bothered by tormenting thoughts, and she also knew that Mrs. West was anxious to help if that were at all possible.

"Norah, I think it would be a nice thing for you to go and visit Benny in hospital and I would be very happy to take you there any evening."

Madge agreed it was a wonderful idea for the two to meet and talk to each other; it was obvious that none of them knew about Benny being at home. In view of all that had taken place, Norah was not so sure about being able to face him and there was the added difficulty that his family was more than likely to be there as well.

"Then so be it, but have you considered that he might be pleased to see you and that your gesture of caring could make him feel good. Please let me take you. It will be good for both of us."

Norah's emotions were beginning to show; it touched her to see that others as well as her dad were so concerned for her well being; she found it hard to hold her tears in the glow of a warmth that was true and blissful. But the generosity had more to give; the Wests were planning a two-week break to a country house in the Yorkshire Dales not far from where the Major grew up. With delightful early October weather, Mrs. West was determined to be traveling within a matter of days and had already told the Major to forget about water carnivals for the remainder of this year. She knew how much he liked going back there for the occasional visit and would eventually fall into line with what she had already planned. Again she looked to Norah with a benevolent smile.

"Norah, we would very much like if you would come with us. I have a special reason for going there this time and I know himself will like it too. I am not going to say anything more about it at this stage but if you can manage to come with us you will be able to see for yourself, and we will be needing you."

Again Madge was quick to concur with what the lady had suggested. She was nevertheless at a loss as to what the special reason could possibly be. But the question did not occupy her mind for an unduly long time. To her, these were a different class of people and who could possibly know their ways? Norah, now recovering from her emotional stir, was endeavoring to cogitate what her employer had just said. For her, this would be an enormous undertaking. Perhaps more than with what she would be able to cope. But the demands of duty must be obeyed. After all, the lady did say, 'We will be needing you.'

"Yes, Mrs. West. If you are going to need me, I will do as you say and

I want to thank you for being so kind to me since the first day I came here."

"That is because you are a good girl and an honest worker too, just like your friend Madge here. But we must not forget about your other friend, Benny. We will go to the hospital tomorrow evening. Then we can head for the Dales with lighter hearts."

"Why wouldn't you go dear girl? It would only do you the world of good and you well deserve a bit of a holiday. Don't worry about me. I can still manage on my own."

In their father-daughter evening chat, Norah related the entire episode involving herself, Madge and the lady of the house to a delightedly attentive Billy Mullen. He was able to tell her that Benny Ryan was back at home since the day before and that was the only place he could be seen or visited. But going to the Ryan home and meeting Benny's parents and sister was not something Norah felt quite ready for. Yet she knew that Mrs. West would not allow such a trivial matter deter her from doing what they had already planned, so refusing to go would hardly now be an option for her. Pulling the last drag out of a fag butt, Billy laughed with an accompanying little cough.

"Norah, it looks like you don't have much choice at this stage but to go ahead. But don't be a bit afraid. These are the nicest and most civil people you could ever meet. You will be able to tell me the same tomorrow night."

It was a short drive down to Coolaghy. Norah had dressed for the occasion but it was not enough to hide an apprehension that was palpable. Mrs. West commented favorably on her overall appearance and that she was the kind of girl that any young man should be delighted to welcome as his visitor.

"As for the others, I should be well enough able to hold them in conversation while you engage with Benny just like you used to do down in the little hall there."

For these somewhat circumspect sweethearts, things could not have worked out better. Just as the well-known Land Rover took the turn below the Ryan abode, they could see a man with two crutches standing by the side of the road. Temporarily dismayed and at a loss for words, Benny just stood there to look at what was the prettiest Norah he had ever set eyes upon. Before a word passed between them, she nervously put a hand on his shoulder and kissed him on the cheek. He responded warmly with a gentle hug. Both of them were now at ease. Just then it only dawned on him to acknowledge the presence of the fine lady who brought Norah to him and he did so with a pleasant smile. With a gesture of pleasance and a smile on her face, Mrs. West handed Norah a tastefully prepared package out of the passenger door that still lay open. "Won't you be needing this?" and then moved off slowly towards the front door of the laborer's cottage.

Benny was still wearing the heavy cast, but well able to amble along with the aid of the crutches. They headed away from the direction of the house and down the road for a short distance. Norah carried the package that Mrs. West helped her to prepare. It contained a variety of fruit and confectionery. She found it difficult to say anything to him about life on the Estate and more so about the events that led to his dismissal from employment there. "Sorry Benny about what has happened to you," was as far as she got before the sobbing muffled the sound of her gentle voice. But to him, it spoke volumes about what was in the heart of this caring being and it made him feel better than he had for a long time. Freeing his hold from the handle of the crutch he took her hand and clasped tightly over it saying how good her presence made him feel. By this time the pair were walking back towards the house where the Lady of Elmwood was drinking tea with her hosts in the warmth of genuine friendship.

She was well able to articulate her thoughts and say what she felt needed to be communicated in the light of recent developments. She had no agenda beyond expressing her sorrow and sympathy to all of them for what had happened. The line of reasoning she had once given to the men in the harvest field about the after-effects of the break-in and, of course, the Major's William Turner, was being played anew to a receptive audience. Without a trace of bitterness or blame, the Ryan family understood and was pleased to learn that the stolen items had been recovered. They found their guest to be very much a woman with the common touch. She was friendly and kind and they deeply appreciated her coming to their humble house. Benny's future was their deepest concern. This fine lady understood, but was unable to comprehend, the implications of a lost footballing career. In their civility, they refrained from over-stating how this was causing much distress to Benny, and indeed, to all of them.

Benny was not for allowing this heavy cross to disturb the sweetness of his precious time with Norah. He knew it was going to be short, and wondered if it would ever happen again. Their talking to each other became more comfortable as the atmosphere between them was of absolute goodness. She told him about her going over to England with the Wests in a couple days time and that she would write to him from there before the end of the two-week stay. He was pleased about having something so nice to look forward to and hoped that it meant more than a simple gesture of friendship. But he liked the way she looked at him as she spoke. They were almost back at the old Land Rover in front of the house. He was looking into her eyes and then they kissed before going in to join the others.

Norah's apprehension about meeting his parents and sister were quickly put to rest. She was indeed worthy of the glowing praises Mrs. West had attributed to her: sweet, pleasant, honest and competent. They made her feel at home and totally at ease in their company. They knew her father and remembered her mother too and were not in the least surprised at her having such high qualities. All six of them spent close to another hour in pleasant conversation and the ease of its flow made the time pass much too quickly. For Norah, this was an accomplishment that relieved much of her worries and Benny wondered would anything further develop from it. They all said their good-byes in the quiet autumn darkness, outside the door of this secluded country cottage. As a parting gesture, Mrs. West turned to Benny saying she hoped in time to be in a position to rectify the damage that has emanated from the mistakes of the past. Leaning on his crutches and looking towards the ground, he failed to response due to an acute twinge of emotion. But the atmosphere was conducive to speedy recovery, as Benny moved closer to Norah and asked would she come to see him again?

Chapter Eleven

She stayed over in the Big House the night before their morning departure. They were taking the early train for the first stage of their journey to Yorkshire. It was a lush and fertile countryside they arrived at, late in the afternoon. The house was close to a quaint village, a few miles outside the old Roman-style city of York. In comparison to Elmwood, it was but a small two-storied dwelling with a rustic, tiled roof. Off the back yard, there was close to a half acre of garden and orchard that appeared to have been well looked after during summer. Many windfall apples and pears lay on the ground beneath the leafless trees that gave them birth and the half- lifeless insects were trying to extend their time feeding off the decaying blackberries along the hedges. It had all the appearance of being a quiet and peaceful kind of place, where the upper class could be at total ease for a couple of weeks.

There was a man waiting to greet and show them the run of the house as well as the local services available; perhaps a local man employed by the Major's friend who owned the property. But the Major was not in need of any such instructions for he had grown up not far from where they now were, so the area was quite familiar to him. It certainly looked an attractive place to be spending a holiday and the weather looked promising to them that liked the outdoor adventure. He pointed out a number of places that he thought might be of interest to Norah, including a large scenic park less than half a mile from the house. They were all a little tired and hungry after the traveling and unpacking. First they would rest for a while before going to the village restaurant that had a reputation for the quality of its food and the efficiency of its service. The meal was leisurely and enjoyable. They spent more than an hour savoring the fare and chatting at ease before returning for an early bedtime.

The Wests were very much at home there and were known by many of the people around. As for Norah, it was all so new and interesting. She had every intention of enjoying her break. That is what she was advised to do by the lady herself that brought her here. They were having a cozy chat in the living room just before retiring for the night.

"We wont be wanting breakfast until after nine in the mornings and that is about all the cooking you will be expected to do over here. There will be other people coming from time to time and some of them may be staying over as well. Tomorrow you will be meeting our son, Stanley, and he will be staying with us for the entire two weeks. In fact, there will be somebody coming with him, but we do not intend to allow any of that impose extra responsibility on you."

This was the son that never once came to Elmwood in the nearly two years since they took over the estate; indeed his name was seldom mentioned by anyone during all of that time. Norah wondered why this was being said to her. After all, preparing breakfast for a couple of extra people was neither here nor there. But nothing further was said about this before going to a strange bed that night; nor was a word spoken in relation to it at the breakfast table next morning. Norah, with her strong work ethic, kept herself occupied all of the forenoon cleaning and tidying around the house and then walked the short distance over to the park. It certainly was a nice place to visit, occupying vast acreage of green grassland as well as lakes and woodlands; the bloom of the flower beds had faded to the brown of autumn as were the leaves falling from the trees. Many people walked the pathways and sat on the bench seats, all of them endeavoring to capture some fleeting glimpse of the ebbing summer.

Most of these people were of an older age group and appeared to be on holiday, just like Norah. Hard to believe she was now one of them. Some of them suffered some form of disability that hampered their movement; one young woman was in a wheelchair and it made the plight of Benny Ryan seem less by far. "Must write that letter to him not later than to-morrow. Better if he gets it before I get back," thought a solitary Norah as she savored the magic of this delightful place. Never before did she have the pleasure of time to herself. There was no compulsion on her to leave the precious moment and answer the call of duty. It was a far cry from the turbulence of everyday life; the fishing dispute with the Major that led to her poor dad almost being criminalized and now the sorry plight of her dear friend, Benny. All of these things, as well as her early life, had impacted on her ability to ever be fully happy.

But she was trying hard not to disturb herself about such things over here. This was her first holiday and holidays were surely ordained to give happiness and pleasure. As she sat observing what was going on around her, she noticed that a young man, attired in running gear, had passed her for the third time and him moving at a steady pace. He had a fine athletic physique and seemed to be taking his training seriously, never taking as much as a lateral glance as he surged repeatedly round the circuit. On completion of the fourth lap and him breathing heavily, he came to a halt at an evergreen shrub close to where she sat. From behind the shrub he retrieved a bottle of water and commenced drinking from it. He kept on the move, at walking pace, as he sipped the deliciously cool liquid. He had a warm and friendly look about him as he said "Hello" to Norah and commented on how tough the run was. It even looked as if he knew something about who she was.

"I hope you like it around here and have a nice holiday. You must surely find it a bit different to what it's like back in Ireland. Oh! My name is Michael, by the way. Did you and your friends enjoy dinner with us last night?"

With such an introduction, the dumbfounded Norah was able to deduce that he was part of the staff or management of the restaurant where they had eaten the night before. In fact, she even remembered seeing him serving drinks to customers at the bar, where they had sat for a while before going into the dining room. His personality made it easy for her to talk comfortably with him. She told him exactly what her position was in the Wests household and how happy she was to be in their employment. He, in turn, was able to tell her how highly the Major and his wife were regarded by the proprietors of the establishment where he worked part-time. As a full time student at the local University, the evening and weekend work suited him ideally.

"Although it is not the kind of work I would want to spend all my days doing, it is nonetheless interesting to a psychology student. I meet some interesting people, not to mention the lovely ones like yourself."

This could only happen in an era of trust and openness; how two strangers were totally at ease and willingly sharing their personal circumstances with each other. Apart from work and studies, athletics was his only other consuming interest. He took his training seriously and pursued a kind of lifestyle that was conducive to a healthy body. He gave her a detailed outline of his daily routine from an early morning run followed by a healthy breakfast and then to the college lecture hall. Now it was his mid-day session that he enjoyed immensely before lunch, which was again of a healthy constituent. All in all, Norah concluded that here was a highly disciplined young man, with a manner that was pleasing to her. Then with the empty bottle in his hand, he took off again at an easy pace saying he would be seeing her again, perhaps in the restaurant. This brief encounter had the effect of making the country girl feel more at home than she thought was ever possible, in this strange land.

The short dander back was an easeful one and with a heightened awareness of herself, she counted her blessings as well as the other good things that were now happening in her life. A large black saloon almost blocked her access to the hall door, which lay wide open; it was almost as big as the Major's old Mercedes, back home at Elmwood. Through the open door a number of voices could be heard in conversation and not all of them recognizable to Norah's sensitive ear. Modesty prevented her from going any further through the main entrance or imposing herself upon the company. Instead, she retreated quietly to the rear of the house and into the kitchen through the back door. That is how she was trained to behave from she first entered into the field of domestic service. After all, she was the servant maid that was expected to know her place in the order of things. This would have been how she perceived the situation; it most certainly had nothing to do with the attitude or behavior of her employers on this occasion.

Alone in the kitchen, she set about attending to some minor matters of household impost, when Mrs. West called on her to join them in the living room. The Major was seated on a soft chair opposite the other two on the couch. Mrs. West stood in the middle of the floor and wasted little time in introducing her guests to Norah.

"Norah, this is our son Stanley who will be staying here with us for a while. Stanley, this is our good friend and housemaid Norah and I know she will be your friend too."

A cold shiver suddenly crept over Norah's entire body, as she looked at Stanley and then the matronly-looking lady seated beside him, who was introduced as Miss Barton. Here she was looking down on the son that she knew existed but had heard little or nothing about. Never in all her time of service, did the Wests ever mention Stanley's name to either her or Madge Crawford. It had been mooted a few times at the beginning that this son was attending law school in London, but that was nothing more than idle speculation on the part of one or two workers claiming to be more in the know than their mates. But Norah was now being brought into the true picture of what had been a family secret, as she looked again at what sat haplessly before her. Stanley was certainly not a student of law or indeed any other academic discipline. She lowered to take his right hand that rose laboriously towards her in a gesture of greeting; the arm and wrist seemed a lot distorted, while the left arm and hand seemed stronger and more active. There was a major indentation that ran from his left temple to near the back of his head; he looked at her with his right eye, the only one that seemed to function. Apart from a few muffled groans, there was no intelligible sound coming from his yawning mouth.

Miss Barton was Stanley's nursemaid and had been from the first day he came into residential care following a motorcycle accident that caused him to have severe brain damage. She was a sturdy, single lady in her early fifties and seemed to be of a friendly disposition. There was an obvious bond of closeness between her and Stanley. Mrs. West came back to the kitchen with Norah. She was kindly sensitive to the initial effect that this shock revelation was having on the young country girl. As a means of addressing the issue, she took Norah into her confidence and began to talk openly about her son and all the disturbing details of his sorry situation.

"He was truly our pride and joy; had been a bright eighteen year-old who was full of life and infectious laughter. At high school he excelled both academically and on the sports field; he was made captain of the senior rugby team in his final year and was assured of admission to law school the following year. That was five years ago and now see how all his plans as well as ours have fallen apart; all we ask for is that he be comfortable with whatever he knows about happiness. That is why Miss Barton has to be with him almost all the time; she is expert in caring for his needs and her kindness makes him very dependent on her. She is a woman with a lot of experience working in the field hospitals with the armed forces during the war years; that is how the Major first came into contact with her. Even though she is employed as one of the carers in this specialized residential centre, it is he who pays a sizable portion of her wages. There are a couple of incapacitated ex-servicemen resident there as well but she is assigned mainly to the care of our Stanley. His presence here will not impinge upon you Norah, but we would like if you could spend some time with him during the day or perhaps take him out on the wheelchair for a while each day now that the weather is fine. Although his ability to respond is very limited, we know that he likes being talked to nonetheless and your gentle voice would be a soothing stimulus for him. With the help of someone to lean on, he can manage to walk a few steps on the level, but that is something that Miss Barton or we ourselves will be attending to."

This talk was now beginning to stir the softness of Norah's emotions; drying her eyes with a handkerchief, she expressed some words of sorrow and a willingness to help. With that, they both went back to join the others in the living room where the Major and Miss Barton were still in deep conversation and took little or no notice of their entry. Now well composed and with a gesture of kindness in her manner, Norah sat down beside Stanley on the side away from his nursemaid.

"Now Stanley, you are again making me jealous. You know I can't let this fellow anywhere near the pretty girls," joked Miss Barton as she continued the chat across to himself. Norah gave a modest laugh and the others laughed as well. Then she took a close look into Stanley's face and was able to see that he was pleased by the comment. Mrs. West then intervened by making a few suggestions about how to make the best of their time together. Addressing Miss Barton by her Christian name 'Elizabeth,' she said how Stanley could hardly survive without having her at hand. But at the same time they wanted her to be able to spend some time away from the tedium of this arduous obligation.

"I think that after lunch, Norah might take Stanley out on the chair and let you and I go into town for a couple of hours. Don't worry Norah, himself will be here if you need him."

The Major nodded his approval and Elizabeth gave her wholehearted support to the suggestion that was very much to her benefit. She felt that the change of focus could only be good for him. Then with her winning smile, Norah again looked at Stanley and took his feeble hand.

"Yes, you and I are going for a long walk this evening, and tomorrow we can go to the park and see the many people as well as the little animals and birds, like the ducks or geese that swim in the ponds. How would you like that, Stanley?"

His response was spluttered and incoherent but she knew he was trying hard to reciprocate the warmth and tenderness she was obviously communicating to him. Through the damage that had been done to a vital portion of his brain, Stanley's mentality had been reduced to the level of a child and Norah could see how well Miss Barton was able to communicate with him at that level. She was glad for the Wests that they had found such a wonderful person to look after their unfortunate son and in spite of her matronly appearance, she was a friendly being as well.

Immediately after lunch, she took Stanley away to attend to some personal needs but before long they were back in the hallway with him seated comfortably on the wheelchair. She warned, in a loving kind of way, that he be good for Norah and to enjoy being out with this new girlfriend. Clasping the cold handles of the chair felt a bit odd at first but that had more to do with the strangeness of the situation Norah now found herself in. A severely handicapped patient was being entrusted into her care. The feeling was odd but good. They moved at a slow pace along the road away from the public park. She wanted to save that adventure for the following day, hopefully before lunchtime when Michael might be out for his run. As they eased along, she leaned down and talked softly into Stanley's ear, telling him about herself and all that she did back at home. She was most perceptive in seeing that he liked the sound of her voice. Then she would stop for a while and take his hand or run her fingers through his hair. There would always be something or other along the roadside or in the fields that she could point out and talk about in an effort to stimulate in him some train of thought.

In this line of specialized work, Norah was totally in the dark. Yet she had a belief in the power of kindness and immediately became fond of working with this special young man. It seemed to fulfill in her a need that was not fully in her consciousness, and Elizabeth Barton was encouraging her to no end. In the days that followed, the two became a familiar sight both on the road and around the park. Her line of communication with Stanley seemed to be increasing at a rate that pleased them both. Most days they would have met Michael who was deeply impressed by the amount of attention that Norah was affording to the one in her care. Indeed, for a student of psychology, she could well be an object subject for investigative study and analysis. But that was not the purpose of this particular student's attraction towards the girl from Donegal. He invited her to come over to the college on one of his free evenings for a social gathering and to meet some of his friends. The place was not too far over the road, so he offered to walk her there and back. Norah was somewhat reluctant to go on such a date. After all, she was in a strange land and had only got to know this man through a casual meeting in a public park. But there was something about him that was likable to her and she agreed to think about his offer before the end of the week.

Right then she was having the best time of her life, holidaying with people that cared about her in a setting that was marvelously beautiful. But strangest of all, she was totally enraptured in her temporary role as attendant to Stanley West, with whom she had formed a kind of bond that was good and fulfilling. With well over a week of her holiday still to be enjoyed, she was in no hurry to embark upon other kinds of adventure, especially the sort she was not all that sure about. Here she could allow herself to feel different in relation to her employers and their guests, sitting down at the breakfast table with the family and then relaxing in conversation with them in the sitting room at night. How different it all was to the organized daily routine of her life with these people back at home. Then she got to thinking about home and how her dad was managing without her; she thought too about Benny Ryan and that letter she promised to write him.

By the end of the first week Norah's daily schedule had formed it-self into a kind of predictable pattern; preparing breakfast at nine, then two leisurely outings with Stanley during the day. The closeness between these two was becoming more and more noticeable to the rest of the household, even to the point of concern about how he might react when all of this comes to an end. But Miss Barton, in her wisdom, was able to reassure that she was well capable of handling the situation when that time came. She was well aware of what was taking place in this new rela-tionship and she could see value in it for Stanley. For him, it was a stimu-lating diversion away from the tedium of routine. Norah too was han-kering some misgiving about her own possible reaction when the time of parting would arrive. She had absolutely no doubt in her mind that she was a positive influence in Stanley's life and it was going to be hard to let go of that. She derived a tremendous feeling of well-being from seeing him try a smile when she held his slender hand while singing a sweet verse into his searching gaze. She knew that too soon it would all be over and he would settle back to his old routine and be happy again with Miss Barton. But these remaining days belonged to them and were precious. They would live them to the full and that was all she asked for.

For these reasons she could never get round to agreeing a time for her evening out with the persistent Michael. It would have to be within the next couple of days or not at all. Still in a kind of quandary, she men-tioned it to Mrs. West who happened to know the young man through seeing him work in the establishment where they all ate each evening.

"Why on earth would you not go out with such a fine young fellow who has the mark of cleanliness and decency all about him? Get yourself ready, girl, for tomorrow night."

This was around six-thirty on the Monday evening of their final week. They were preparing to go out to dinner and Norah noticed a familiar looking briefcase in the hallway as she went out to get her coat. She knew that he had arrived and was somewhere on the premises. It was almost a certainty that he too would be going with them to the village restaurant. That he did and he sat himself between the Major and Mrs. West at the specially arranged round table that had been pre-booked. He conversed mainly with the Major in a voice that was deliberately undertone. The three ladies along with Stanley were quite happy to make their own chat, which was casual and relaxed, especially for Norah who knew that Mi-chael was on bar duty. Now more than ever she was determined to have that date with him, not only because the Missus wanted her to but also because that other unsavory character would be lurking about the place. To her there was something about this David that caused her to be ill at ease in his presence and it was something she could not quite understand.

It was a while before teatime on Wednesday when Michael came to take his beautiful date out for the evening. She was dressed in a manner that complimented her attractive appearance. Her dress and make up consultants was none other than Mrs. West and Elizabeth Barton. They both wanted her date to be a happy and memorable one. They peeped out the living room window to see him take Norah by the hand as the two walked slowly out the gate and over the road to wherever he was taking her. They ate in the college canteen or dining hall along with Michael's student friends. it was a most enjoyable sitting to one who had never been to such a place before. The quality of the fare was substandard compared to what she had become accustomed to, since coming to this place. But the pleasant atmosphere and the jolly friendship more than compensated for such a minor shortfall. Then Michael took her on a tour of inspection around the entire complex: the lecture halls, the halls of residence and the sports facilities, where young men and women were partaking.

The ancient city with its Roman walls and narrow cobbled streets, the likes of which Norah had never seen before, was alive to the throng of sightseeing tourists and shoppers. Still holding hands, they made their way around the souvenir shops to look at the items on display and perhaps find something to take back to dad. She found a chain for his pocket watch and was told it had been washed in gold; it was at a price she could afford. Dainty cuff links of a similar grade tempted her further, as she thought for a while about Benny Ryan and that promised letter still not written. With these few thoughts about home and the dear folks back there, she quickly returned to the reality of where she was and whom she was with. He was everything and more than Mrs. West said he appeared to be. He was kind and gentlemanly and insisted that she accept a small gift as a memento of their brief but sweet acquaintance. Being with Michael was having a good affect on Norah. It gave her a feeling of sensual calm, but she knew that all this would pass as would the memory of it eventually ebb away.

They made their own entertainment as only students can back at the university bar. There was music, song and much laughter right through until closing time. They all wanted to make it good for Michael's girl. Good it certainly was, and she told them so as she said goodbye at the time of leaving, to enjoy the pleasure of walking back with such a learned and charming gentleman. As they walked, he lamented the fact that she had only four days of her holiday left and begged her to see him once more before he resumed his working for the full weekend. Norah pointed out that as he would be starting work on Friday evening he actually had only one free night left and that was tomorrow, Thursday. For that reason, she thought it best that they make do with their mid-day meetings in the park, but she would never go there without taking Stanley with her. They both agreed that this was probably the best they could hope for in the circumstances but at least they were now together and alone, standing with arms around each other at the back door of the Wests holiday home. For the first time in her life, Norah felt at ease in this situation and made no excuse about having a time to be back in the house. They hugged and kissed. They even cried like this was the last such joy they were ever likely to experience again.

It was the warmest of greeting she received next morning at the dining room table from Mrs. West. Miss Barton had just brought Stanley in to join the three of them for breakfast. The Major and David were gone since early morning on some kind of business, the nature of which was not to be revealed.

"You were back earlier than we thought last night. Did you not think so too, Elizabeth? Tell us Norah, did you enjoy your date?"

"Yes, I was back fairly early but the time I had was nothing short of wonderful. All of Michael's friends were so lively and friendly. I suppose for me it was a bit unreal but it will always be a nice memory to have. I like Michael a lot because he is nice and good but the world I belong to is totally different to his and that is something I must never forget, even though we truly like each other."

What she said impressed her listeners. It was a responsible form of reasoning and well articulated. She had the mind of a philosopher and perhaps in other circumstances could well have been one of the campus residents up the road. She held Stanley's hand as she talked to the ladies and said to him: "Stanley, I like you best of all and we will soon be going for our walk." With that, she went out to the kitchen and brought in the four breakfast plates from which they ate in feasting togetherness.

It was an easeful couple of days that followed. The Major did not return until Saturday afternoon, but David did not come with him. Norah and Stanley paid several visits to the park and met up with Michael at the same time every day. But now the time was nigh and Saturday would be their last farewell. Although Monday was their day of departure, most of Sunday would be taken up preparing for the journey home. But alas, it was also the day that Stanley would be taken back to his place of care and this was more than Norah's soft heart could bear. In the park, she stood with Michael, close to Stanley in the wheelchair. In their very own special way, each of these young men had affected her deeply and would she ever see either of them again? Stanley looked on as the two embraced for the last time and Norah sensed it disturbed him somewhat. With tears for Michael, she then stooped down to hug the one that needed her most. That beautiful park which represented happiness for both of them was now being left for others to enjoy; she would walk, talk and sing with Stanley on this their final outing, for tomorrow he would be gone.

That tomorrow came on them fast, with Elizabeth Barton in full control. She had Stanley and herself ready to travel well before midday. She was confident and reassuring to all of them that he would easily settle back into his daily routine with her. Of that they had no doubt for they knew her to be a good and caring person, whom Stanley loved and depended upon. Norah did her best to refrain from showing emotion. This was mainly because of Mrs. West, who was having a weepy morning. She certainly did show her softer side that forenoon as she and the Major sat alone with their son in the living room for the final half hour. Then it was time to go and all of them had their good-byes, except the Major who was taking them back in the large car he had been using since the day after they came to the Dale. It was not until the three had gone off and out of sight that the two left behind were fully free to express their heartbreak, and that they did in each other's arms. Now empty of tears, they both sipped tea until the atmosphere began to brighten. Then Mrs. West rose to her feet:

"Norah, we have had such a happy time together here and I hope for you it was happy too. Now it's time to pack our things. Home is calling once again."

Chapter Twelve

They were home in time for the last week of the potato digging. There was a big squad of gatherers, both men and women, working in the field next to the river. The crop had to be got out of there before the autumn rains saturated the porous soil, or worse again, the danger of a heavy flood. It was the morning after before the Major appeared on the scene and was satisfied at what he saw; the yield was as heavy as the quality was good. Yet, he saw fit to reprimand a set of gatherers for leaving too many good ones on the ground. He thought that Vincent should be keeping an eye on such things. His presence was not seen as a serious imposition on the workers as they knew he did not look like a man that would be staying with them all that long. But before leaving to let Wilkie get on with it, he noticed the presence of young Chris Harrigan in the squad and wondered how this came about. Vincent was well prepared for the predictable reaction and said Mrs. West had given him permission to give the lad a start, as she was not the sort to hold a grudge.

The woman herself verified the story unapologetically; she felt it was high time they thought about moving on from the antagonisms of the past.

"That boy is little more than a child and by all accounts has not been given a great start in life by way of opportunity. And I see there is more trouble brewing for us in relation to the fishing rights."

She drew his attention to the letter that lay on the bureau unopened and on the back of the envelope was the name O'Donnell and Company Solicitors. It was not the kind of reading that give pleasure to either of them on the day after returning from a relaxing vacation. The note was short and deliberate, that the company was giving notice of its intentions to initiate court proceedings on behalf of Mr. William Mullen who was being denied access to the River Camus through a lawful right-of-way. It also stated that the law had an obligation to defend the right of the individual to use such accesses.

This was a totally new development from what had been decided upon by Pauric O'Donnell and Hat McGivern, where the case was to be taken against the Fisheries Board.

But it later emerged that, unknown to McGivern, the young O'Donnell, in his legal wisdom, came to Billy Mullen with a new proposition and asked him again to be the front man. In his professional opinion, the right-of-way question needed immediate attention and he felt the two proceedings should run concurrently. So in short, Billy Mullen would be suing both the Major and the Fisheries Board in a test case on behalf of the Portneill fishermen. She looked over his shoulder as he perused the letter thoroughly without making comment.

"This is the sort of thing that is making life rather unpleasant for us here and I happen to think that most of it is quite unnecessary as well. In my opinion, you are holding out on this against your better judgment simply because you cannot allow yourself to concede the fact that your judgment was flawed."

The two were alone in the living room so the old soldier was free to raise his voice in authority and told her in stern tone:

"I am not going to be lectured by anyone, not by you or by these people you seem to be having such a rapport with. Nor will I be influenced by the threat of law from a young whippersnapper of a lawyer from the back country."

His disparaging reference to the place where Mr. O'Donnell lived and worked would have been influenced by the colloquialism he had obviously picked up since coming to live in the area. The report was loud enough to be heard by the servants back in the kitchen. It was not something they were accustomed to hearing from this pair and it disturbed Norah much more than Madge. She had just got settled back to her working routine after having such a wonderful time with these people who treated her like one of their own. There had to be something seriously the matter between them to cause the Major to raise his voice to that extent, she thought. But the storm passed and the Big House returned to its tranquil state. The Major took off in the car and Mrs. West went to the potato field to see how the work was progressing. Norah related to Madge all the exciting details of her holiday and in trustful secrecy, the tragic story about their son Stanley. It was a story that Madge knew a little about from a chat she had with Mrs. West over a glass of sherry the previous Christmas but it was a brief mentioning without going into the extent of the boy's incapacity.

"I could see it was hard on her to even mention his name and it was something neither she nor himself ever talk about beyond themselves. For that reason, I was sworn to secrecy as well."

"Well, I have been working a lot with Stanley while I was over there and found it to be the most rewarding experience of my life and I cannot understand why they are so loathe to talk or even bring him over here. But we have to respect their wishes and feel sorry for both of them as well as Stanley. It is hard for all of them. A wonderfully good lady called Elizabeth Barton cares for him and does so in a way that makes him happy. I hope to God that the poor soul was not the cause of them arguing in the living room."

Little she knew, poor girl, that it was her dear father that ignited the spark on this occasion. Billy told her nothing at all about his leading the case on behalf of his fellow fishermen, which involved taking Major West to court. In spite of his stubborn resistance to the pleadings of his wife, the letter did have the effect of creating a degree of uncertainty in the Major's determination? That was why he took off and away from the heat of angry exchanges with his more sagacious spouse; he headed north in pursuit of legal counsel. Whatever advice he got there, he kept very much to himself and she spent the remainder of the day in the potato field with Wilkie and his squad. The only thing he did disclose to her later that night was that the case was unlikely to be listed for hearing before the month of February at least. That was also the information given by Pauric O'Donnell to Billy Mullen on the day he first put the proposition to him. But the important thing for both sides was that the contentious issue would be dealt with before the commencement of the next fishing season and all of them would have time to prepare their cases.

Taking action against the Major was a strategy that would have found most favor amongst the rank and file of the fishermen, but O'Donnell advised Billy against divulging the plan to any of them. To do so, he said, would only fuel the train of speculation and that could very well play to the advantage of the opposition. So what was being initiated would have to remain confidential between the plaintiff and his counsel, the exception of course being the Wests who would have to defend the charge. What made this somewhat easier was the fact that the case against the Fisheries Board was common knowledge and allowed the people to speculate at will. Although it had ceased to be a popular topic, Billy had the admiration and support of everyone for what he was trying to achieve in taking the Board to task. But through it all he remained steadfast in his silence about the second lawsuit, even to his daughter whom he knew it would upset. Mrs. West must have suspected that this was the case in relation to Norah, for never once did she mention the unpleasant subject to her.

The friendship that had recently developed between Dr.Clarke and the Major was now progressing at an agreeable rate; they had succeeded in gracing the golf course together on more than one occasion. They seemed to get on well together in a friendship that was based upon mutual respect. It appeared that the doctor had given up on trying to nudge his friend towards a more reasonable approach, in relation to the dispute with the fishermen. They were able to converse in joviality about most other topics and found that their views were never too much incompatible. But in spite of this fraternizing, he was not the kind of man that could easily be bought away from the cause of his people. So another approach must have been on his mind. Through his daily interaction with the people, he was well informed as to what was taking place and that Billy Mullen was taking action against the Fisheries Board early in the New Year.

This, he knew, could very well force the Board into taking the kind of action that might put them on a collision course with the Major and eventually led to a resolution of the dispute. He figured that the Major, being a clever and perceptible man, must surely have considered such an eventuality. There was another significant factor at play here as well; the main protagonist happened to be none other than the father of his excellent housemaid, Norah. Both he and his wife had grown immensely in their fondness for this modest and competent servant and it was a fondness growing even more since their time together in England. For these reasons, it was not a comfortable situation to be in and could drive him to a state where he might want to share his anxiety with a friend. That friend would be ready and waiting when the time was right, hopefully to take advantage of a more enlightened mind-set. Dr. Clarke was a patient man who believed in the power of reasoning; time and reflection were the important ingredients in nudging people towards the realm of reason.

Apart from the minor stir of receiving a solicitor's letter, not much was likely to happen during the intervening period, which could be for the duration of three to four months. This would allow for a winter of peaceful calmness, where nothing mattered beyond earning a decent living with occasional thoughts about family and the coming Christmas season. Norah had a lot to think about and it was mostly of a pleasant nature, her darling Stanley West and the bonny brief romance with Michael in the park. Now back to thinking about Benny Ryan, she wondered had he received the letter she had written with the fountain pen that Michael had bought her on the evening of their date. With all that

105

had happened over there, she had just about managed to write and post it a bare two days before coming home. She felt a bit bad for allowing herself to be so distracted from thinking about him amidst the glamour and excitement of her holiday adventure. Still, she had a nice little present for him and would be sending it with his sister Kathleen after Mass on Sunday. She also wanted to ask about him and if his injuries were healing satisfactorily; it was now almost three weeks since that evening Mrs. West brought her to see him and she wondered how he was coming to terms with his situation since?

For Benny the letter was indeed a welcome diversion away from thoughts that were still troubling him; it was a shortish note but long enough to reassure that she thought and cared about him. A brief mention was given to the holiday in England but nothing at all about either Stanley or Michael, as one of them was the Wests' family secret while the other was her own. She looked forward to seeing him again but that would probably have to wait until he was well enough to be out and about again. He kept the letter close to his person and re-read it several times over the following days when he thought that no one was watching him. It pleased his people no end to see the good effect this was having on their Benny and him thinking about when he would ever see her again? The novelty and excitement had just about subsided when Kathleen handed him the dainty package that contained the gold-washed cuff links that were brought with affection from the town of York.

It was nearly eight weeks before either of them heard from each other again and that was done through the exchange of Christmas Greetings cards. That was about as much as Benny's financial circumstances permitted him to do; Norah fully understood this and made up her mind to go and see him before the holy day would come. Now in a position where she was not so shy about asking Mrs. West for modest favors, she wondered if she could be taken to Coolaghy for another time.

"I would be more than happy to take you over there whatever evening you say but remember there are only four days left before Christmas and you should get him a specially nice present this time. Don't be thinking about the cost, for the boss and I have agreed that you and Madge are deserving of a special bonus at this time of year. Would you like to come shopping with me tomorrow after dinner? You need to get something nice for yourself as well."

Then with a devilish laugh she asked Norah about the nice watch she got in the summer from Christy Flood and why on earth did she never wear it. Norah was not amused but manage a passable smile.

"Yes, and he keeps asking me that as well; I have worn it a few times but only in here and that was just to please him, and you know, the more I do that the more he keeps after me. Only the other day when he called here nothing would do but I go with him to Derry on Sunday evening to see this film, 'The Quiet Man', and maybe a bite to eat afterwards."

Christy was still pursuing her and even more imposingly so at this seasonal time of year. Over the years he had acquired considerable means and would have been well able to outbid any of his rivals. He even gave visual effect to his superiority by trading-in the old van for one that was new and of a more modern design. This was a man far apart from the common young *lochsiuil* "that hadnay the nails to scratch his arse." But Norah was also acquiring a degree of independence that was enabling her to withstand and even ward off such imposing attention. In spite of her innate disposition towards gentleness and courtesy, she was beginning to learn that certain situations demanded from her a response that was not always in keeping with the wishes of others. So she plucked up the courage to tell Christy she was not for going to Derry or any place else with him and would be grateful if he could leave her alone in future. This ultimatum was mainly to thwart what she knew he was planning by way of an over-elaborate Christmas Gift.

Norah was left at the Ryan home early on the night before Christmas Eve; Mrs. West said she would collect her again closer to bedtime. It was Sunday and Kathleen was preparing to go on a night out with some friends, but the visitor was warmly welcomed by all four of them. From a shopping bag she took out a small package and handed it to Mrs. Ryan. It was a larger and more decoratively wrapped item that she gave to Benny whom she barely recognized. He had grown a massive beard that was now concealing his fine features. Even though it was clean and with a glowing sheen, Norah took an immediate dislike to it. Why, she wondered, why would a young man with attractive features go out and about with that disgusting thing attached to his face and upper lip? In the circumstances she had little option but to keep her opinion unspoken; she did not have Benny to herself, but perhaps later on they could take themselves for a walk.

On the good side of things his leg was improving and becoming suppler; he was now able to walk with the aid of just a walking stick and his mental state was better too. As for the beard, well, it was nothing more than something he was trying out of curiosity during his housebound days; he had no intention of keeping it beyond that. Though perhaps not fully aware of it, she herself had been his greatest remedy. What she had been communicating to him was precious in terms of self and purpose. Her coming to see him did more for his sense of well-being than anyone could have imagined and he told her so as they stood outside with arms around each other. One could not but be enriched at being paid such an endearing compliment but Norah was still somewhat circumspect in these matters. She certainly did not want to be Benny's only reason for wanting to find a new direction; she could not be sure about her own readiness for such closeness. Still, she found it hard to part from him at the end of the night. The sound of the old Land Rover coming up the road was telling them it was over until heaven knows when.

It had been a good Christmas for both Norah and her father; they spent it together in the cottage. She had received cards from both Stanley and Michael, to say they were missing her a lot. The Wests seemed to have had a good festival as well. But they were more into celebrating the New Year, hence another house party had to be arranged at short notice. There is little more to be said about the parties in Elmwood House; the usual people, including the Clarkes, were there. It was by no means an elaborate affair, so Madge and Norah were able to prepare and serve the food without additional help. As usual, Madge went home after the tidying up; Norah was staying overnight and again had the pleasure of being invited to join the guests in the sitting room. The New England Grandfather Clock chimed the midnight hour as everyone rose to welcome each other into the dawn of another year. Everyone present exchanged a greeting with each of the other guests and it was done in a spirit that was warm and pleasant. Even the cold David managed a hug for Norah that conveyed more strangeness than warmth to the sensuality of her being.

While still on their feet the Major moved to the centre of the floor holding a glass head high.

"Friends, I want you to take your glasses and drink with me to the health, happiness and prosperity of all of us for the year ahead."

Everyone concurred by raising his or her glasses chanting, "To all of us."

"Yes, indeed," intoned Mrs. West, "and I sincerely hope that it is a less turbulent year than the one we have just moved out of."

Few of the people from overseas would have known what the good lady was referring to, but it was her way of making her feelings known to them that did know. But considering all that had taken place since that morning when the right-of-way was first closed off to the public, it had indeed been a turbulent time. Dr Clarke took a discreet glance towards the Major who showed little signs of being itched by his wife's intervention, yet he wondered if it might just touch a chord. Time was marching on; they were now into a new year and the contentious issue would soon be back to command their attention once again.

Chapter Thirteen

It was the morning of St. Patrick's Day and the March wind was blowing cold from the east; the people were on their way to ten o'clock mass for the celebration of the national feast day. Few of them were wearing the authentic shamrock; a sprig of clover was about as much as the bare ground could yet provide. Cycling two abreast was Billy Mullen and his daughter Norah; they had just passed the main entrance to the estate when they were distracted by a voice that sounded like Laurence Keatley.

"Hey Mullen, come and tack a look at this and what the hell do you think it means?"

He was standing at the gateway of the second entrance that accessed the contentious right-of-way to the river which none of them had trodden for almost a year. To their amazement the heavy padlock had been removed from the gate and in its place a neatly printed sign that read PUBLIC RIGHT OF WAY TO RIVER and signed Major S. West. Very soon a number of other mass-goers had joined the three in wondering what had brought about this unexpected turn of events. The court cases involving Billy had still not been brought before the judge, even though they had been filed for hearing since the previous Autumn. Keatley was of no doubt that this was the yellow streak showing itself on the part of West.

"The cowardly hoor," he laughed.

That was Keatley's take on it but it was hardly the correct one. There had to be some other force at play to bring about this apparent change of heart. Few people had much doubt that Mrs. West was the major player in bringing wiser counsel to bear on her husband's thinking. She was vehemently opposed to him going to court to defend his actions against the local people, just as she was opposed to what he was attempting to do from the outset. But in addition to that, there was a growing uncertainty on the part of the Major himself about how to handle the inevitable pressure that would be coming from the Fisheries Board. It was Dr. Clarke who, as a friend, advised him that the court would have to instruct the Board to exercise its duty in relation to the rights of licensed fishermen.

As for the case about access to the right-of-way, of which the doctor had been informed in confidence by the Major, he was not in a position to give legal opinion on it. At the same time, he could not remember a time when people did not take that route when going to the river.

To reason in the spirit of friendly advice would be the most effective strategy to employ against this headstrong man from the ruling class. This was the considered opinion formed by the quiet medical man right from that very first evening when he and Mr. McGivern first met the Major. From there on he had gotten to know him better than most others in the neighborhood and their regard for each other had grown considerably since then. Much deliberation took place quietly between the two over a period of many months; it would have happened on the golf course as well as in the big house where Mrs. West continued to speak her mind. She would have worked in cahoots with the doctor whom she was beginning to see had a better way of getting through to her husband than she herself could ever manage to do. If this was a flaw in their marital state it was not one that bothered her too much right then; if this man could deliver the prize of neighborliness and peace of mind. In the end, it was the combination of these forces that eventually impacted upon the stubborn determination of an authoritarian army officer that had a habit of getting his own way.

So the bitter dispute that so upset a peaceful community and was the catalyst for some violent and criminal activity had finally come to an end. As a consequence of it, a young man was still serving out a prison sentence while two others were under probation and bound to the peace. While most of the credit was due to Mrs. West and Dr. Clarke, not many of the local people were yet fully aware of how hard they had actually worked to soften the Major. Hat McGivern wasted little time in promulgating his own slant on how the resolution came about. It was through his initiative of involving the doctor at the outset not to mention how well the two of them presented the case on behalf of the Portneill fishermen.

"Ya did in yir fuckin arse," said Keatley. "If it hadnay a been for the doctor tellin' that big English hoor that he hadnay a hope in a court o law, we would still be locked oot and a think maybe she was keepin' the owl thing aff him isweel, but you would know nathin' aboot that."

To this McGivern made no reply, perhaps the comment was beneath the dignity of a man who reads Dickens. They were all in the Poachers Inn for the traditional drowning of the shamrock. Apart from Keatley's outburst, it was a friendly neighborly kind of gathering where they talked about the new fishing season that was now about to begin. Most all of them were pleased and wanted nothing more than to leave the bitterness of the past behind them. For a few, it was considered a time of good craic and something to talk about, whereas the majority saw it as a vexing time they were happily consigning to history.

An episode in history it certainly turned out to be, for within a matter of weeks, all the parties were back to doing the things they did best and without controversy. The fishermen were again casting their nets and rowing their boats on every shot of the Camus without fear of reprimand from anyone. A much better atmosphere prevailed amongst the workforce of Elmwood Estate; Mrs. West was out again in the fields with her men; they were busy in the midst of the spring sowing and planting of crops. She talked to them about her great sense of relief on being able to meet and chat with her neighbors knowing that the obstacle to them trusting her had finally been removed. The men were most reassuring that no blame had ever been attached to her. On the contrary, they all knew of her tireless efforts on the side of reason.

"A think it's high time we all quit chatting about it, never say Keatley." Vincent Wilkie was throwing a bag of wheat seed into the hopper of the old broadcast sower and looking down towards a flock of wild geese that had brought an air of peacefulness to the lowland meadows.

"Are they geese or swans?' inquired Mrs. West, as she ran her hand through the hard dry grains of seeds.

"Whatever they are Missus, they look to be happy and content, not a bit bothered about the things we be squabbling about. Tell me Missus, when do you think are the most feathers on a goose?"

"I don't honestly know, Vincent, and I am sure you are going to tell me anyway, but there is one thing I can tell you, neither the Boss nor Christy will be pleased to see them; it seems they soil up the grazing land and the cattle won't eat it."

"When the gander is upon her," retorted the devilish Wilkie.

Christy Flood was again making frequent visits to the farmyard; he and the Major would inspect the pasture to see if it was ready for the first consignment of heavy grazers. He had not quite given up on Norah Mullen and would seldom leave the place without paying a visit to the kitchen where the bite to eat would always be there for him. Norah would do her best to be busy in another part of the house at such times; experience had taught her that he tended to overstay his welcome when she was around. Nor was he likely to let the occasion pass without making some kind of suggestion about how their relationship might progress. He had heard through Madge about her holiday romance with a young English student called Michael and that they had actually exchanged gifts and greetings at Christmas. Needless to say there was quite a bit of exaggeration in Madge's reporting and it was done with a purpose in mind; this man's persistence had gone beyond being a joke.

Now there was talk about Benny Ryan being out and about again, not fully recovered from his lameness, yet talk of his re-emergence was enough to disturb Christy's happiness. Beyond seeing him at Sunday Mass, Norah had very little contact with Benny since the time of her Christmas visit to his house. This was in keeping with her policy of not allowing herself to over-invest in the man stakes, lest it might impose a closeness she was not yet ready to take on board. She still maintained a friendship with his sister Kathleen who was able to keep her informed as to how he was coming along. He had still not made it back to the dances, not even down the road to the wee Coolaghy hall, of a Sunday night. The loss of his precious footballing career he was still finding hard to come to terms with, and for that reason, they were anxious that he should get out again to meet people and perhaps find interests that are new. Kathleen knew of his deep affection for Norah but did not go so far as to impose upon her the responsibility of having such knowledge.

It was being partly aware of this that kept her from going back to see him, even though she held feelings of longing that made her want to do so many times. Now amidst better days of pleasant goodness, she had other things to be doing and thinking about. The approaching days of summer were more conducive to hope and promise. Her hard-working father was availing of what spare time he had down at the river with his friend Laurence Keatley and enjoying considerable success as well. Heavy catches were being reported from all quarters during those early days; it had all the signs of being a bumper year for all that were engaged in the business. This was good news for everyone as it was bound to bring about a healthy and fluid cash flow throughout the district. The fishermen were never shy of spending a pound or in sharing the fortunes of their success in the years when the river was good to them.

The fish merchants too were busy on their daily collection rounds with an element of competition between them that would normally be seen as the life of trade. But as the season moved on and the summer days brought bigger catches, the market supply increased to a stage where these buyers no longer needed to compete with each other. What follows from that situation is a fall in demand and the inevitable lowering of prices. Then it is the merchant that becomes the main beneficiary of the high-yielding salmon season and that is achieved at the expense of the fisherman. It would be true to say that these operators had over the years done exceptionally well out of the Portneill fishing industry. No one more so than a certain Darby Deeney who was thought of as being nearly the best of this frugal fraternity; he had a habit of quietly paying a penny or two more per pound than his rivals.

Very much a routine man, his northern registered van would arrive at the houses most days at around mid-forenoon when the men folk were either at the river or at work. It was always cash on delivery transaction where the women supervised the weighing operation and collected what payment was appropriately due. Then for some reason or other Deeney introduced what he called a more efficient method of doing the business and for their co-operation would pay an extra penny per pound. It meant that the fish would still be collected at the same time and in the same way; the only difference being was that payment would now be on a weekly basis on Saturday mornings. Both the fishermen and their wives were an agreeable lot. They did not see the new arrangement as being a serious imposition on their way of life and it would make Saturday a day to look forward to with money in the morning and shopping in the evening.

The system was put into effect immediately and the weeks that followed brought little or no complaints against it; it was really a great old time with money in everyone's pocket. So assured were all of them that little notice was taken of the Saturday morning that a different young man came in the same blue van to collect the fish. He introduced himself as Deeney's son and said his father had to go to Killybegs on some other kind of fishy business but would be calling round with the money in the afternoon. Nobody was overly bothered when it passed the nightly hour of nine and them concluding that the man had probably been delayed in the execution of his business. It was the same young fellow that came on Monday saying his dad had to go back to the Donegal fishing port where he was negotiating a deal for the supply of other kinds of sea fish. Midweek saw the return of Deeney with a plausible story about his expanding business and his ever-increasing need for a greater supply of various species of marine life. He apologized for not getting round with the money on Saturday and would appreciate if they could now manage to hold on until the coming weekend.

The following Friday was the last time any of them ever set eyes on Darby Deeney. He had done a runner, leaving a huge debt owing to the fishing people of Portneill. The amount owed to one particular family amounted to almost five hundred pounds, a huge amount of money for the times that were in it and there seemed no way of retrieving any of it. A few of the more militant went after the rogue, but alas to no avail. He could never be found and no one seemed to know where he had gone. Had it not been for the resilience of these honest thrifty people, many of them would have given up and sold off their boats and nets. Giving up on a way of life that they were so committed to was not an option entertained for very long. After all, it was a good season with a fair part of it still to come. They would have to bear the pain of their loss and let all bad luck go with it; a costly lesson had been learned and it was one not to be lost on them as they decided to carry on. There was good money still left in the deep waters of the Camus River.

The lesson that is learned from a bad experience is often of most benefit; this was essentially true in the case of these callously defrauded people. Apart from their resolve not to be deterred by the actions of a heartless scoundrel, they also began to think about the industry as a whole, particularly in relation to the market side of it. No longer were they simply content to be casting their nets in the hope of landing a good result and then selling it on without question to boost the profits of the middleman. There was a strong resolve on the part of some to take a more active role in seeking out other and hopefully better markets and this resolve was augmented by the knowledge that their stance against the Major had eventually won the day. This again became the cause for another meeting in the Poachers Inn. On this occasion Dr. Clarke was in attendance, thus preventing Hat McGivern from assuming the presiding role. The doctor was thoroughly annoyed about the contemptible behavior of the villainous Darby Deeney towards his hard-working neighbors. He wanted to support them in finding a way of getting the best possible return for what they and their families had worked long and hard for.

These were the kind of sentiments he expressed when accepting his elevation to the chair. He was a popular choice by the simple process of acclamation; no other names were suggested. The meeting was lengthy and friendly but little noticeable progress was being made by way of setting out a concrete course of action. Some unworkable suggestions were made, like the withholding of the product as if it was an imperishable good that could be kept indefinitely or had an alternative use. McGivern sat in silence for a good part of the time but showed his appreciation when asked by the chair for his informed opinion as to what might be a practical or workable course of action for them to explore further.

"Explore, explore," intoned McGivern. "I am glad you used that word, for in truth that is about all we can do right now or indeed for the remainder of this season. Yes, by all means go out and look for other markets but that is where you are going to need some responsible person that knows the business as well as the markets."

"Aye, somebody like McGivern," came a kind of scoffing voice from the back.

It sounded like it came from the direction of where Laurence Keatley was standing. The chairman called for order and thanked the previous speaker for his contribution, then went on to ask for other suggestions that were somewhat slow in coming. Apart from hinting the desirability of the 'responsible person', McGivern did little more than state in his long-winded way the reason why the meeting was being held in the first place. No inspiring wisdom seemed to descend upon the gathering and with the evening wearing late, the doctor gave mention to the idea of a fisheries co-operative. The thinking behind such a venture was that ideally it should be owned and controlled by those engaged in the fishing industry and no one else. There was however one major obstacle to such an undertaking and that was the important matter of finance. Any such body would need to be in possession, not only of a sizable cash flow, but also have the backing of a reputable banking organization as well.

With the exception of one small farmer who had an interest in the river as a means of supplementing his meager income, very few of the others were prepared to take the risk of venturing into the unknown. Most of them felt it was much safer to carry on as they had been doing. It would certainly be less complicated and there were plenty of other buyers ready and willing to take over from Darby Deeney. Faced with a high degree of circumspection, the chairman was left with little option but to draw the proceedings to a close and he did so on the grounds that the people needed time to think things over. Though disappointed at the lack of initiative, he fully understood why these people were so reluctant to face a challenge that was vague and hard to measure. Still, as previously experienced, Dr Clarke was not a man to abandon a cause he felt strongly about and this was one he felt deserved further exploration. He decided not to engage in the futile exercise of holding another meeting; instead he began to explore other avenues that might involve a small number of people where one or two of them might be prepared to invest.

There was little doubt on his astute mind that a viable business could be launched in the area and that it would be favorable towards the interests of the local suppliers. With close to two months of the season still remaining and it a good year he knew it would be worthwhile getting something up and running fast. Enthused with faith and confidence in his own plan, he discretely approached two other people with a proposal for them to consider. The small farmer, Robert McElwee, was very impressed by what the doctor had outlined to him. He was a man that knew through his farming experience, something about the merits of co-operation and the benefits that can accrue from it. He was also relieved to learn that no monetary investment would be expected from him. His name as a solvent member of the co-operative body was the only thing required. Being an intelligent man, he enquired as to how this could be and was informed that the third partner would be the main sponsoring agent.

Robert was not overly surprised when the persuasive doctor told him who that partner was to be. He and Major West were fully on board for providing the initial finances and accommodating what they hoped to call Elmwood Fisheries Co-op. The Major was already out and about seeking reliable outlets with the assistance of friends and associates, including Mr. Orr from the Board. In the circumstances, it would have to be run on a profit-making basis but they were absolutely certain of being able to pay a much better price than the people were used to getting. This was the surest and speediest way of getting what should be a very satisfactory arrangement up and running. The Major, being a clever man with an eye for a good deal, was able to see that this proposition had the potential of growing into a thriving and lucrative enterprise. As for the doctor, all he wanted was to recover his initial investment along with a modest dividend; his main objective was the provision of a satisfactory marketing facility for the benefit of the people. In truth, this venture did not have the properties of a true co-operative, as its official membership was limited to three people with one of them being the major sponsor and consequently the beneficiary. That said, the other two names did give it the semblance of being so, and that might just be enough to placate the curious public.

Very quickly, the shrewd Major had one of his small secure sheds converted into a serviceable depot from where the business operation could be conducted. It consisted of a main weighing and grading area, which opened out to a side road that accessed the slipway. Off that, there was a sealed cold storage compartment, which became known as the ice room; this was because it was kept cool by using dry ice. Office space was not required, at least not in the short term. A simple writing bureau in the main area was quite sufficient for the purpose of records and accounts. With all systems ready in record time the only other requirement

117

was the good will and support of the local suppliers, many of whom had still not forgotten the happenings of the previous year. But not surprisingly, the vast majority of them were attracted to the prospect of getting a higher return for their work and in spite of their feelings towards West, they knew that the business was in the hands of creditable people.

With some difficulty, Robert McElwee was persuaded to man the depot for the remaining weeks of the season. Being a farmer and part time fisherman, he did not really have the time to do this. At the same time, he accepted the Doctor's reasoning that his presence there would give credence to the bona fides of the new operation as a genuine Co-op. It was indeed a busy few weeks for Robert who let it be known that he would be glad to see it over and had no intentions of repeating the exercise for the following year. But from a business point of view, it was a success far beyond their expectations. So much so, that West was already making plans not only for the year ahead but also with thoughts of continuing to supply a market that was viable and secure. This, he knew, would require the sourcing of supplies from the seaports during the lengthy off-season and most definitely the purchase of a van and a man employed to drive it.

For obvious reasons, the impetuous Major wasted little time in getting round the fishing ports in an exercise of research. With somewhat less enthusiasm, Clarke and McElwee went along with the idea, feeling assured it would not impinge upon the primary objective of their precious Co-op, which was to help the local fishermen. They knew full well that this man was for going ahead with it in any case and that he would do well from it, no doubt. That was the benefit of being in a position of power and wealth, but from their point of view, it was being utilized positively and to a wider benefit. It was a benefit the people could recognize and were appreciative of. They were being paid a price that was just, in a market that was right beside them. There were but a few dissenting opinions uttered during the early days; one of them being Laurence Keatley who could never see himself entering the premises while West was in occupation. Not wanting to be the odd man out was the one thing that eventually brought Keatley into line with the others. He could also see that his partner Mullen was favoring the so-called co-operative venture.

The atmosphere between the Major and his popular wife had improved considerably since the days of the fishing dispute. Now she was constantly hearing about his move into the world of buying and selling. While she was dutifully supportive of her husband and tried to show a shared enthusiasm with him she had already decided not to involve herself in the workings of it. She had a strange apathy towards it and that was certainly not like Mrs. West. That was until the morning after one of their many nighttime discussions about this consuming topic; she could recall that he mentioned the employment of a van driver. Uneasy thoughts about Benny Ryan still resided with Mrs. West. Had it been in her power she would have done her utmost to help that young man to a better life. Now, she wondered was this her chance to make amends or would she be able to coax her husband anywhere near to her own level of benevolence? She knew that his pet project had him in a high state of mind and she was not for letting the occasion pass without giving Benny's cause her best shot.

That evening her enthusiasm for the entire project was noticeably greater. Both of them talked about it as if nothing else in the world mattered or merited serious attention. Then, in the height of it all, she broached the delicate subject of the unfortunate youth who had suffered unjustly for the sins of the guilty.

"His willingness as a worker has never been in doubt by any of us and as for his character, well, I don't think there is any need for us to look any further into that. Neither I nor anybody else has ever heard an unkind word spoken about that fine young boy or his hard-working parents."

This woman's determination grew with every utterance and she could see clearly that her words were commanding the attention of the listener; perhaps she was stirring in him a latent guilt?

"My dear woman, I do not disagree with what you say, but what happened back then was not all my fault; the circumstances of him being in the house with Miss Mullen created a suspicion in all of us, including the police. As you jolly well know, dear wife, my background does not allow me to entertain anyone that is under the least suspicion and need I remind you about our own state of mind at that time?"

"Yes indeed, I need no reminding and yes again, your reaction was understandable, but none of this alters the fact that a terrible wrong was done to Benny Ryan. For the sake of noble honor and in the interest of common decency, I think we should grasp the opportunity of putting things right with these decent people. Decent people they certainly are, for I had occasion to visit their home once last Autumn when Norah, like myself, was feeling low about what had happened to Benny and their simple friendship touched me deeply, I can tell you."

There was potency in every breath of her conviction and the Major could see that the premise of her contention was creditably true on all accounts. He made no attempt at putting another slant on any of the points she had put so elegantly to him. In truth, it looked like she had brought him along to her own way of thinking.

"Yes, I can see the truth in every thing you say and if young Ryan should come to me in the pursuit of work, I will certainly give him a hearing; that is about all I can promise at this time".

"You can do better than that. You are a good man and no one knows that better than I do. Just promise me you will take him on and leave the rest of it to me".

That was the sum total of Mrs. Wests involvement in the affairs of Elmwood Fisheries Co-op and two days later the young man with a slight limp was welcomed with a warm handshake by Major West. He was introduced to Robert McElwee who gladly showed him what had to be done by way of weighing, grading and recording. The new van had not yet arrived but Benny needed these final two weeks of the fishing season learning the business from Robert, the expert. A fast learner Benny turned out to be. He liked working in the little depot with this friendly mentor man and as the salmon season drew to a close, he was looking forward to getting on the road to continue the business in a different way. His return to the work scene was welcomed by everyone not least the workers of the estate. Although his new role afforded him little contact with any of them, he still needed their friendship and support. He even received a welcoming and congratulatory call from his rival, Christy Flood, for whom it was a conscience thing, emanating from the memory of an ignoble deed. Flood was satisfied that contact between young Ryan and Norah had practically ceased since the goings on of last Christmas and hoped it might stay that way, even with him around the place again. It was obvious that Benny's return was causing some degree of unease in the mind of the enduring suitor and Norah was now getting attention to the point of near despair.

Chapter Fourteen

In the strangest of ways, Norah's problem with Christy Flood came to a sudden kind of end shortly after the re-employment of Benny Ryan, though Benny had played no part whatever in it. Apart from her love for the land, there was definitely something odder still about Mrs. Wests lack of involvement in the affairs of the Fisheries Co-op. She was genuinely pleased to see it coming into being and that her neighbors were deriving benefit from it, especially its lone employee. Her slight apprehension was that it might impinge on her plans to develop an interest of her own, which was the uniquely beautiful Connemara Pony. Of recent times she became preoccupied with a determination to purchase breeding stock of these particularly attractive equines. Her husband too had shown an interest. That was until the other business distracted him. Now her main worry was whether this distraction would cause him to lose enthusiasm for the horsey business and perhaps pull back from proceeding with it.

The annual Connemara Horse Fair, which focused mainly on this particular breed of pony, was due to take place the following week and the Wests had already made plans to go there. True enough, the Major's interest had evaporated somewhat. In fact, he had totally forgotten about the pre-arranged trip to the annual pony show and fair in Clifden, Connemara. Very soon he became aware of his wife's displeasure at his waning interest in what she was so passionately committed to pursuing, so he had little choice but to re-kindle his ebbing zest. The keeping and breeding of horses was not an unusual kind of leisurely pursuit for people from the higher accolade of society, especially them that resided in mansion-type dwellings. However, for the Wests there was a slight problem. Neither of them knew enough about this line of business to be investing in it without the assistance of some knowledgeable person and for that there was only one place to go.

Christy the cattleman was not so sure about his expertise in this specialized field and thought for a moment about giving them the name of his friend, Jimmy McGurk, a decent man with vast knowledge of quality bloodstock. Yet, a jaunt to the far west was much too good to be handing over to someone else, so Christy quickly decided to withhold this information and again nominated himself to be a kind of expert.

"I don't know a lot about this particular breed, but I have been to the fair of Clifden a couple of times before and I know the dealers fairly well. There is one thing I can tell you; it is something both of you will enjoy. It is a wonderful place to be and it is there you will find the best stock in the land."

So said ever-obliging Christy who also happened to be the ever-ready traveler when such an opportunity would sometimes present itself. This would be yet another self-fulfilling mission for the man in whom the Major had an abundance of trust. He was the one to see that their investment was wise and informed. He was of absolutely no doubt that they would easily find what they were looking for at this event and that it would be of the highest quality. As this was going to be a stay over for two nights, some preparations had to be attended to before the day of departure. One such requirement was the booking of accommodation for the two nights somewhere in or around the Clifden area. Another was a visit to Andy Mossy's forge to have a tow bar affixed to the old Mercedes for the purpose of pulling a twin horse box. Christy was able to tell them that good quality transport boxes would be on sale at a premises not far from where the fair was being held and it might be better to check out the horse trade first.

With everything and everybody ready, the party of three set off on their long journey towards the west. It was mid-morning of a sunny August day. Christy sat in the back wearing meticulously washed flannel trousers that complemented his tweed jacket and long-legged red boots that were the authentic mark of a livestock dealer. He also carried the characteristic bamboo cane to further augment his bona fides. In length, it was about waist high with a wrap binding of black adhesive tape on two places. They were going to make it a leisurely journey and were happy enough to be getting to the hotel in Clifden at around evening teatime. It was Christy's pleasure to point out places of interest as they traveled along the way, from Barnesmore Gap to the tabletop mountain of Benbulben and the grave of the legendary Queen Maeve on top of Knocknarea.

Like Donegal, the land of the western counties was varied from good to marginal but none of it seemed to have the richness they were used to along the banks of the Camus River or anywhere in the Roughan Valley. He explained to them the story behind the holy shrine at Knock and its significance to the faithful here in Ireland and to many from other parts of the world.

"Let's stop and pray here," said Mrs. West. "I think this should be good for all of us and maybe bring success to our mission as well."

Further on and to the west they were able to see the high hill of St. Patrick, outside the town of Westport where many people still walk the penitential way of the national apostle. These stories were most intriguing to them that were not familiar with the cultural and religious traditions; Christy explained them informatively and had the benefit of two attentive listeners. In the Mayo town of Claremorris, it was time to break the journey and have some light refreshments. The Major was feeling a bit tired from the driving and was having nothing more than a soft drink. Christy was having a sandwich and asked for a cool pint, fresh from the wooden barrel and herself said "Why not? Just give me the same." She accepted her husband's quietness was due to tiredness not only from the journey but also from the amount of work and stress he had put himself under of late in setting up that fish business. Now what they needed was something new and interesting, something that could pay its way but at the same time be pleasurable and relaxing as well.

Christy agreed that they were moving in the right direction by getting into quality horse breeding and for that reason should only go after top quality in Clifden tomorrow. It was close to an hour later before the Major felt rested enough to continue the journey and was very relieved when his wife suggested that she or Christy might take the wheel for part of the way. With the two men swapping places, commenced the final stage of their advance towards the rugged landscape of Connemara. No better way to revive the weary body than a period of easeful reclining across the comfortable and softly upholstered back seat of the prestigious Merc. Fortified by their sandwich and Guinness, the other two continued with their chat and admiration of the more fertile Galway countryside. Mrs. West was very taken by the quality of the flat farmland and further intrigued at how the fields were separated by stonewall boundaries that were built with precision and excellence. Not a sound could be heard coming from the back seat.

Through the beautiful village of Oughterard, with the glint of the evening sunshine reflecting on the still water of picturesque Lough Corrib, they were making fast headway towards their destination. The narrow road to Clifden was busier than usual as many others were heading that way as well. They were lucky to have booked accommodation beforehand. Almost there and the Major looking well refreshed, he asked to be taken to the place where the horse box trailers were on sale. It was still early in the evening and it might be a good idea to take a look around the place. There were five or six of these things on display and all of them looked suitable for the purpose. Christy tested each of them for what he called 'weight on the drawbar'. He did this several times and then the Major began to follow suit only to discover that they were much heavier than he thought; his observant wife noticed he did not look all that well.

Again she put this down to tiredness and fatigue. this man, she said to herself, needs to learn a new lifestyle; one that is less stressful and more recreational. That would be a tall order for a man so economically obsessed. Unlike her, he could not content himself to the simple pleasure of being in a tillage field or amongst the livestock thriving on summer pasture. So many other things he had to be doing, like attempting to take over part of the river against sound advice and now starting into a business he knows very little about. There was yet another less talked about involvement in the world of stocks and shares for which he relied so heavily on the agency of the frequent visitor, David. A man in his sixties with a highly productive farming enterprise plus his army pension should be well able to live in peace without the pressure of having so many irons in the fire.

It was a sedate family-run hotel in the centre of Clifden where a man who looked like he was the owner of the establishment greeted the three of them. Quite a few others were checking in as well and the dining room staff looked like they were stretched to the limit serving the evening meals. At the dinner table, Christy spoke over to a man who was seated across from where they sat. He was a prominent horse dealer and they knew each other well. It soon became obvious to the newcomers that the vast majority of the hotel patrons were there for the same reason as themselves and they would soon get to know each other. By all accounts, the initial business of the famous horse show had already begun. Christy assured his friends that a very interesting night lay ahead. After dinner many introductions took place and the Wests were fully inducted into the equine fraternity. They were touched by the friendship of these people and looked forward to having drinks with them later in the evening, but first they would like to rest for a while. Christy took a stroll up town to help digest his food.

During his time away, he met a few more of his acquaintances and with them visited more than one licensed establishment. For him, this was a real holiday. He was totally free with no set time for returning. Even at this stage, on the eve of the event, there was much bargaining in progress throughout the town. It had all the signs of being a lively affair. Later than intended, he arrived back at the hotel bar with a couple of friends. It was fairly crowded and the theme of discussion was much as he expected it to be. Before he had time to order a drink, the bar attendant told him to go to reception where the proprietor wanted to talk to him urgently. The man addressed him as Mr. Flood and had signs of concern about him. He said that Mr. West had taken suddenly ill and that his wife had gone with him to the hospital in Galway. It appeared that he had suffered some kind of seizure in his room where he and his wife had gone for a rest shortly after dinner. She immediately alerted reception and the doctor was sent for. Fortunately there was a locally based ambulance near at hand and little time was wasted in getting him to hospital. The doctor was not overly concerned but felt it was best to have the patient examined more thoroughly. The man told Christy that the lady would call from the hospital later in the night and it would be advisable for him to be available to talk to her when she gets through.

Christy was not the excitable type and would be seen as a man who could hold his composure in the face of most situations, but on this occasion he did show concern. It later emerged that one of his concerns was that she might ask him to bring the car into Galway to collect her or maybe the two of them at a very late hour. This, he feared, would put a damper on his planned night of enjoyment. The drinking and merry-making he knew to be good and perhaps there'd be a woman that might oblige him. He was a good man at the bottled Guinness and slipped back quietly to the friends that were waiting for him at the bar; he related the story to them and hoped that the night would not be spoiled. On that count he was re-assured shortly after eleven when the call came through from Mrs. West. She said the doctors had given the Major a very thorough examination and so far had not found signs of any serious disorder. They would know better in the morning after they had carried out some further tests. She was for staying overnight and would call again in the morning, hopefully with good news.

It was coming close to ten in the morning and it the day of the horse fair. Christy sat anxiously near reception hoping for the phone to ring. He wanted more than anything to get up the street and into the business of the fair but his orders were to wait for the call. The night before had been hectic enough, mainly through heavy drinking into the late hours and, through no fault of his own, he remained chaste throughout. Then came the "ting-a-ling" and Christy gets to his feet. The girl at reception says, "Mr. Flood, it's for you." Good news from Mrs. West; all tests completed and the doctors could find nothing about the Major's condition that was cause for alarm. She went on to say that, as a matter of routine, he was being kept in hospital a further twenty-four hours for observation. That meant they would have to stay over for another night but that was not a serious inconvenience, as they more than likely would have done so in any case. Her main concern was that Christy should proceed with the purchase of the two mare ponies that were of the best quality and in foal. Both of them trusted his judgment.

It would probably be after mid-day before she could get back to join him at the fair as she had some shopping to do for himself before catching a train out to Clifden. The old Major was not at all happy to be missing out on the experience of this famous horse show but on the other hand very pleased to have gotten a clean bill of health. He looked forward to seeing the purchase next day. By the time she got back, Christy had completed the bargaining for two of the finest looking animals at the show. They were both alike, of a reddish roan and she looked at them as a child would at a new toy. The two horses were given a distinctive mark and taken to a holding paddock where they would remain until it was time to transport them home to Elmwood Estate. In making the purchase, Christy did not rely totally on his own knowledge of horseflesh. Before declaring an interest, he discretely sought the advice of his more experienced friends. So for that reason he could confidently assure the purchaser that she had got value for money and that the trip to Connemara was well worthwhile.

"Now Christy, its time you and I had some lunch. Let's go to the hotel and I think you deserve a drink as well. Indeed both of us do."

In the midst of her delight, not a word was spoken about the man who still lay hospitalized. It was Christy who broached the subject at the dining table. It was such a relief for her to know that he was sound and healthy and she was just as glad they were keeping him in for another night, as she was pretty sure it was the rest he really needed.

"Mind you, I don't think he will see it quite as I do; he will not be at all happy at missing out on all that is going on in this wonderful place."

Christy nodded in agreement. "Yes, it is a pity all right and you are dead right Missus. This is a wonderful place to be and you know the best of it is still to come. We had great craic here in the hotel last night; you would fairly have enjoyed it. Mind you, I am a bit tired today but I tell you it was well worth it. Don't worry Missus, it will be even better tonight. I don't suppose it will be the same for you without himself being there as well; but then again, I don't think he would be very much into these late sessions."

Then it was back to the paddock to have another look at their precious purchase; this time they looked even more appealing to the excited lady from Donegal. At the showgrounds, there was much on offer to capture the attention of the eager onlooker; there was very little that Mrs. West did not take in and the friendship made it even better. Strange men and woman kept coming to her; all of them asking about her dear husband and a genuine sorrow that he could not be with them on this festive day. To her, it appeared the entire hurrah was for her alone and that she had awakened this little place on the western seaboard from a lengthy slumber. There were friendly pubs too where Christy felt she had to visit in order to get the real flavor of what this unique event was all about; it is in them that the true language of the horsey culture is spoken and enriched with wit. They spent a while in each of these before returning to the hotel for dinner at seven. But first, a phone call to the hospital to make sure that all is well.

Reassured on that account, the Major said he never felt better and was anxious to see the ponies next morning. He hoped for them to get on the road good and early. That, she assured him, they would endeavor to do even though it was hard to think about leaving such a heavenly spot to which she promised they would return. To her this short adventure represented what was best about her adopted country and it was a country she had no desire to ever leave. Out on the street the crowds were defying the lateness of the evening and an occasional horse trot could be heard making its way out of town, some going back to where they left and just as many to pastures new. The atmosphere would linger late around the town with a deal or two yet unfinished; a row breaks out and the crowd looks on; it's the dying kick of the pony fair.

Christy carries a sack of horse feed through a quiet town over to the paddock where the two animals were waiting to be fed. With that minor duty attended to, he was now moving into the closing act or epilogue in the hotel lounge.

The place was crowded and the heat intense. Most of the people were already well inebriated from the ablutions of the day. Mrs. West, wearing a light dress of cool fabric, held a seat for him at the top end of the spacious room. but first, he had to mingle amid wild drink and chat where mirthful mischief was alive. The seats were not far from where the piano stood and she was being called upon to play a tune to get the party into motion. She was by no means an accomplished musician but her rendition was well enough received by this particular audience who showed their appreciation by buying drinks for both her and Christy. It was truly a place of merriment and the best of friendship; songs were sung and stories told; recitations that were funny brought laughter galore.

Christy sat snug with his bottles of stout. He would rather be entertained than to entertain. He took the occasional glance in the direction of the women folk but noticed that most all of them seemed to be attached. He could feel a kind of an urge come over him from the memory of his first visit to the Clifden fair; she was a Connemara woman who had sold two fillies and he helped her to make the deal. She gave him five shillings for helping her to get that extra two quid out of the tough tangler that was trying to wear her down, then a couple of bottles and the bite to eat. Later in the night he found her in one of the crowded pubs. Then, accepting her gratitude once again, took her to the hay barn at the back of the paddocks. That was a few years ago when Christy was a fitter man. He came back the year after but nothing the same was in the offing. No mating calls, no fleshy thighs, nothing now but Arthur and the craic. There was no shortage of that on this occasion. He had consumed a massive amount of the black stuff over the run of the day and him simply living it to the full. His staying power was much admired as he told them stories about wilder days long before good sense endowed him.

It was well past the hour of midnight when the people started to gradually move away, most of them heading for their homes or other places. For Mrs. West, the fete was over; all good friends were heading off with promises to meet each other again next year. Her emotions stirred with the aid of gin and tonic water, she seldom felt such good before. Her voice gone husky from over-use, singing songs in chorus that she did not know, even from a song sheet a poor attempt at Galway Bay. A couple from Clare and another from Cavan were all that was left to keep her company as the curtain was falling on this grand event. They were the sorts to whom she could easily relate, but in that they were not unique as she felt the same about all the rest. Another drink or maybe two. It was wearing late and there was nothing more left to be taken out of this dying show. Christy had already taken leave from the company. He had had enough.

There was a gentle breeze making a whistling sound through the ivy that clung to the outer wall and around the window of his room. Christy looked on to an empty street. He thought about relieving his bladder out the window but thought again before going up the corridor to gill it into the piss-stained water of the shiny loo. On his way back, he could hear that familiar voice coming up the stairs. She was having another try at Galway Bay, as the other couples were saying good night. He had nothing on but the long tailed shirt, so he gathered speed back to the bedroom door. Safe inside, he lit a fag and a flash of thought about Norah Mullen. Enough of thought to cause a rise, he wondered if she ever would? But sure he might as well go chasing after moonbeams or light a penny candle from a star. That was the message coming from the corridor outside his door. She was singing her way to a bed that eluded her the night before and the one her man never got to.

Christy opened the door just about enough to let his head peep through.

"An early start in the morning Missus and we have to collect that horse box first. Say eight o'clock?"

"Ah Christy, is it you? Hope my singing hasn't disturbed you. Ah yes, the morning. And what about it Christy? Not too early I hope. Christy, you think of everything. How could we ever do without you?"

Then, with a warm hand, she ran her fingers through his graying hair.

"A good man Christy. A very good man."

Pushing the door more open against him, he falters back , aware that he was half undressed. The room was dark except for the little light that beamed from outside through the ivy- shadowed window. Resting both her hands on his shoulders and gripping the fabric of his shirt, she pulled his porter-stained lips into her open mouth. They pressed heavily against each other and she could feel the truth in everything that Vincent Wilkie told her about this man. He was all of that and even more.

Christy awoke as day was breaking. he could sense that the naked body beside him was awake as well. There they lay silently and aware of each other. She was a few years his senior, but he had no complaint, nor had she. They knew that time was wearing thin but there was latent passion still in reserve. So waste not, want not. As his living motto, he was ready again for another go. Ready too, she laid it on and thought again what Wilkie said; "This randy rogue has got it all, so better me than someone else." In the stillness of dawn they made love again, only this time with more sober and conscious intensity and, in the afterglow of post satisfaction, talked freely about the pleasant atmosphere of the fair, the ponies and the long drive home, just as if nothing had ever happened. The Major's name did not come up. It was hardly the time or indeed the place to be talking about the man who was a safe distance away from the hot and heavy scene. What is not known can never harm and that is how it was going to be, both of them were assured of that. It was pleasure wild and at no cost. They would both return to their banal ways and be like friends in most every way, as the purveyor of livestock;

none better than Christy Flood. To the Major, he was the trusted friend.

The tedious journey had now begun. They were out of Clifden on the Galway road. Christy drove at a modest pace, as the load on tow was new to him. With some kinky mysteries thus unveiled; they knew much more about each other; would this deformalize their dealings where deference would be no more. would it still be Missus or 'Florence Girl'? Not just now with the Major on board. It was back to what it had been before. He was looking good and liked the ponies. He apologized for causing a fuss. Mrs. West sat behind and related most all the happenings of the fair to his listening ear; how the deals were bargained out, in what to her was dramatic form. The entire show was a grand affair; the pretty animals were a sight to see and the side events were fun as well; she was really sorry he had to miss it all. Silent Christy at the wheel was praised for the comfort of the ride. They would stop two times or maybe three to air the ponies at a quiet spot or two along the way.

A great relief at the sight of home. Back at Elmwood shortly after six and no one there but Norah Mullen, the ponies were taken to the wee acre behind the house. Norah prepared an evening tea for the weary travelers while Mrs. West relayed to her most all that had happened in beautiful Connemara, at least all that was safe to tell. Major West, looking quite relaxed, talked a little about his scare and glad it was nothing more than that.

"I have missed out on what these two seem to have very much enjoyed and for that reason I am hardly likely to forget my brief stay in scenic Connemara."

"Yes, but the important thing is that you are well and will no doubt be going back again next year," spoke the reassuring wife.

Christy gave a nod of approval to what the lady said; he seemed a bit tired and had good reason to be so, as only the Missus herself would know. He mused over what the Major said about his not forgetting. Yes indeed, he thought. It was fair comment, but little he knows, poor man.

"Her and I have reasons too."

Norah cleared the table after tea and took all to the kitchen. She was trying hard to get away before Christy had taken leave of his hosts as he might be on for leaving her home. But such a thought was not on his mind and never again would it re-occur. Yes, for some strange reason, he bothered her no more. To her, it was a relief and to Madge a mystery. They even mentioned it to Mrs. West who give a giddy laugh and said, "Maybe he has found someone else?"

Chapter Fifteen

It was wearing close to another Christmas with a more than usual amount of mail coming the way of Elmwood House, most of it from overseas. Mrs. West could easily recognize the handwriting on the one addressed to her husband; Elizabeth Barton was the sender but it did not look like a greeting card. Miss Barton was writing to voice concern about Stanley's condition. She felt it was a pity they did not come over for a couple of weeks like the previous year. They had only managed about two long weekends with him since that time. While the doctor could not see any noticeable decline in his medical condition, she nevertheless could see in him a big loss of interest in the things around him. He was slow at responding to any kind of stimulus. He had recently suffered an epileptic attack that was not too severe; it was an infrequent yet recurrent condition that they were well used to dealing with. She was by no means the alarmist type, but the Wests knew her well enough to take note of what she had to say when it comes to Stanley's welfare. Many times she would remind them about the amount of good he derived from having had that couple of weeks with them in the Dales and how he had taken to that lovely girl, Norah.

The news was a bit discomforting for the two of them and coming at an awkward time with Christmas and the New Year just around the corner. Mrs. West called Norah and Madge into the living room and related everything to them about what was in the letter; she said it looked like they might have to cancel the New Year's Eve party and spend it over there instead. Though Madge had never seen this ailing son, she nevertheless felt pity for him and expressed it with sensitivity as best she could. Norah had often thought about Stanley and wondered if he still remembered her or the little things they used to do together during those lovely autumn days the year before. She stated her candid opinion that Stanley was a lot more important than any celebration could ever be. Her advice was for them to get over there immediately, or better again, bring him over to spend Christmas or perhaps the New Year with his parents here in Elmwood. The lady was silent and appeared pensive. She was obviously taking cognizance of what had been put to her so frankly.

She then took a more consenting look at Norah. "Dear, you do speak a lot of sense and that is what I would like to do, but there is a problem about taking him away far from the Centre and he does feel more at home there than anywhere else."

"He feels at home wherever Miss Barton is and surely she can come here along with him. I know from our time in York how dependent he is on her, but I too can help as well you know."

On that assertion there was no disputing and it was stated clearly in Elizabeth Barton's letter. Not that the Wests needed any reminding of this obvious truth. As they were talking, the Major was in conversation with Elizabeth on the telephone. She assured him that Stanley's condition was not a cause for immediate concern. It was just that she thought he might benefit a little from having new people around him for a while. She suggested they might consider coming over in the New Year to spend a while of patient engagement with their son and perhaps bring that sweet girl as well. After coming off the phone he came out to where his wife and the two housemaids were still talking. They all listened to his account and what he sought to do about it. Norah was not so ready to express her feelings to the Major about what was best for Stanley and for a while was taken by the thought of going for a few days to England. But her concern on this issue was real and genuine; she was a kind-hearted person who wanted more than anything to bring a bit of comfort and cheerfulness to this unfortunate man-child.

No decision was taken right then in Norah's presence, but she was pretty confident that the woman had taken heed of what she said and was likely to give it more thought, as well as mention to the Major. She did not have too long to wait for an answer to her desire; Mrs. West came that evening to say they had both agreed it was time Stanley was brought here to stay with them for a while in the family home and that the boss himself would be going over for him and Elizabeth shortly after Christmas. This news made Norah feel rather good about her gaining influence in the Big House. She had just played a part in nudging these people in the direction of doing what was right. As for Stanley, she hoped he would remember and be glad to see her. It would be much the same as before, taking him around in his wheelchair and amusing him with chat and song.

Very quiet was how this particular Christmas had been described by most of the people. For Norah and her father, it had been that as well. She had received an extra special gift from the wage-earning Benny Ryan. In the accompanying card, he again expressed his affection for her and in truth it was what she wanted to hear from him. Even though he was now working on the estate, they were seldom ever in contact with each other. His place of work was at the furthermost end of the farmyard, well out of view from the dwelling. Another reason for them not having much contact could well be that Benny was now having a much fuller life through being a lot on the road with the van. He was mixing with many people, both men and women. As for Norah, the best she could manage this time was to send him a greeting card. She still had a problem about allowing herself get deeply involved in a relationship so personal as a steady boyfriend. She had a definite liking for Benny and thought about him many times, but was fully content in being with her father and in the service of people that valued her contribution. For her it was an uncomplicated, and at times exciting, kind of life. She had no desire to change it, at least not for the time being.

The Major left on the morning after Christmas Day. He was going to be away for three or four days. He always seemed to have business to attend to over there and it would more than likely involve his friend David. As usual at such times Norah would be staying over in the Big House so as not to have the lady totally on her own. Apart from this, it would be an easygoing time and she could spend a good part of the daytime attending to things in her own home. She liked the relaxed nature of her evening chats with Mrs. West. They would have a glass of wine or two, as it was the festive time and the name of Benny Ryan would surely get a mention. It was always an early bedtime, seldom later than ten o'clock. Norah's room was to the rear of the house, over the kitchen area and closer to the farmyard. In the mornings she could always hear Vincent Wilkie's voice when he and the other men would be attending to the wintering livestock and their exchanges were always calmly jovial.

Even though it was regarded as the eerie house among the trees, she always slept at ease in it. There was never a sound to disturb the night. That was why she thought it strange to hear what sounded like a side door being closed at around the hour of five in the morning and stranger still the sound of a motor vehicle leaving the yard shortly after. Duty prompted her to leave her room and go over the long corridor and through a library room to the main section of the house to alert Mrs. West. There was a dim light in the main corridor outside the half-open door of the master bedroom. Norah could see that the lady was securely asleep and perhaps better left undisturbed so she retreated quietly back to her own quarters. It was not so easy for her to get back to sleep, though she felt assured that all was well and the workmen would soon be arriving for their morning chores. She took a book to read herself back to slumber.

"A hell of a long time to go without, but it was well worth the wait," thought a very fulfilled Christy Flood as he drove home in the glow of sheer contentment. He could scarcely believe that it was over four months since they had their romp at the Connemara Horse Fair and it like a bloody famine ever since. Back in the home territory this kind of thing was not so easy to do. Here he had to be ever so discrete and the Florence girl warned on his life to be just that. "Never say Keatley." This was to be their dark secret that time was not likely to ever reveal. They were both expert at playing it cool and casual when in the company of other people, never giving a hint as to what was going on. The thought of any such suspicions coming the way of the gossipy workers was inconceivable as far as either of the two was concerned. To the Major, Christy was an invaluable asset to his farming enterprise; a trusted friend that he could depend on and that was how it had to stay.

Stanley was brought to Elmwood on the eve of the New Year; it was a bitter cold evening with snow showers blowing in from the east as darkness was descending. Norah put her two arms around him and looked closely into his face. She could see that some change had come over him since the time they were together more than a year earlier. But it was still the same Stanley she was holding in her arms. It was a joy for her to see him again and sweeter still when he smiled and said her name. He was immediately taken into the living room and set before a glowing fire along with his parents and Miss Barton. Norah stayed with them for a little while before going back to her duties with Madge and the other woman who helped at set times. They were busy getting things ready for the party that would be taking place later in the night. The party was not intended to be a big or elaborate affair; no overseas guests this year, not even the strange fellow David. Just Dr and Mrs. Clarke plus a few friends and associates that the Major had got to know through his business and golfing connections. The late arrival of Christy Flood made it a slightly more local affair but it was a select gathering nonetheless.

Again Norah was invited to join the party after the food had been served and the other ladies had gone home. For a change she no longer had to worry about Christy who seemed to have given up the pursuit of her. For the first time she was asked to sing a song, something she certainly did not want to do. It was Miss Barton who made the request, saying how she loved hearing her sweet singing voice the many times she did so to entertain Stanley. The sweetness of the melody brought total silence and Stanley looked at her with tearful eyes. He was again living in the memory of a time that was special when she was doing this for him and him alone. All the others quickly observed his reaction to Norah and to her it was a clear indication that for the days ahead most of her time would again be devoted to him. This time it was going to be different though. With quite a bit of snow on the ground it would not be possible to take him out and around the place in his wheelchair. What a pity, she thought. Even though it is the dead of winter there are still many places and things that she could have shown him if only the weather had been a bit more compliant.

In a house the size of Elmwood with its many rooms at both levels she would have to find other ways to engage his interest until the weather softened enough to allow them venture outside. Part of his daily routine was to be walked with the aid of a person or two. This, Miss Barton said, was most important for his blood circulation and muscular preservation. It needed to be done twice daily at least. Norah watched carefully at how the expert one went about this task and marveled at how easy she made it look; it was a skill to acquire and she was ready for it. In spite of protests, Norah insisted she was well able to do this on her own and no one doubted that she could. It was just that the Major and Mrs. West thought it unfair to impose such a burden on the girl. But for this particular girl it was certainly not a burden. Her fondness for Stanley and the knowledge that he was reciprocating her goodness, made it a duty of pleasure. By the end of the first week the two of them were walking the entire ground floor area of the Big House as many as three or perhaps four times daily and the signs were encouraging.

She quickly reattuned her hearing to the sound of his discordant speech and very soon was able to decipher the plethora of words he never seemed to grow tired of speaking to her. The number of board games that were already in the house further aided their communication. There were a variety of these that was suited to all levels of mental agility and much fun they derived from them. There was a lot of curious interest coming from the men folk on the first day that Norah wheeled him down the yard to view the livestock, particularly the two Connemara Ponies. Few of them ever heard much about Stanley apart from the occasional chat in the earlier days about the mysterious son who was studying law in England. As a preparation for his arrival, Mrs. West thought it best that these men should know what to expect and advised Madge and Norah to convey the message tactfully to them. Christy, in whom she had confided on the night he kept her company, was also talking casually about the visit of young West and the terrible misfortune that had come over him. These mostly hardened men were moved by compassion they could not disguise as each of them came to shake Stanley's pale hand and wished him to have a happy time. With the proverbial ice now broken and the winter one dissolved under milder weather, they wanted to discover more about the outdoor side of things for what was left of the days ahead.

With the fields and hedges now bare and lifeless there was nothing much that Norah could show him while nature rested for the winter; it was not the best time for him to be here. Why, she thought to herself, could they not have done the sensible thing of bringing Stanley over here when the Estate was lush and alive with so many things to see and do. This was a thought she intended giving expression to at the first opportune time. She was confident too that it would be heard as her effect on Stanley was already showing. Instead of going in the direction of the muddy fields, she decided to keep on the solid ground of the farmyard and go across towards the slipway to watch the flow of the river. In order to get there it was necessary for them to pass by the fish depot where Benny Ryan was busy washing the inner walls and floors. The white van was parked outside

"Benny," she called. "Come out and say hello to Stanley. I am sure you have heard about him being here with us on holiday. Stanley, this is my friend Benny."

Like the others, Benny too offered him a friendly hand and said he was pleased to meet him. He failed to comprehend Stanley's muffled utterance, which Norah interpreted for him as 'Thank you, Benny.' Turning to Norah, he asked what Christmas had been like for her and did she do anything interesting over the festive time. Mindful of the nice gift he had given her and feeling less than worthy for not having returned the generosity, she mentioned how busy she had been on account of Stanley coming so soon after Christmas.

"You see, we only got word about this a few days before Christmas and from that on little else was done or talked about until the Major went over for him. I am sorry for not getting you something but to tell you the honest truth Benny, I never got out as much as once to do any shopping."

Managing artfully to hide his hurt, Benny shrugged his shoulders and turned towards Stanley saying he understood and not to be worrying.

"Stanley, aren't you the lucky man to have such a beautiful girl as Norah all to yourself and here is poor me not able to see her any more."

Her reply to both of them was a smiling gesture and to Benny it was a luring one of which he would have liked to analyze for fuller meaning.

She was still the one he longed for most. But right then her main mission was to bring brightness to the dismal life of Stanley West and that required being extra sensitive to his perceptions. She would do or say nothing to disturb his happiness. Her feelings for him were born out of pity for his sorry plight. That was the kind of nature that resided in Norah Mullen. But more than pity, she was able to see within this broken body a real and gentle person who was safe and easy to be with.

For whatever length of time he would be staying here with them, it was going to be her pleasure to do what was expected of her. To her it was truly a labor of love and her reward was in seeing a smile come over him. On that understanding, her feelings for Benny Ryan would just have to stay on hold until a time that was less demanding in terms of duty and emotional call.

They did not make it as far as the slipway on that occasion. There was coldness in the air and she thought it best to bring him back to the indoor warmth where there were other things that they could do. The card and board games they found easy and relaxed. Stanley seemed quite familiar with the rules pertaining to them. Miss Barton had obviously been working on that aspect of his rehabilitation. He had yet another talent which was revealed on the night of the party when, with one hand, he played part of a tune on the grand piano. Whatever about the quality of the music, it was a moving experience for them that were there. So Norah insisted that music would have to be part of their daily routine from there on.

"First, Stanley, you must play me a tune on the piano before we do anything else and don't forget you promised to teach me how to play before you go away again."

Talk about going away, she then realized, was not conducive to the atmosphere she wanted to create but she had the gift of immediacy and recovered the mood by singing gently to his vacant glance. She watched attentively as he touched on the ivory with the fingers of that left hand which had reasonable function and holding power. The right one was almost powerless.

Although Elizabeth Barton was mainly assigned to the care of Stanley, she also had an area of responsibility in the nursing home where he was kept and for that reason could not be away from the place for too long. It was also a fact that Stanley could never come away for any of these breaks without her being with him or at least close at hand. Her life was a demanding one for which she seemed well suited. That was why the Major willingly contributed towards a large part of her weekly salary and was glad that Norah was able to give her a deserving break. All of them could see benefit in this arrangement and the main beneficiary being Stanley himself. Now everything about him seemed better by far.

There was absolutely no doubt that Norah had a way with Stanley that was good beyond words and whatever it was should be availed of on a more regular basis. Norah was very much in favor of the idea, when Mrs. West put it to her. She talked about the many places and happenings on the estate that she would like to take him to, more so during spring and summer. The suggestion obviously found favor with Mrs. West but she had to point out the necessity of having Elizabeth here as well and that may not always be possible.

"Norah, I have absolutely no doubt that you and I are quite capable in most respects, but there are certain things with Stanley where Elizabeth is essentially better suited, like in the case of him getting an epileptic seizure. Yes, by all means let us bring them over as often as we can but what we were thinking is that perhaps you could go over a time or two during the year as well."

Norah could see no serious difficulty about agreeing to this proposal. Her dad was well capable of managing on his own for a week or two and she would be doing what she thoroughly enjoyed. She could also sense from the conversation that Stanley's time of departure was nigh at hand and that their time together was close to an end; Mrs. West was downbeat.

"However, as it is now mid-January and Spring not all that far away, we will try to have him over to see the planting and sowing of crops as well as the new batch of grazing cattle going out to pasture and not forgetting the two pretty ponies. Their parturition time is around the second and third week of March so hopefully we will have two lovely little foals going out to grass at that time as well. Mid-April and into May should be a very good time, don't you think Norah? And May first happens to be Stanley's birthday as well? That, after all, is not too far away, so we don't have to think about sending you over until summer and perhaps again in the Autumn because we can clearly see how good you are for him."

Norah, too, was downbeat and even more so on the days following Stanley's exit from Elmwood. That morning as they were leaving to go, he held tight to her hand and was stubbornly reluctant to let go his grip. Miss Barton assured that all would be well again in a day or two; she would also do her best to get back in the spring. It certainly was a time of ebbing spirits around the place; the gloom even visited Christy for a time as he learned that it was the Florence girl that had gone back with the visitors instead of the Major. Not to worry Christy, for this good lady would surely find a way of making it up to him in the days ahead.

Chapter Sixteen

A filly and a colt were born within a week of each other. The first one arrived late evening St. Patrick's Day. Andy Snodgrass, the veterinarian, delivered them safely. Except for the Major who was in with a cold, there was a lot of excitement around the place and Mrs. West was certainly showing signs of being the most affected. This was her very own enterprise and she was off to a flying start. Christy was very much on the scene for these important events. Indeed, Florence and him spent what could be called a fair amount of time over in the stables, most likely seeing to it that everything was in order. Their interest in this was not at all surprising considering that these animals held a special resonance for both of them. All of this had now taken place without the participation of Major West who was confined to bed under Dr Clarke's orders. He had contracted a bout of influenza that seemed to be lingering longer than what was considered normal. The doctor had called with him a few times and was concerned enough to suggest sending him for further investigation, but that could wait until the patient was back on his feet. Without being over alarmist, he suggested sending him to a Dublin Clinic to be examined by an eminent heart specialist who happened to be a friend of his.

"Most likely this man will find absolutely nothing wrong with you. But, for your own peace of mind, it is better to have it checked out just in case something might be starting. It might also be advisable for you to think about taking things a bit easier from now on; you have been going at a fast pace ever since you got here and I can well imagine the amount of mental anxiety that goes with all of that."

"Yes, I agree. It has been quite hectic here at times over the past three years and I suppose you could say I brought a lot of it on myself. But thankfully now we have moved on and away from the acrimony that beset us for so long. I also realize that we have an excellent workforce and regretfully, I was too slow in seeing that at the start. My good wife is better by far at handling that end of the business. As for the fish business, that young man Benny Ryan is doing a first class job. I certainly have nothing to worry about in that department."

As they were talking, Benny was preparing for the start of the local fishing season. The spring fish were on the move and the net men were out to catch as many of them as possible. This meant he would have to be more about the place from then until the end of summer.

He was quite happy in his role as manager of the Fisheries Co-Op. That was the title he liked to give himself from time to time but only when he was out of earshot of the local suppliers. They would tend to deride a young man's harmless fancy. Norah was beginning to pay him the occasional visit at times when she happened to have a few minutes to spare, and now with him working on the estate there would be no objections to her making him a cup of tea from time to time.

"Nothing," he said, "could please me better than to have a cup of tea that was made specially for me by you; and as the Major has been generous enough to allow me take the van home with me I would like to take you to the pictures one of these evenings."

Norah graciously accepted the invitation saying it was something she too would very much like to do and would be free most evenings after work now that the Major and Mrs. West had gone to Dublin for a couple of days. She then went on to tell him about plans for her increased involvement with Stanley West. It was envisaged that he would be coming here on a more regular basis and that she would occasionally be going over to England as well. This was most likely her tactful way of telling him not to be counting on her availability for a steady relationship. While there was no doubting her fondness for Benny, there was still something or other holding her back. It was so much easier for her to involve more fully with the helpless and dependent Stanley West where nothing was being sought beyond human kindness.

They sat with their arms around each other in a van that was washed clean both in and out, but still carrying a fishy scent to the unaccustomed nose. This was by no means a deterrent to the one who was out with a young man so besot by her beauty and gentleness. She was fully trusting of his goodness. In a pleading way, he expressed the depth of his love for her and hoped that she too could feel the same for him.

"Ever since that first Sunday evening I met you at the Coolaghy Hall, my mind has seldom been free of thoughts about you. So long as you are around I will never be able to go out with anyone else. Norah, I want to love you."

This to Norah was a kind of pressure she felt very ill at ease with.

"Benny I like you very much too and I want you to know that. But please understand, I am not yet ready for what I think you are asking from me, Benny, I am sorry it has to be like this for the present. I am terribly fond of you but I need more time."

Benny then realized that further persistence was not going to work on this gentle yet uncertain being. He again expressed his love for her and would still be waiting for her readiness. They then spent close to another half hour of tender attentiveness that did not involve over-intense physical engagement, the kind that she was obviously afraid of. This was the one thing about her that he had difficulty in attaching meaning to, yet he knew enough to question in his mind why it was that this special one was so different from all the others. At the end of their sharing, he accepted her invitation to come in for a nighttime cuppa. Feeling quite at ease in the presence of friendly Billy Mullen, he sat down by the blazing fire where the kettle hung a bubbling. Billy and he had much in common and had a lot to talk about through their involvement in the two ends of the fisheries business. Norah watched and listened as the two engaged each other in chat, while she was preparing the tea. For a moment she thought how this cozy bedtime scene was appealing to her but just as quickly dissolved the thought.

A valvular condition of the heart was how the Dublin specialist described his diagnostic findings to Major West in the company of his wife. In simple language, he was not a well man. On the positive side, he knew many with a similar ailment that are living a normal enough lifestyle; the secret of this is to avoid tasks that are strenuous or situations that are stressful. It was disturbing news for both of them and would most likely put paid to many of their long-term plans for the future of Elmwood Estate. For the present. they were for keeping the news strictly to themselves. He would be going on a prescribed medication for the rest of his natural life and decisions about the future would be taken wisely over the summer months. There was nothing unusual about Mrs. West playing the major role with the workmen out in the tillage fields. After all, this is what she has been doing since shortly after their coming here. At the same time, she could see problems ahead with him not being actively involved in the running of the show. He was not the type to rest easily in the passive role.

Now that the crops were sown and the grazing stock purchased there was nothing for it but to carry on as usual for the season ahead. There was time and plenty for thinking things through. It was past the middle of April and Stanley was on his way along with Elizabeth Barton. Norah was helping the Missus prepare for their arrival. To her it seemed only such a short time since he left them that cold January morning. Now was a much better time for him to be taken out and around the estate and she was determined to make the best of the fine spring weather that was in it. On this occasion Elizabeth had managed to get him here on her own. Neither of the two parents was quite up to the traveling at that particular time. Stanley showed his delight at seeing all of them again and especially delighted when Norah took both his hands to raise him up out of the wheelchair to begin a walk across the rear exterior of the house. Again she insisted on doing it on her own by holding his limp arm tightly around her neck and her bearing the entire weight of his defective side. The onlookers marveled at how easy she made it look. She possessed a unique skill that was born out of a need within her. It was a labor of profound fulfillment.

"Mrs. West, I don't think we can let Stanley's birthday pass without a proper celebration of it. This is an occasion for the biggest party ever held in this house. You and the Major would both like it to be grand, I know." Norah put this to the lady with a conviction that had to be heeded. To her, this was an event of much greater importance than the many things they had been known to celebrate in the past.

"Indeed, it's one of the few times since his accident that we will be celebrating his birth with him. We will certainly be having a party to mark the occasion but as for it being a grand affair, well I am not so sure?"

Like all the other members of staff, Norah was completely in the dark about the state of the Major's health. Perhaps if she had known about this, her approach would not have been so forcefully stated. Nevertheless her sentiments were well received by Mrs. West who was going to have a quiet talk with the ailing boss, now endeavoring to accustom himself to a less engaging lifestyle. He was in total agreement that the event was certainly worthy of celebration but in the circumstances had some reservations about doing so in an all out big way. He would have to take time to think it over and of course time was something he now had plenty of as his wife swiftly reminded him. At the same time, they would have to decide soon as the actual date was less than two weeks away, so the party would have to be held in or around that time, perhaps the Friday evening nearest to it. She had her answer before bedtime that very night. Yes, his thinking was much in line with what Norah had suggested. As grand, if not better than anything that was before. The only difference was that he would be taking little or no responsibility for any aspect of it but said he would like the usual overseas guests to be invited, even at this late stage.

The ever-supporting wife assured him that all would be taken care of and that their good friend Elizabeth was willingly ready to share the burden of responsibility with her. These two ladies set about the task with enthusiasm and Mrs. West ruled that all the workers as well as some of the neighbors were going to be included in the guest list for this special occasion. She had fond memories of that first ever party to mark their arrival at Elmwood; the warmth of goodwill that existed on that occasion was still there and only waiting to be retrieved. The days that lay ahead promised little idle set for any of them. For Elizabeth Barton, it was a diversion away from the tedium of a demanding routine thus allowing Norah Mullen to be in her sweet best as the sunshine of Stanley's days.

It was Friday evening, the second day of May, and a number of English visitors were already gathering in. Two additional local women were drafted in to assist with the catering. There was little doubt that this was going to be the grand affair that Norah had hoped for. On this occasion, she was playing but a minor role in the food and drinks department, as her duties to Stanley were of paramount importance. The Major left the comfort of his warm study to have a word with the friends from overseas that had gathered into the sitting room. Both he and his wife were keeping faith with the policy of saying nothing about the state of his health. All of the male employees, along with the few invited neighbors, assembled in the everyday living room that lay between the kitchen and the large sitting room where the Major and his friends were. It looked like this kind of segregation was happening unintentionally but in truth it was the sort of arrangement that suited both sides best.

Out of courtesy and thoughtfulness, Norah insisted that Miss Barton be the one, along with Major and Mrs. West, to present the guest of honor to all that came to celebrate his birthday. Later on she would bring him back into the living room where he would be more likely to get a laugh from the likes of Vincent Wilkie or even Christy Flood. Once again Billy Mullen failed to make his appearance. In spite of much persuasion from his daughter, he stubbornly refused and went to the river with Laurence Keatley instead.

"Daughter dear, I think it might be more profitable for me to go down there than to sit with that crowd and have to watch that fucker of a David into the bargain. I would still find it hard to keep my hands off him after what he said to me yon morning."

"Daddy, do you not think its about time we left all that in the past where it belongs? Mind you, I am not in the least happy being anywhere next or near that man, but he is their friend and that is something I just have to live with."

"Yes, and for that very reason I am staying well shot of the place tonight. Good night my dear, and enjoy your party."

A variety of beverages were there in abundance and the effects were being heard throughout the building. Norah sang her party piece for each of the groups and was highly commended by both. Even after dark it was still a mild and pleasant evening outside. Two men and one of the helper ladies sat smoking on a bench seat at the side of the house. They also held drinks in their hands. They were being observed by the stealthy David who was by far the best dressed of all the men folk. He was out for a breath of the fresh country air and walked alone towards the front lawn. Norah then joined Madge and the other two helpers in the kitchen for the washing and tidying up after the feasting had ended. Along with them was a little girl. She was the daughter of one of the women and was lending them a hand. She might have been aged twelve or less and her name was Monica. As the chores were being attended to, the women were still able to hear the banter of fun coming from the living room. Wilkie was inebriated and giving a best performance. There was a quieter and more subdued affair going on over in the big sitting room where local wit would surely have been lost like a grain of pollen in the desert air, with the Major entertaining a higher caliber of guest.

Mrs. West who could make herself equally at home with either group brought Elizabeth and Stanley in to share the goodness that was the source of merry laughter. All of them were deferential in kindness towards the junior Mr. West, who looked around in search of Norah. He had missed seeing her for a good part of the time. At the same time, he seemed captivated by the sound of strange tongues and the amount of unquelled laughter that went with it. It was a happy place to be and he wanted it not to end. The little girl in the kitchen with the working women was more anxious about getting to see the new foals out in the wee acre behind the house. She was not having a lot of luck in persuading her busy mum to leave the atmosphere and go outside with her in the dark of night. Norah, in her kindness, did not like seeing the child disappointed so she took her little hand and retrieved a battery torch from the kitchen shelf. The two departed through the back door.

Like their mother, the elegant equines of Connemara were docile tame, obviously from the amount of attention and pampering they had been getting all of the six weeks since their birth. After spending a good fifteen minutes stroking and patting them, Norah could not get the little one away form the tiny ponies. "I could stay with them forever," she said. When they eventually got back, the kitchen was almost deserted. All of the ladies except Madge had moved into the living room where the craic was rough and ready and still going strong. Christy did not like being outshone by the likes of Vincent Wilkie but was content enough sitting in the corner nourishing his belly with frothy stout. He looked like he had a bit of an edge on, taking the occasional glance in the direction of the Missus who was again wearing that summery frock to complement her protuberant bosom. Yet he was sober and wise enough to know that there was nothing more on offer for him on this occasion. He would just have to wait his chance and that he would surely do.

Stanley was at his happiest with Norah seated close beside him and her asking how he was enjoying himself while squeezing his hand in an affirmative gesture. She had just finished the singing of "Lovely Derry" when Madge came to the room door and beckoned her attention. Norah then followed her back to the kitchen. Not appearing to be overly concerned, she enquired where the wee girl Monica had gone. She had been with Madge for a while after coming in from the ponies but then disappeared again. Her mother was enjoying a relaxing moment that was well deserved and seldom ever came her way. She was feeling the uplifting affect of Sandyman Port and nobody there begrudged it to her.

"It's okay," Norah assured, "I think I know where she is. I see the torch has been taken. Don't say anything and I will go and fetch her."

Norah went back to the wee acre gate and in a low voice called, "Monica, are you in there?" Getting no response, she thought about other likely spots the young one might have stolen away to. Turning away from the gate she thought for a moment of hearing a faint gasping kind of sound. It sounded like it came from the top end of the field where there was an open shed that the horses had access to. At this point Norah could not fully trust her hearing as to what the sound represented or indeed did she actually hear anything discernible at all. The best thing was for her to check it out before looking in other places.

She did not want to make a fuss about what was nothing more than a curious wee girl slipping out to have a look around. As she made off over the pathway towards the shed her foot hit against an object on the ground. She was acutely alarmed to discover it to be the battery torch that they had used earlier when viewing the ponies. Expeditiously fast, she made it to the shed that contained a quantity of straw bedding, but it also housed a scene that was horrific and one that she was ill prepared to deal with. On hearing the sound of activity inside, she stopped for a brief moment before entering. Clearly she heard a voice that was only too familiar and it speaking words that reawakened in her a latent and hellish torment. Monica was crying.

"Do not be afraid my dear beautiful child. You are so beautiful I could not harm you. Come now. This will make you into a real woman. yes, a real and even more beautiful woman."

Norah ran inside and screamed for Monica to come to her. The frightened child ran towards the bright torchlight and into the arms of her rescuer. The hideous ruffian turned away from the blinding glare that was beaming upon him like he had been debased far beneath the level of human dignity. Through Norah's timely intervention, he had not gotten quite so far as to violate his innocent captive. But a more damning reality was just about to reveal itself to him. Holding the little one tightly with one arm, Norah continued to keep the predatory pervert under the spotlight While the drag of regression was taking her back to her own childhood days in the farmyard of that old monastery. Her story was not one of being rescued like Monica had just been, but of being subjected to vile abuse by a man robed in black. She thought his name was Brother Thomas and here he now stood in ignominy before her.

"Brother Thomas, if I might call you so. I don't suppose you remember me, the wee girl that brought the tea to uncle Jack in the farmyard of Tirkeeran Monastery?"

Still holding the strong light straight into his bewilderment, she could see the look of petrified anxiety that had totally engulfed him. He was now a fallen creature.

"I am fairly certain that neither the Major nor Mrs. West know exactly who or what you are but will no doubt be interested to hear what I am going to tell them as well as the guards in the morning. Consider yourself lucky that my father is not here for me to tell who exactly you are."

David remained mute throughout all of this, as there was nothing he could usefully say in his precarious predicament. But then in desperation, made the serious blunder of suggesting payment for her silence along with a promise to be gone for good early in the morning. Still maintaining a show of strength and composure, Norah retorted with resolute promptness.

"Things are different now. Your ill-begotten money can never buy my silence nor can you force silence on me with the threat that something terrible will happen to me; just as you did when I was an innocent child like this wee girl is."

With a degree of uncertainty about what was best to do, Norah took Monica back inside. The child seemed none the worse for what she had been through.

The fact that she had been rescued in time made her somewhat oblivious to the intensity of the perilous situation she had just been freed from. Norah held her silence and decided it should remain that way until morning at least. Then, with a chilling onset of fear and nausea coming suddenly over her, she sat alone trembling in the kitchen. The abuse that happened to her occurred over a period of several months when she was about eleven years old and then, to her relief, the said Brother Thomas was suddenly gone from the place. While no reports of wrong-doing had ever been made against this man, the senior priests of the order began to have serious doubts about his suitability for the priest-hood. He had joined the order on what was called a late vocation and in the hope of eventually becoming a priest was ordained a deacon with the title Brother Thomas. It was a tribute to the wisdom of the prudent men that were charged with the responsibility of assessing his worthiness that they judged him to be unfit. He was born and reared in England, the son of half-Irish parents and it was believed he went back there after leaving the confines of Tirkeeran. He was never heard of since.

The little girl Monica had gone back to the living room where her mother, along with Christy Flood, was dancing an old time waltz to the music of Jamesy Connolly on the button-keyed melodeon. With music and craic galore, Stanley's birthday party seemed unending as he sat in the midst of it all, wondering where Norah had gone. Choosing to be in her aloneness, from the kitchen Norah could hear the sound of unfet-tered merriment. For most of them all troubles were on hold for that little while and it would have been a pity to disclose anything that would put paid to their pleasure. However, she made up her mind not to stay over for the night. The thought of being in the same house as that man was anything but comforting and she would have to find some way to avoid it. Benny Ryan was about the last of the late arrivals to the party. He was exceptionally well groomed and had obviously been out for the night on some other mission. He had come to realize the futility of him pursuing Norah Mullen, at least for the present time. Yet to him, she was by far the most desirable around. But in this her inner thoughts were negative and relentlessly persistent when faced with the challenge of fac-ing what her heart was endeavoring to nudge her towards. He looked appealing on the night and she pondered that in secret. It was him she wanted to take her home, just as a friend and nothing more.

Although a little surprised, Mrs. West did not question Norah's wish to leave the proceedings and go home with Benny. After all, the girl had been giving a lot of her time to Stanley of late and was probably tired. It was not the usual chatty Norah that sat in the van beside Benny on their way up the road. He did not comment on this to her, nor did she question him as to why he was so late in getting to the party. She had not been seeing him very much of late. In fact, she had never once taken Stanley over across the yard to see him since the time of his winter visit. Perhaps this had to do with her wish not to be seen as ever available to this likable man and having to endure the discomfort of declining his goodness. Needless to say, little time was spent at the time of parting outside her cottage home. She expressed her gratitude to him for continued friendship and trusted kindness.

From his bed, Billy Mullen called out, "Is it you Norah and how did your party go?" Not getting a reply, he spoke again to enquire if his daughter was feeling all right. She entered the room and sat on the edge of his bed. Immediately he could see that something was seriously the matter and asked her to tell him what it was or what on earth could have happened to his little girl. Through wailing tears of profound distress, she began relating the nauseating story involving child Monica and then the grim discovery that ensued from it. Telling the story was a painful ordeal for her to contend with. It took her on a backward journey of distress, fear, and violation, but it was the empathy of the listener that made it so much the easier. It was a story she had shared with him in the past but at no time with anyone else. He understood how deeply it had affected her life and how it colored her perception of the male of the species. Her tears and sobbing distressed him untold but for her sake he managed to quell the rage that was surging within him. Calm was what she needed and he was sensitive to her need.

Billy got up out of bed to attend to the fire that was still smoldering. Soon it was fully alight with the kettle bubbling over it. Norah was feeling the better for having talked to her dad. Most of her tension was easing away as the two chatted late in an atmosphere of loving peace. In spite of all that had happened, she enjoyed a reasonable nights rest and appeared to be fast asleep when Billy peeped into her room before going to the river very early in the morning. They would not be seeing each other until after work in the evening.

Dr. Clarke's car was parked near the side door that Mrs. West had left ajar for his convenience. Madge informed Norah that the Major had not been feeling very good during the night. Perhaps it was due to the excess of the night before. She then switched to how Norah was feeling or was there something the matter that she had to go and leave such an enjoyable gathering. That was also the opinion of the overnight guests that were seated around the breakfast table. Norah was quick to notice that David was not among them. She would check his room later to see if he had gone. So much the better if he had. She certainly did not want to be bothering her employer at a time when there was sickness in the family. In any case, it was a subject she would find almost impossible to talk to them about or to face the distress of being questioned in relation to. By the time she had finally satisfied herself that he and the briefcase had definitely taken off, she was better ready to commence her day with Stanley and to free her mind from turbulent thought.

In the days that followed Norah continued as before while making a conscious effort to forget all that had taken place and even that the scurrilous David ever existed. The fact that she had been given the opportunity of bringing him down to the level he deserved set in motion within her a renewed process of healing. Although it was an era where such incidences were seldom, if ever, reported, at the same time he was aware that she now had the power to make things rather uncomfortable for him and by extension had the added satisfaction of putting fear into him. There was nothing unusual about him making a quick and unannounced departure. This time it was no exception. He was up and away before the others were out of bed, only on this occasion he would not be returning.

Norah held her secret and was pleased to be reasonably contented once again. The incident was never talked about by anyone. Obviously, the little girl Monica had held her silence too. Billy Mullen seemed to be the most affected by what had happened. He too maintained a silence that was uncharacteristic and his dutiful daughter became increasingly worried about what was happening to him.

Chapter Seventeen

The Major returned to what his wife called a satisfactory state of health. Stanley and Elizabeth Barton had already gone back on a promise that Norah would be going over to them for a couple of weeks in July. There was little doubt that she was having a very positive affect on Stanley's form. With her support he was able to walk from the hall door up to the end of the avenue. Her days with him were tiring and demanding, but for her, there was benefit in it that only she could attempt to quantify; going to England would be more a pleasure than a duty. As for the farm workers, they were happy enough operating under the direction of Mrs. West and all things were being thoroughly attended to in every respect. At the same time there were unsettling rumors circulating among them about the future of the estate; it was being said that for health reasons the Major might be retiring at the end of the season. Such a move would result in the land being either sold or rented out and most of them losing their jobs.

Not one of them had the courage to question Mrs. West about the rumor, and in spite of many hints from Vincent Wilkie, she never once gave the slightest indication as to what was likely to happen. There was little doubt on any of their minds that she was more than capable of running the entire operation better than he could ever have done. But they also knew that he was the owner and boss, so perhaps with an uncertain medical condition, his enthusiasm could be very much on the wane. This conjecture was also sowing a seed of unease in the mind of their trusted friend Christy who was noticing the Major's declining interest in the livestock herd. He was now making more frequent visits to the place and could always find a plausible excuse for calling to the house in relation to matters of common interest. His concern about the Major's condition would have been genuine enough. After all this was a big part of his bread and butter, not to mention the side benefits that sometimes went with it. That was why his visits to the ladies in the kitchen had of late become less and less. Neither of them could quite understand why this detachment had come about, especially at a time when Norah no longer felt uncomfortable in his presence.

All of this was happening in an era of greater cordiality between the residents of Elmwood and the neighboring community. So for that reason, the Wests were becoming the object of enquiry from sincere well-wishers. They were seen by most as the bringers of life and vibrancy to a people that was finding it hard to hold on to its young people in an existence that was hitherto banal in the extreme. In spite of past difficulties, few would deny the positive aspect of their being here. Apart from the employment generated by the estate, there was a marked improvement in the fish market in terms of prices and grading. Young Ryan was a fast learner and soon had the total confidence of the suppliers. His personality and efficiency were highly regarded. The Major however was the controlling figure in the business and the rumors that were circulating were causing alarm bells to sound in that direction as well. So it would be in everyone's interest if the Major's illness was neither debilitating nor life-threatening.

Dr. Clarke was ever so attentive and was making house visits on an almost daily basis, but the question that seemed to bother most of them was whether he was calling as a family friend or to render aid to a sickly man. Then a most welcome sight was observed one sunny morning in June when the sprightly Major came out the side door carrying a bag of golf clubs and pitching them into the back of the doctor's car. Later on, out in the hay field with the Missus, Wilkie and the others said how pleased they were of seeing him out and about doing the things he liked to be doing. Thanking them for their concern, she talked of how hopeful they all were that her husband would continue to improve as he had been over the past few weeks. They had finally gotten him on to a medication that was not only agreeing with him but was very beneficial to his condition as well.

"Hopefully, this will continue and bring him back to what he once was and serve as a reminder for him to take life at an easier pace from here in."

For whatever the reason, there was unity of purpose amongst her listeners; all of them shared in her sentiment. From it they deduced a more positive outlook. It did not now appear that any major change was likely to happen on the estate beyond the one that they welcomed. He would not be pestering them any more. It was, by and large, an uneventful summer and had all the possibility of being a fruitful one as well. The crops were heavy and the cattle were thriving from the fat of the land. Norah had left for England around the middle of July and would not be returning until the second week of August. One of the occasional helpers was brought in as a replacement for the period of her absence. A longer than usual stay away from her father was the only thing that bothered her about leaving. She knew he was quite capable of managing on his own but for some reason or other seemed not his usual good self of late.

For him it was like all the other summers; work days that were long and tedious along with nights and early mornings down at the river with Laurence Keatley. Keatley had long given up on talking to him about the affairs of Elmwood Estate or its owner. It was highly unlikely that chat about the Major's state of health had eluded him, yet he never once mentioned it to his friend Billy. The fact that he was one of the beneficiaries from the establishment of the Fisheries Co-Operative tended to make him less hostile towards its chief executive. Both he and Billy Mullen were regular suppliers and had reason to call to the depot on an ongoing basis during the salmon season. Although not admitting such, he always put an effort into avoiding the Major on these occasions while trying to give the impression that the opposite was the case.

"A can tell ya fir nathin, it's him that's keepin oot o' my effin way for a hay the cow o the bastard, not that a would iver dee any herm tay a seek man."

Laurence Keatley could never be seen as the one bending the knee in any kind of gesture towards a long-standing enemy and perhaps it was best to leave it that way. He was not the kind to be easily intimidated by anyone, not even by his archenemy Rusty McKeague, who had recently appeared back on the scene. After being released from Sligo Jail he came home to a coolish welcome and not long after took the Derry boat over to Glasgow where he met up with the hefty woman that was now back with him in Portneill. From the observations of the local people, it appeared that he had mellowed somewhat and seemed eager to engage more cordially with them and showed his worth by buying drinks for all the patrons of the Poachers Inn. No one spurned his generosity; it was their sincere hope that he had learned a useful lesson and that all of them would be big enough to treat him with a degree of common decency. The two young friends that he had led into trouble with him in the past had now matured into honest, working adults with an admirable sense of responsibility. So McKeague had returned to a community that was more at ease with itself and if he decided to settle back, there would surely be a place and a welcome for him.

It was well past the middle of August by the time Norah got back from England. She had a lovely time staying with Elizabeth Barton in her sedate country cottage not far out of London, situated on a sunny spot adjacent to Elizabeth's place of work, and what was for Stanley, his home and sanctuary. There was a quaint peacefulness about this cottage, described in detail by Norah to her father in a letter that was poetically inspired in its descriptive content; it was her Eden Entire. Her morning routine was to bring Stanley to the cottage after breakfast. Elizabeth would already have had him ready for collection and it was a relief for her to know he was being left in capable hands. It was the sheer beauty of the place, as well as the pleasure Norah derived from the work she was doing, that made her want to stay on for that extra week. It was indeed a memorable week, one that she would be unlikely to ever forget.

After a month's absence, it was a matter of getting back to the usual routine and the entire household of Elmwood was feeling the benefit of her uplifting presence. The Major looked like a man that was very much back to his old self, taking a renewed interest in the affairs of the estate and doing so without over-imposing himself in areas where his intervention was neither needed nor sought. Mrs. West told Norah that he had been to see the specialist in Dublin during the time of her stay in England and the news was encouraging enough. At the same time, he did have a heart condition that had the potential to worsen if he put himself under any kind of severe stress, be it either physical or mental. By avoiding these, along with taking his prescribed medication, there was nothing to stop him from living a normal kind of life. For that reason she was trying to encourage him towards giving more time to interests of a recreational nature such as his golfing days with Dr Clarke and perhaps a spot of fishing on the river.

"Why, only the other day, Christy Flood and myself were putting these points to him saying how good it would be for him to get away from the place for at least one or perhaps two days a week. It would do him the world of good you know and to tell the truth, it would be a benefit to the rest of us as well."

Benefit indeed, and few of the working team would have disputed the assertion; they were by far a more efficient workforce and capable of higher achievement in his absence. As for Christy, well, his contribution to the enterprise was of a different nature. Being a trusted agent that knew his trade, the question of supervision did not arise. The trusting Major considered him a most valuable asset to the estate. As for herself, she could not agree more. Christy was reliable and always available when needed. To his great disappointment, there was no talk from any of them about going to the Connemara pony fair; the Major's unstable condition had obviously put paid to any plans of that kind. But shortly after that time of year came the good news that no change was going to happen in the farming practice of Elmwood Estate; they were for carrying on as usual.

Summer had passed and they were into the darker evenings of autumn. Overseas visitors continued to frequent the place on a regular basis. Seldom a month would pass without a number of visiting guests being entertained to dinner. The absence of David from all of these gatherings did not escape the attention of Madge Crawford. She commented on this a few times to Norah who choose the option of silence on the subject. She was pretty certain he would never be back to bother anyone again. In any case, she had gotten over the effects of that horrific encounter involving the little girl Monica. In a sense, she found the final confrontation with this man to be liberating, like she could feel the weight of some kind of demonic curse that had beset her for the best part of her life now being lifted off her. Now it was she and she alone that knew the reason why the despicable creature would not be coming back. It was one occasion when she knew more than her employers but on that she was going to hold her council.

Only once did Mrs. West mention his name to her two housemaids and that was to express her dismay as to why he had abandoned them for so long. She went on to say the Major had been trying to contact him at a London address but all to no avail; with several addresses from Gibraltar to Hong Kong, he could well be described as of no fixed abode. His continuing absence did not appear to be causing any degree of anxiety in the West household. He had been a friend to the Major through their shared interest in the stock market but nothing more than that. So even if he had gone off to seek out pastures new, none of them would be any the poorer. Major West was a sagacious operator in that sense and well capable of protecting his own interests, particularly in relation to matters financial.

From the master bedroom, Mrs. West could hear the sound of a motor and noticed the lights of a vehicle dance against the window blinds; someone was coming in the front avenue. Not wanting to disturb her sleeping husband, she went out to the landing to see who or what it was at such an early hour of the morning. To her it looked like Dr. Clarke was the man getting out of the car. Through the open window she spoke down, as he was about to press the doorbell, "Is that you John? Is there something the matter?" In the gentlest possible voice he asked her to come down and let him in. There was something he had to tell her and her husband together. She opened the front door, wearing a heavy nightgown to fend off the chill of early morning October.

"Florence," he began, "I am going to tell you this before we both break it to himself. Your friend, Elizabeth Barton, called me about half an hour ago asking me to be the bearer of bad news to you. I am sorry for being the one, but your son, Stanley, suffered a severe attack during the night and unfortunately did not come out of it. For the sake of your sick husband, I want you to show the fortitude I know you to be capable of. I will be at hand to render whatever support I can to both of you. Shall we now go up and talk to him?"

As they began the ascent, the Major addressed them from the landing,

"John, I gather that the news is not good. I heard enough to know it's to do with Stanley. He is dead; you come to tell us?"

Dressed in a heavy robe, he led them into the living room and put a match to the preset coal fire. A two-bar electric fire was also switched on.

The kind doctor spent close to an hour with the bereaved helping them to come to terms with this new situation and they remained remarkably calm throughout. It was the kind of news they had more or less conditioned themselves into expecting. They had been sensitively advised that Stanley's life expectancy was going to be relatively short. Their failure to show any outward signs of emotion could have been taken to represent a degree of callousness on their part, but truthfully speaking, that was not the case. They had already come through a mourning that was severe and protracted. Many times during the days and weeks after Stanley's accident they thought to themselves that the sparing of his life was indeed a doubtful blessing. Yet in their hearts, they felt sad and even bitter that fate had dealt them such a cruel hand. He was their only child and how different it could all have been.

Elmwood Estate was in mourning. No major work operations were entered into for the next couple of days; the digging of the potato crop had been completed a few days earlier so no urgent duties were beckoning. The parents went over as quickly as they could after getting the news. Norah declined their offer to take her with them for the laying out and interment. She was dreadfully disturbed and could not see herself being able to withstand the pain and distress of participating in the midst of such profound grief. There was too much on her mind right then. Instead she went home to rest and think things over for the few days that they would be on the other side. She was last to leave the Big House that evening. Madge had already gone home with sorrow in her heart and would also avail of the couple of day's respite. Some of the workmen were busying themselves doing a spot of tidying up in the farmyard.

They were using yard brushes, shovels and a wheelbarrow. There was no one to bother them, no deadline to be met.

Norah had walked to the end of the avenue when she heard the sound of the fish van coming out the right-of-way. Benny had also closed shop owing to the death in the family. She was glad to see him stop and offer to take her home. To her there seemed an air of gloom about the place they were leaving behind. It was a relief to have a friend to talk to. Never before had she felt such warmth in his presence. Had she at last reached the stage of being freed from what had restrained her for so long? Was she now ready to give or was it too late? Her warmth however did have the effect of projecting itself across to Benny as he kissed her sweet lips before they parted. He then suggested they go out on a date to which she replied, "Perhaps later on when all this has passed."

There was little by way of joy around Elmwood in the days or even weeks that followed Stanley's death; it was well on into the month of November before things returned to near normal. The Major and the Missus were understandably downcast. They were going to need space and time to grieve in their own way. Yet it was Norah that seemed the most perturbed and Mrs. West was beginning to take notice of her distress. Recalling her close attachment to Stanley, she could understand the poor girl was in need of being talked to. Madge too was kindly supportive. She understood how a good-natured person like Norah could quite easily be consumed by what she had been doing for that sadly afflicted being. She advised her to put all of that behind her now and to get out again with friends that would willingly help her back to living the fun-life that was deserving of the young.

"Stanley is at peace now and what you have done for him is immeasurably good. Nobody knows it better than his parents, so be assured they will in gratefulness endeavor to console your grief."

Not a word was spoken about the festive season and them into the second week of December. The occasional bout of laughter could be heard coming from the potato shed where the men were filling an order for shipment. They were being allowed to get on with it on their own initiative; it was unlike Mrs. West not to be heavily involved with such an operation but she had not been seen in either the yard or fields for some time. It was an easy time for the domestic staff as well. Madge was taking most responsibility in the kitchen and was doing so out of consideration for Norah whose sorrow seemed to be subsiding. Then, out of the blue one morning after breakfast, the lady herself came to Madge in the kitchen to announce that Norah was going over to work with Miss

Barton in the care home. She said it was Elizabeth's idea, that this girl had a special suitability for working with these kinds of people and it was a talent that should not go to waste. She would be leaving the next morning and had already spoken to her father who was understandably upset at the thought of losing his precious daughter but at the same time pleased she was getting this opportunity.

The post, she said, was being offered on a trial basis to see how it would work out for both sides. Madge was of little doubt that Norah's ability and intelligence would make her ideally suited for any post of responsibility. All of them agreed it was an opportunity to be availed of, but with sadness, they thought about Billy Mullen being alone once again and it all happening just two weeks before Christmas.

Chapter Eighteen

There was a black frost wind blowing down the valley. Wilkie and his men were busy trying to prevent it from penetrating the door and windows of the large potato shed where twenty-five ton of seed spuds were ready for the assessment of McGinley, the Department Inspector. It was the coldest of January days but the work was necessary in order to protect the valuable product from the destructive harshness of the severe frost. Just as they had finished, the Major arrived and asked for two men to go over and fetch a heavy oil heater from the house. He was a man that had to be surer than sure. He waited for the two men to return with the heater before thanking all of them for a job well done. It was a gesture of gratitude they thought unusual for him and thoughtfully put it down to his state of health. Then with a look of vexation, he continued by saying he had something important and indeed difficult to say to them.

"As you men may already know, I have not been enjoying very good health for some time now and added to that is the death of my son, so I have been advised to take things a bit easier from now on. So in order to facilitate this easier life style, Mrs. West and I have, with reluctance, decided to cease farming the estate except for a small enterprise just as an interest or pastime. Regretfully this decision does not come easy for most of you people as it means that nearly all of you will have to be laid off. Just one workman can adequately attend to what we have in mind. Consequently I have instructed McKinley and Co., Auctioneers to set a suitable date for the disposal of machinery and implements as well as letting the vast bulk of the estate. It is with a deep sense of sadness that I bring this kind of news to you. As a team of workers you were all that one could have desired. So again, I thank all of you most sincerely and may good fortune be always with you and your families."

A shock announcement it surely was, especially when such speculation was totally discounted less than three months earlier. Now it was real and happening. The good time was over. It had been a good time and of that there was no doubt; the work was organized and the pay was generous with every hour of overtime accounted for. Seldom is such good fortune appreciated at the time of its giving. More clearly do its merits reveal to them that have lost them. Five of these men would be losing their jobs. Knowing that he was the one most likely to be retained, Vincent Wilkie was first to reply stating how satisfying it had been working for a decent man.

"Hear, hear!" shouted the other five, all of them hoping that perhaps they might be the lucky one. Then the timid voice of wee Dickie Boyle sounded a gladness that the Major and his wife would still be living in the locality.

"We wish you many more years of health and happiness in this lovely Elmwood House," he spluttered with quivering emotion.

The word spread rapidly throughout the countryside. The grandiose estate had ceased to maintain. Now after these few short years, it was all but over. Hughie McGuire, from the era of the Miss Walker's, was not in the least surprised. The place was simply not being run right. There was not a knowledgeable man about the place since the day he was let go. Nor did he feel in the least sorry for the ones that were losing their jobs. As far as he was concerned they were nothing more than a shower of arse lickers for the gentry. Another quietly displaced man was Christy Flood. As the sole purveyor of livestock for the estate he would surely stand to lose out on commission. He was slightly peeved by the fact that the news had been delivered first to the workmen instead of him. This, Mrs. West tried to explain, was because he had not been to the place very much since Christmas. But she did manage to reassure him that they still intended to continue grazing a number of cattle over the summer months.

"Needless to say, Christy, this will be on a vastly smaller scale than before but your services will still be required nevertheless. You will always have reason to call here and you know there will always be special times as well."

Christy was known to be a shrewd operator when it came to earning a handy pound so no one was in any doubt that he would easily make up the shortfall in the course of his business. Things were not going to change all that much for him.

Crowds from far and wide had assembled in the front field where all the machinery items were on display. It was a cold bright day at the end of January and McKinley stood on a high platform. The bidding was brisk and competitive. A substantial sum of money was realized from the disposal sale. All of the items were sold off within an hour. For the land letting, there was hectic competition for every inch of it. The rich loamy soil of the estate was ideal for either tillage or grazing. It was what

160

every farmer and conacre man was seeking after. When the business of the day was finally transacted, McKinley and the Major along with the auctioneer's clerk sat down to tea with Mrs. West after which a rough assessment was carried out. The results were most impressive. From the letting the projected return for the following November was estimated to be as high, if not better, than what had been realized from the entire enterprise the previous year. Forty acres of the best pasture was being kept for the grazing of heavy cattle as well as the four Connemara Ponies that they hoped to increase in numbers before the end of the year. All in all it looked like it was going to be a very cozy setup and Vincent Wilkie had got what his neighbors called a handy wee number.

None of the new arrangement appeared to be affecting Benny Ryan. The fisheries business was totally separate from the estate and had the appearance of being a Co-Operative venture. In any case, it was a job he was well capable of running on his own. The only thing the Major involved himself in was banking and the provision of ready cash. As the main investor, it could not be any other way. It bothered Benny somewhat that Norah had gone away, apparently for good. She had left without saying a word or even as much as goodbye to him. He wanted to write and openly state the depth of his feelings for her but again had second thoughts when considering that over the few years he had known her she repeatedly retracted from his pursuance. Yet she was the one he wanted and it was painful to think of her being the object of attention from some man across the water that was more socially accomplished and her succumbing to the glamour of it all.

This was a subject he could never see himself talking to the Major or Mrs. West about. If he could ever get the courage to put pen to paper, it would have to be soon so the only other place to get the address was from her father. Still the closed season for salmon fishing, he would not have Billy Mullen calling to the depot until after St. Patrick's Day which was a full two weeks away. When Benny called to the Mullen cottage, he found Billy not quite the man he had known him to be. It must have been that Norah's leaving was having a severe effect on him as well. Although seemingly a bit downcast, he was nonetheless welcoming to his visitor; their talk was mainly about the onset of the new fishing season and what to expect by way of market and prices. It was a normal enough kind of engagement for two people that were involved in the industry and it was best to get it over with at the start before moving on to the burning issue that was obviously afflicting both of them. Billy said how hard it was for him to settle into the idea of her being gone and away after him being so used to having her around.

"The loneliness is so hard to take," he said. "Anyhow, with the longer evenings and the start of the fishing it should get a lot better and according to her last letter, she expects to get a few weeks holidays in August."

"It's a hell of a long time until the month of August and a hell of a lot can happen between now and then," thought Benny to himself, as he drove alone back to Coolaghy.

At the same time, he now had her English address in his pocket and was determined to put time and thought into a written expression of what was on his mind, all because of his love for her. Before the work was finally completed he had written and re-written several trial drafts. It was a strenuous effort for one so unaccustomed to conveying the tender sentiment through the medium of the pen. But what he stated was from the heart and his deepest wish was that it would affect. It was timed so as to reach her a week before St. Patrick's Day, in the hope of stirring an awakening emotion, and on the day before the national feast, he received a card that contained a seasonal emblem and a terse written message, "Happy St. Patrick's Day Benny, Love from Norah."

It was hard to draw any kind meaning from a communication of that sort. It made no reference whatever to his letter or the sentiments contained therein. Was this confirmation of his worst fears? Had she met someone else and was now in a steady relationship, something she persistently refused to engage with him. His doubts and apprehension were enough to make him lay off the trail. Norah had gone to a new life and it very much seemed she was moving fast beyond his depth. On his way home from the holiday mass, he, for the first time in his life, entered the premises of the Poacher's Inn. This was the day for the drowning of the shamrock. Being new to the pub culture, he was treated over-generously by the friendly patrons, especially them from the fishing fraternity. It was a totally new experience and he enjoyed it thoroughly. What a costly experience it would eventually turn out to be, for within six months he was known to be a habitual heavy drinker and it was downhill from there on. He continued to engage himself actively in the affairs of the new fishing season and partly succeeded in erasing all lingering thoughts about Norah Mullen from his ponderous mind. This was his second full year in the employment of the Fisheries Co-op and he was in what could rightly be called a secure position. The money he was earning was considered good by local standards. The local girls saw Benny in a very favorable light. He was popular and handsome according to all of them. There was certainly no reason why he should remain unattached amid such seeing eyes.

But it was unattached he continued to be and instead courted what Joyce described as the 'vile decoction that ruined many a heart and home.' Never an evening of that summer did he return from work without paying a visit to the Inn. Except for the occasional caller offering a few salmon to sell, life was rather quiet around the estate. There was no noisy banter about the farmyard, just Vincent Wilkie on the wee Ford Tractor. Mrs. West continued to drive the old Land Rover through the few fields that were kept. Each morning would see her out counting and checking the thirty-five grazers just as she did when things were more intensive. This was her own small enterprise and with Christy's help, she ran it well. She was happy galore to watch them thrive on the summer grass. The four ponies were her pride and joy. They were as tame as the fireside cat through the amount of time she spent with them each day. "Florence Girl," said Christy, "you will have no excuse for not going to the Clifden Pony Fair this year and I suppose he will be wanting to go as well." Her answer was very much in the affirmative. It was something she and the Major had already been thinking about but as the event was over two months away nothing yet was definite.

Another feature of the more relaxed atmosphere about Elmwood was the drastic reduction in the number of overseas visitors. Just one dinner party in all of the eight months since the time of Stanley's death and it just three days after the Major and Mrs. West returned from being in England. It was for a small group of little more than ten guests that included a couple who were introduced as Steve and Stella West. They appeared to be in their early to mid-forties and were definitely first time visitors to Elmwood. It was a very subdued affair and held on the second weekend of May; the only thing significant about the timing was that it happened to be in or about one year from the date of Stanley's party. Madge Crawford, along with the other casual helper who seemed to be about the place more often since the departure of Norah Mullen, adequately attended to the catering end of things. Now a year on and never a mention of the name David, he like Norah had well and truly gone from the scene. There was never a hint that any linkage ever existed between them. Perhaps the little girl Monica may at some stage later in life recall the occurrence in the farm shed, but in the age that was in it and in the absence of the culprit she was more likely to hold silence.

Chapter Nineteen

Norah arrived back around the middle of August, after being away for two thirds of the year. Except for a delighted father, her return was scarcely noticed. It was when the fishing season was at its peak and Billy, along with his friend Keatley, were to be found at the river both late and early. For those that had seen Norah, they commented how she still looked pretty but seemingly less lively than before. It was at Sunday Mass she met up with old friends and all of them were keen for her to come and join them for a lively night out. "Yes, but not tonight," was how she put it to them, and then proceeded to explain that she was going to be around for a good few weeks and would definitely be joining them on one of these dates. A noteworthy observation on Madge's part was made two weeks after Norah came back; it was that never once in that time did she pay a daytime visit to Elmwood House. Nor did there appear to be any willingness on the part of Mrs. West to talk about or attach much importance to the fact that her once favored housemaid was now back at home.

Madge's curiosity brought her up to Mullen's cottage on Sunday afternoon.

Norah was glad to see her, as was Billy, even though he would soon be heading for the river. There was much to talk about in relation to what had taken place on the estate. All of the changes were brought in shortly after Norah's departure from the scene and life was certainly moving at a slower pace since then. Madge reported the entire scene with detailed account. Wilkie, along with the Missus, were now doing it all on their own, except for the odd appearance of Christy Flood. When she had finished relating the goings on at the estate she switched attention to the wider community and all that was happening within it; not an evil word was spoken about friend or neighbor. There was little joy for either of the two when attention was turned to the subject of Benny Ryan and his retrogressive behavior. What a terrible turnaround in such a short time and sadly happening to the finest of young men. Her father had already given the disturbing news about this to Norah. He was still working for the Fisheries Co-op but already some negative soundings were being heard.

"Let's hope and pray," said Madge, "that God, in his goodness, will deliver Benny from this destructive habit before it becomes a chronic affliction. Have you ever seen him since you came back, Norah?"

"Never once, not even at Sunday Mass and I find that very strange indeed. He actually wrote to me as recently as last March and to tell the truth I did not return the compliment, save a flimsy card. Whatever is the matter I have to say it is so unlike Benny and I hate to think of the effect this must be having on his good parents and sister. Yes, I promise to pray for all of them."

The focus continued on the unhappy story for longer than Madge had intended. She was by now more anxious to hear how Norah had made out in England as well as what her future plans might be. On the question of England, Norah commented little beyond saying it was a nice place and Miss Barton was a wonderfully good and helpful person. As for the future, she was not too forthcoming, simply stating how much her daddy had missed her and how that was making it hard for her to think about leaving him again. She had no definite plans for a departure date, causing Madge to wonder what kind of employment contract could allow her such a lengthy and indefinite period of leave. Madge was not the probing type. Endowed with the wisdom of knowing when to pull back, she tactfully switched the focus to something of a more casual nature. Norah thought about asking if her name ever been mentioned by Mrs. West at any time since her return from England, but then decided against it. After all, that lady knew enough already through her contact with Miss Barton. Nor did she disclose anything about her present relationship with her former employer.

By the end of October Norah was still around and had applied for a job in what was then called the County Hospital in Lifford. She had been highly recommended for the post by Dr. Clarke who visited the infirmary every morning. It was now finally settled. England was not for her and Billy would be cured of his loneliness. It would be pretty much back to what it had been like for the two of them in the old days. The bond that existed between this father and daughter was known not only to the doctor but the wider community, all of who were pleased to see that they again had the support of each other. Wards maid was the job description attributed to Norah's work. She very quickly settled into the daily routine of what was involved and, not unexpectedly, her caring qualities were noticeably impressive. Through their friend, Dr Clarke, the Wests got to hear about the new hospital appointee. They were not in the least surprised at hearing how highly she was being rated by her supervisors.

Nobody knew her worth better than they did. As a housemaid and cook, Norah had given them exemplary service but that was now in the past.

For whatever reason, Norah had no intentions of ever re-acquainting herself with Elmwood House. Her involvement with these people was well and truly over and nothing was likely to make her change her mind. Apart from her unquestionable competence, she had gained considerably in confidence as well. She could now make a positive assessment of her own worth as well as her contribution to the needs of society. Had Norah Mullen been give the opportunity to avail of the required schooling, what an asset she would have been to the nursing profession. That was the observation of the professionals to whom she was subservient as well as her working colleagues and the patients she endeared herself to. Now at twenty-seven, the likelihood of her ever progressing to a meaningful level beyond the ranks of servitude were slim to say the least. Still she was thankful for what she had, doing the kind of work she obviously had a leaning towards and with the added benefit of being near to home and the father who needed her.

In the month of April of the following year, Benny Ryan sought permission from Major West to move back into the workers' living quarters down in the farmyard where only one occupant now resided. A more forlorn atmosphere now prevailed there compared to the high days when all the building and renovation was in progress. At one time as many as six men resided in that joint with a servant maid specifically assigned to the catering requirements that were essentially demanding. This move came about as a result of Benny's addictive behavior. His parents and sister had at this stage reached breaking point. They had tried everything from the kindest of reasoning to threats of disownment but all to no avail. For them it was a family crisis and they were totally unequipped to deal with it. Their hearts were breaking for the loved one they seemed to be losing. It was he who took the initiative to move out and the Major agreed to facilitate him along with a warning that his timekeeping and attention to duty were becoming a cause for concern. Benny, in his sickness, forsook the love of family, perhaps in the mistaken belief that his drinking might be more enjoyable away from the nagging atmosphere of home life. The speed with which the addiction progressed was quite phenomenal. In a period of just fifteen months from the date of his first drink, he was close to the bottom. Now in this so-called life of freedom, he was poised to decline at a more rapid pace, with heavier and longer nights of drinking, along with a less sustaining food intake. The question was, how much longer could he carry on?

The answer was revealed to Norah on the first Sunday morning of June when she arrived into the male ward of the hospital and saw the screens around one of the beds. Dr. Bannigan and a nurse were with the patient.

"His name is Ryan, Benny Ryan, and he is in a very bad way," said the nurse who appeared from behind the barrier and addressed her comment to the startled Norah.

The nurse also informed her that his parents and sister were in a distraught state down in the day room and as yet were not being allowed in to see him. He had been brought in by ambulance in the early hours of the morning from the scene of a horrific accident where the van he was driving crashed into a tree. Hard as it was for her to do, Norah went straight to the day room to show her concern for these good and troubled people. They acknowledged her kindness with gratitude that was expressed more by gesture than words. It was too early for the doctor to say exactly the extent of Benny's injuries. The only thing he was sure about was that the right jawbone was broken along with considerable damage to the chest region. There was also the added complication of his stomach being swollen full with alcohol. Very little could be done until that was removed and out of his system.

The family remained on the premises for all of that Sunday; Norah brought light refreshments to them a couple of times during the day. They were eventually allowed in to see Benny for a brief moment. It was not a pretty sight that lay broad backed and motionless before them with a gurgling noise emitting from deep in his throat. Later in the evening the doctor returned to talk to the family. Nothing new to report except to say that the patient was maintaining a steady heartbeat and would be better left alone until the morning. John Ryan suggested to his wife and daughter that they all go out to the Green Café for something to eat and it might be best if the two of them then went home to avail of some rest. There was no sense in all of them spending the night in the hospital and he felt himself to be the one best fit for staying on at that stage. He would more than likely walk down to Harte's for a bottle of stout before his all night vigil began.

He got through the tedious hours by nodding off now and again in the comfort of a soft chair in front of the fireplace where dying embers still smoldered. The two women re-joined him sometime after ten in the morning and were just in time to see Benny being taken by stretcher to the awaiting ambulance. He was being sent to Dublin for specialized surgery. For the family, this was encouraging news. Dr. Bannigan was kindly reassuring; that the stay in Dublin would be of short duration.

"I expect he will be back here again by the middle of the week. he is going to pull through this time so don't be worrying. Just go quietly home and get some rest."

True to the doctor's word, Benny arrived back in Lifford late on Wednesday evening. An eminent bone specialist had put him together again. The work to the facial area was delicate but successful. The chest injuries along with the broken ribs were being left to the mercy of time and him kept bedded in an easeful position. After the nurses got him settled back as comfortable as was possible, Norah went up to see him and what a sight it was, like a man who had just come through the ravages of war. His eyes were hidden behind a swollen thick of bruised and broken flesh. His head was held steady in a plaster cast that extended round his chin. Speech was totally suspended. She placed a warm hand on his pale and moist forehead. "Benny, this is Norah and I am glad to see you back here where we can take good care of you. I am so sorry to see you hurting Benny, but I know you are going to get better fast and I am going to help you to." Though his response was mute, she was able to sense a reaction in the rhythm of his breathing. He had heard the sound of her soft and gentle voice and would remember the words forever.

It would be another six weeks before Benny was deemed well enough to go home but after a couple of weeks he was able to move at a slow pace within the confines of the ward. Having had previous experience of the hospital routine, he was again able to be the model patient. He was tidy, agreeable and undemanding. At the beginning and due to lack of mouth function, his sole source of sustenance was in the form of high protein liquid, which had to be administrated frequently and carefully. Norah, with her acquired experience in working with the likes of Stanley West, was allowed by the nursing staff to execute the task on this special patient. It was a number of weeks before Benny fully regained the uninhibited faculty of speech and that was something he found frustrating, especially when Norah was working with him. As a result of what happened along with his behavior over the past year and more, he had become a somewhat disturbed young man. His emotions were over-heightened and he tended towards self-pity in a most pathetic way. He was now at a stage where the understanding listener had a vital role to play.

Through the demands of her overall responsibility, it was not possible for Norah to be that listening ear at the rate he expected and this was at a time when such support was not readily available on a professional basis. However, here was a girl with a tendency towards the plight of the afflicted and perhaps with a special gravitation towards that which was still the object of personal feelings. Most all of what was her free time she spent sitting by his bedside on what could have rightly been called the counselor's chair. Repeatedly she heard his plaintive plangency about all that had gone wrong for him; two serious accidents both of which could have been avoided and added to that was the loss of the job he was happy in. At no time in the course of their talks did he ever allude to his current and most pressing problem, that of his addiction to alcohol. Like most people so afflicted, he was totally blind to what it was doing to him.

Like everyone else, Norah knew right well that drink was the sole cause of him being where he was and he in such a debased state. At the same time, it was a subject she knew little or nothing about. All she knew was that its destructive power had the capacity to ravage and ruin the lives of the best of people.

He talked morbidly about how his life should have been so much different had it not been for the unfortunate events that befell him from the start.

"My involvement with Elmwood Estate has not been a happy one. Not only did I get the sack from my first job there, but also accused by the Major and the Guards of being in with the robbers that burgled the house. That was a terrible time I can tell you, and then, as you know, much worse was about to happen with the accident that ended my hopes of ever achieving my dream of being a professional footballer."

"Oh, yes, Benny, all our lives could have been so different. 'If only,' you could just as easily say. If you had not met me, none of these terrible things would have happened and your dreams would have been fulfilled."

On this conjecture he pondered for a while and reasoned it to be one he could not readily concur with. Never could he see Norah Mullen in a light that was other than goodness. A goodness that was constant and unconditional. It sustained him throughout the long weeks of recuperation right up to the day he was finally discharged from hospital care. Physically and cosmetically, Benny was well on the road to recovery, but more importantly, so was the mental state he was now taking back to the home where love awaited him. He said his loving goodbye to Norah on the night before the morning of his departure. He expressed his love openly to her and she, for the first time, reciprocated willingly. His expectation was for her to come and see him at his home, just as she had done before, to help him through another dark period. That, he said, was the only thing good about the last time he was confined to the house.

"The memory of you coming to see me still gives me a feeling of goodness about that time, so please remember how much it means to me."

Now repatriated in the family home, Benny was better able to appreciate the comfort and security that is too often taken for granted, living as he did in the workers quarters of the estate had taught him that much at least. Accepting the grave consequences of him losing his job was not an easy thing to do and made even more torturous by knowing the reason why; he was the author of his own misfortune. As yet nobody had replaced him in the fisheries job, Vincent Wilkie was managing to look after the depot as well as his other duties and the business was being limited to the local supply.

Mrs. West, and sometimes Vincent, was able to transport the boxes of fish in the back of the old Land Rover. There seemed to be no urgency about replacing the van that was wrecked beyond repair. The truth of the matter was, the Major no longer had the drive to engage himself in the everyday hassle of running a business enterprise and the same could have been said about the silent partnership of Dr Clarke and Robert McElwee. So it looked as if it was going back to serving what was the original purpose of setting up the venture, namely to provide a dependable market for the salmon hunters of the Camus. That was really all that mattered to the local people. It was a handy outlet right beside them and one that offered them an honest deal. There was a lot of sympathy expressed about the misfortunes of young Ryan, a popular and likable young fellow that had brought ruin upon himself and now facing an uncertain future.

The sympathy of the people was sincere and heartfelt, yet few of them knew enough about the potency of the affliction that had taken hold of their likable friend. For him there was one mighty challenge still to be faced. It was the crucial test of how to face a world that was no different to the one he had been sheltered away from for the two months before. All of the rich goodness was still there for him to savor, but so too were the vices. It was going to take resolve and willpower to carry him over the quagmire that awaited him. His desire was to do the right thing and he knew right well what that was. Norah had shown him the way towards seeing himself in a more favorable light, and that seeing could well be the seed of his redemption. The struggle would be mighty but the goal was achievable. Would he have the strength to unlearn a habit that was all too leisurely and grand, like a ride into the illusionary fairyland on the chariot of Bacchus?

Norah visited him many times over the weeks that followed and the effects were indeed encouraging. Their talking to each other was at a level they never before experienced. More and more was their closeness growing with a tenderness that was soothing and empowering. Each time was becoming ever more engaging. It looked like they had at last found what had eluded them for so long. Norah had been freed from the demons of the past. No longer were they controlling her actions and desires. That was one undeniable benefit of having been in the service of Major and Mrs. West. It was now two and a half years since the David incident and she was living the benefit of being rid of that diabolical haunting that robbed her of her childhood. Her deliverance was in being afforded the opportunity to face the source of what had bedeviled her for so long, although it was regressively traumatic at the time. It all became good for her in the end. The strange man David, misguided as he was, would have to pay a price for the freedom she had gained, never again to set foot on the paths of Elmwood, forgotten by everyone.

Chapter Twenty

Mrs. Ryan received her annual and belated Christmas greetings from Philadelphia on the eve of New Year Day; it was from her brother Paddy and his wife Catherine; they had been there for almost twenty-five years. The only thing different about the written message was that they were thinking about coming over for two weeks in the summer and would be in touch about the arrangements later on. By this time the courtship of Benny and Norah Mullen was common knowledge throughout. Everyone saw them as the perfect couple that was ideally suited. Although still unemployed, Benny's misadventure had all but been forgotten about. He had made an admirable recovery in all respects. This, Norah and he, were attributing to the power of their love for each other. They were now set on a course of planning a future that had to accommodate them being together and that undoubtedly required the male of the partnership to be in employment.

There were certainly no signs of any approach being made to him by either the Major or his wife. They had well and truly adapted themselves to the easier lifestyle and were unlikely to disturb it by inviting back what had previously been a problem. It was not quite what he wanted, but Benny was pleased enough to take a laborer's job on Mulrine's farm. The pay was fair but not near what he had been accustomed to earning from the Co-op. He had moved from a high to low status employment. At least that was how he read the situation; less money in his pocket and without the perquisite prestige of being in charge. On the positive side, he was living a cleaner and healthier kind of life. What money he had was being spent wisely. He now had a reason to aim for a higher goal. That reason was Norah Mullen, the darling love of his life, the one that loved him in return and accepted him unconditionally. They were going to be together come what may.

Financial restraints ruled out any thoughts about marriage for at least a year or perhaps two; Norah had a job that she liked and knew it was only available to her while she was in the single state. However, as a gesture of their commitment to each other, they opened a joint savings account in the local Post Office. The weekly input to it would not be heavily augmenting, but the idea was that in being faithfully consistent with whatever was affordable, the accumulation could be fairly substantial in the end. They were setting themselves a target date of twelve months hence and with a resolute determination on Benny's part to seek a position that was worthy of his talent. Now in the security of a meaningful relationship, he was swiftly regaining his self-confidence, and in such a blissful state anything was possible. Apart from all of that, he had already achieved something more precious in finding himself living in the tranquility of contented sobriety.

He was put severely to the test on the August evening he came back tired from work to be introduced to uncle Paddy and his Scottish-American wife. They were seated with his parents and enjoying the contents of a large bottle. Their manner was pleasant and inviting. They were keen for him to partake of their goodness and unwittingly moved to do so with the best intentions in mind. In the circumstances, the temptation was strong and could have easily been succumbed to, but the resilient Benny prevailed and came out a stronger man. His condition was an incurable one, only he happened to be blessed with the wisdom and fortitude to understand that he lived on the brink, just one drink away from the grip of disaster. Though his material fortune was relatively small, he was happy with what he had and was not for putting at risk the prize he had struggled for years to acquire.

Benny, the home bird, was not all that taken in by the high appraisal Pat the Yank was affording his adopted homeland. It was definitely the place for the young and ambitious, he said. Unthinkable that he would suggest such a move to Norah who had to be near her father. It was her intention that they move into the cottage with Billy when the time was right. For them this was going to be a sizable benefit that would allow them to get married much sooner than if they had to acquire living accommodation for themselves. So for that reason, the invitation to Benny and his bride to be was never taken seriously, nor was it going to be a considered option for sister Kathleen either. She was in a serious relationship with a young farmer from the neighboring townland. The attachment of the Ryan parents to their son and daughter was as close as was that of Billy Mullen to his Norah. Parting with any of them would be unimaginable in the extreme. No doubt there was a lot of truth in what the good-hearted uncle was telling them about life in America; a hard working and sober young man could make good in this land of opportunity.

As a gesture of his appreciation, Benny did say that he might at some later date consider their offer but only if he failed to secure a decent job for himself at home. Both he and his intended were working hard towards achieving that and were reasonably confident of succeeding; neither of them had any inclination towards living abroad. The guests were staying in a boarding house near Raphoe and were intending to do some traveling around Donegal over the next week or ten days. They would be calling to see them again at least one more time before they leave. Paddy was a couple of years younger than his sister who was married to John Ryan; they were born and reared in Coolaghy along with two other sisters and a brother. They had lived a meager existence in their childhood days and talked a lot about it on the evening of their first get together. By all accounts, Paddy had done well for himself in the material sense. He had a well-paid job and drove to work in what he called his Ford Saloon. Even though in his late forties, he had only been married to his attractive wife for about eight years and it turned out to be a childless marriage. He observed how the home scene was changing but at all too slow a pace. But John was snugly content with what he had, living in reasonable comfort with the assured support of wife and family.

These were blessings much greater than wealth, and Benny wished for nothing more than for him and Norah to create a home like the one he had the good fortune to grow up in. Fortune, alas, did not come his way so readily in the job market, for twelve months later he was still in the menial role of farm laborer over with old Mr. Mulrine. The prospect of their October wedding was not very encouraging. Owing to the shortness of her service, Norah was going to have to leave her work with a gratuity that was paltry. None of this however was going to dampen their resolve to execute their nuptial intentions. They were highly pleased at the amount of money realized from their savings account over the eighteen-month period. They would be able to afford a modest wedding celebration with family and friends. The advantage of having a ready-made home to move into was not to be lightly discounted. The important thing for both of them was that it was, at last, happening. Their love for each other had brought them through many a challenge and they were confident it would eventually lead them to even greater things. For Norah, the greatest thing right then was in becoming Mrs. Benny Ryan. They had come a long way and seen many changes in the years that had passed since that first Sunday night they danced together in the wee Coolaghy Hall.

The wedding was a dignified affair; just a few friends and neighbors joined the two families in the old Portneill Chapel. It was a pleasant October morning. After the ceremony, all of them went back to the Mullen Cottage where Madge Crawford and a couple of other women had a simple but tasty meal prepared for them. Beverages of the common type were in ample supply. Madge was still the main cook at Elmwood House. Both the Major and Mrs. West were in England at the time. Their absence from the guest list seemed strange considering that Norah's association with them had been so involved and for so long. The years that had passed since she left their employment seemed to have distanced them beyond regain. The question people were asking was, "How could this have happened?" These were not important issues to be bothering about on a day of celebration. Benny and Norah were now happily united and savoring the delights of being the focus of attention from friends and well-wishers.

It was a happy winter they spent in the cottage with Billy. Norah, in her role as housewife, was ever so caring towards her two men, both of whom went off to work early in the mornings. Their combined income was sufficient to maintain for all of them a comfortable standard of living; at the same time Benny was showing signs of discontent about his inability to secure a more prestigious posting. What he had, he considered to be but a stopgap until such time as he found his true niche. Now he was beginning to doubt that this would ever happen. Just when things seemed at their bleakest in this regard, the local County Councilor, Corney Doherty, sent word to him through Billy Mullen that the Council had a vacancy for the post of cottage rent collector in a neighboring district. This prospect sent a flurry of excitement and expectation that was hard to conceal. Both of them set about getting the relevant information in relation to the recruitment criteria. References were sought from all possible sources, including Major West, who made it clear that he harbored no animosity towards his former employee. He was not in the least reluctant to recommend Benny Ryan for whatever position his qualifications made him suitable.

The reference to qualification turned out to be a relevant consideration as Benny and Norah were to learn from the communications that was being forwarded from the recruiting body. The selection procedure involved a written examination in the subjects of English and Arithmetic; this appeared too much a challenge for a young man with a poor enough National School record. However, with the encouragement of a supportive wife and the fact that they had both pinned so much hope on him getting this job, he decided to give it a try. As it turned out, that decision was an incorrect one. Not only did he see the job given to someone else but had to suffer the affront of being deemed a failure. His confidence was deeply shattered as was his sense of self worth. It was the love and devoted attention of his sweet Norah that saved him from what he could have easily fallen back into.

The consequences of him succumbing to such a fall would have been a disaster of the highest magnitude and at a time so early in his married life. He thought about his new kind of life and reasoned it to be one that was by far more valuable than anything else society could ever bestow upon him. Winning the hand of Norah Mullen was what he had devoted the major part of his adult life in pursuance of, and in that, his endeavors were rewarded. He had succeeded where it really mattered. Sometimes it takes a more heightened sense of value on the part of the downcast to enable them to calculate the worth of what they already have. The blessing of such insight is enabling and can empower the vanquished towards a new appraisal where endeavor will undoubtedly follow. Benny put the bad experience behind him and decided to give up on the pursuit of the better job. He turned his thoughts to America instead.

He went back to working on the farm but only as a means of carrying him over until he had found a way of getting Norah's blessing on what he had in mind for all of them. All of them were to include Billy Mullen who would be kept in the dark until the feasibility of the plan was properly assessed and deemed to be practical. Contact was made with uncle Paddy, whose response was predictably encouraging. There would be no problem whatever in finding suitable employment for a young man that was willing to work. Benny's plan was for him and Norah to get over there as quickly as possible, get into a secure job and hopefully find suitable living accommodation soon after. Only when these basic requirements were procured could they think about bringing Billy out to join them in the new world. That was how the proposal was put to Norah who listened attentively to a detailed outline of what she was being asked to consider as a future for life.

Her love for her man was total and complete. If this was what he wanted to do, her support was assured. This was made easier for her in the knowledge that what now seemed likely to happen did take account of her dear dad as well. He was still a young enough man to make a life for himself in this supposed land of plenty, and with Norah and Benny over there with him, what was left at home for any of them to pine for? With these reassurances, her initial caution gave way to outright enthusiasm. They were for up and away and nothing was going to stop them. It was after Sunday dinner and them in their risen state, they jointly put the case to Billy who was casually unprepared for any such upheaval. To their very great surprise, he did not rule out the suggestion as being wildly impractical. In fact, he said it was something he had thought a lot about in his young days.

"Norah, had I not had the good fortune to meet your kind sweet mother, that is probably where I would have ended up. But life had another route for me to take and it was good for a while. Then I lost her and almost you as well, so I hope both of you can understand I don't ever want to be far away from you again. Yes, if it is possible, I might indeed consider going with you to America. No question about it; I would miss the place I was born and grew up in, not to mention the many friends I have around here, men like Laurence Keatley."

Wiping away her tears, Norah proceeded to give a broad outline of the proposed sequence of events that would eventually lead to all of them being out of the country by September or October.

"Daddy, if all goes according to plan, Benny and I will be gone by the beginning of June and we will allow a further three months to find a place of our own. Yes, I know it won't be easy for you to leave your home and friends, but the good thing is we are going to be together and perhaps in a couple of years time all three of us will be able to come back here on holiday."

Billy's compliance had to be understood in that he chose not to live out his days separated from the one that mattered more to him than all of his precious homeland. But secretly, he had another reason, something that had been troubling him a lot over recent years. It was a dark secret known only to him and would remain so until death relieved him of it. Hard as it was for the parents of Benny Ryan to see their only son go so far away, they at least had the consolation of knowing that daughter Kathleen would be living not far from them. Yet it was a decision that Benny did not take lightly. From his own experience of people that had gone to America, the chances of them returning within the foreseeable future was slight indeed. However, circumstances were such that he wittingly discounted all the negatives relating to what he had made up his mind to embark upon. They were going to be part of the bigger world, setting up home in a land they were trusting to deliver on what it had promised to give them.

On the second day of June, just before the onset of the intense humid heat of the American summer, Paddy and Catherine welcomed Benny and his ever-pretty wife to Philadelphia. There was a vastness about the place that was mesmerizing at first: heavy traffic on the streets with everything moving at a much faster pace than either of them had previously been accustomed to. The friends and acquaintances made known to them by Paddy and Catherine helped in making their settling down to life in a new land that bit easier. True to his promise, Paddy found suitable work for the two of them within one week of their arrival in the States. Suitable, insofar as both of them were working for the same employer, one as a storeman with potential to becoming a van driver, the other in the catering department of the workers' canteen. The joint income was promising as a means to achieving the goal they were aiming for: to have their own place by the end of summer. On that, they succeeded well ahead of target. With the help of friendly workmates, they were settled into their cozy rented house in early September. Back home in a crowded Poacher's Inn, a lively party was being held to mark the departure of a decent man and good neighbor; they were saying their fond farewell to the upright Billy Mullen. Its liveliness did prevail in spite of many tears, most noticeably from the hard-skinned Laurence Keatley who cursed America for taking from him his best and truest friend.

Chapter Twenty-One

Elmwood Estate had, by now, succumbed in many ways to the state of the doldrums. The Major's health had deteriorated considerably and except for the more frequent trips across to England, he was showing little interest in the outdoor life. No longer the social gatherings and dinner parties that had been synonymous with the Big House, they had all but come to an end. Just the occasional few might come to spend a weekend, one or two times a year, but noticeably absent on all of these occasions was the mood for celebration. A number of conacre men were using the land and farm buildings albeit in a much less organized fashion. Mrs. West, with the assistance of the jovial Vincent Wilkie, continued in operating the small enterprise that was considered more therapeutic than profitable. The Connemara ponies had now increased to six and continued to be an important part of that operation. Yet, there was still enough going on to warrant the involvement of Christy Flood who was faithfully available whenever his service might happen to be required.

As far as the local people were concerned, there was definitely one regrettable change happening. They had been informed through Vincent that Major West was ceasing the operation of the Fisheries Co-op. At least this announcement came at the end of the fishing season and might allow the industry enough time to re-organize before the commencement of the new one. There was no animosity being directed towards the Wests for taking this not unexpected decision. Everyone understood the Major was no longer up to the responsibility of such a task. At the same time he had the graciousness to advise that the business was lucrative enough for any group of responsible people to set up and continue as a proper co-operative company. The advice was heeded and set in train a flurry of activity that was reminiscent of the days, many years ago, when all of them were locked in bitter dispute with the same Major West.

A number of meetings were held in the Poacher's Inn, this time in total concurrence. Here was an opportunity for them to take control of the marketing end of their business. Foremost amongst the initiators were once again Dr. Clarke and Robert McElwee, and strong in support was

Laurence Keatley, who was pleased to see the depot being moved to another location. With the sudden and unexpected departure of Billy, his friend and fishing partner, he had become full owner of the boat they had both shared for many years. He had also been given responsibility of disposing of the Mullen assets. Not unexpectedly, Hat McGivern was more than enthusiastic about the new venture. Though he did not go so far as to suggest himself for the job, there was little doubt he had designs on the seasonal post of depot manager. As a means of advancing his claim, he tentatively offered the use of his premises to be the central location of the Portneill Fishermen's Co-Op. That turned out to be the final agreement; everyone was satisfied enough to proceed. They had the winter months ahead of them to prepare for a new and hopefully rewarding season.

As a pledge of solidarity, the new partnership vowed to work within the limits of the law and would actively seek to discourage the practice of off-season poaching. That was going to be a tall order, indeed, as there were a few within the group not overly bothered about compliance. It was a case of old habits dying hard. However, the main body of the gathering were adamant that this kind of activity should not be tolerated, especially within its own membership, and that some or all of them should be prepared to act as vigilantes against those so inclined. They were not for setting themselves up as bailiffs or policemen but merely to be there, making a forceful presence and statement of determination against the wrongdoer. The plan was eventually put into practice and was, by and large, seen as a positive gesture. As expected, some opposition was encountered from known quarters, but seldom did a fracas go beyond the doling out of verbal abuse.

Big Harry Doran along with McGivern were on lookout duty at the hour of six in the morning. It was nearing the end of October, a few days after a time of heavy rain. The swell of the river had subsided enough to perhaps attract the lurking looter of which there were still a few. Keatley had little to say about the culture of compliance. He seemed more concerned about finding a junior partner to replace Billy Mullen. Beginning at the top end of the valley, both men walked quietly together down along the riverbank. All was peaceful on the water, not a scamp to be seen. By the time they had made it as far as the deep holes just above the Major's slipway, daylight had broken and the mission of duty had come to an end. As they were heading towards the right-of-way that would take them out to the main road, it was necessary for them to pass by the top end of the slipway. Doran stopped suddenly and spoke:

"What the hell is that I see down at the edge of the water? It looks like the bones of a dead animal that has been washed down with the flood."

The discovery warranted further investigation. The cool McGivern took an inquisitive look and a heavy inward drag from the Sweet Afton that protruded from his mouth.

"Harry, my lad, these are not the bones of an animal and unless I am far mistaken they look like the remains of a human being. Don't you think we might be better to report this?"

Within a matter of two hours, Elmwood Estate was once again the focal point of community interest with a heavy Garda presence as well as technical personality descending authoritatively upon its grounds. The skeleton remains were taken away for tests and ascertainment while the Garda commenced an intensive investigation through re-examining the files relating to missing persons. It was established through the pathology report that the remains were that of a male person and that he had died from causes unknown. The neck joint appeared to be dislocated but in its decomposed state it was nigh impossible to ascertain when or how this could have happened. This rare find was for a while the talk of the Parish but after a couple of weeks and the Garda investigation getting nowhere, local interest faded. After the due-deliberative requirements of the law had been executed, the body pieces were taken to the unconsecrated portion of Portneill graveyard for an unceremonious burial.

For a while after, a number of Sunday Mass goers did stop to say a prayer at the grave of the unknown. They prayed that his soul be at rest and that the mystery of his identity may one day be made known.

It was a perplexing mystery that light would never be shed upon. There was only one person in the entire world that knew who it was that once fleshed these skeletal remains. Three thousand miles away in a cozy Philadelphia home, Billy Mullen read the gruesome report in a Donegal Paper. An item from home that had been sent regularly by Madge Crawford to his daughter Norah. He declined to engage with either Norah or Benny, both of who were preoccupied with interest in the bizarre story. This was his dark secret. The one that made him so readily amenable to the suggestion that he forsake his beloved homeland. The burden of guilt he would carry alone never to be imposed on the daughter he had to protect. There and then he made up his mind never to return to the place he called home. He had found a job that suited him. The pay and conditions were such that he could live out his life independently and in comfort.

As comfortable as his troubled mind would allow, hardly a day had passed since that fateful morning that the memory of what had taken place did not come back to haunt him. Every cursed detail of what had happened that night and morning over five years earlier were now surging through his head like never before and it was something that would never subside. For him, it all began on the night Norah came back home after Stanley Wests birthday party. Her sobbing state, as well as the story she related, disturbed him more than anything had ever done before. After spending a sleepless night paying close attention to her and when she finally went to sleep at an early morning hour, he made off in the direction of the river. What was on his mind as he walked out the door, only he himself, could tell. At the same time, there was nothing unusual about him paying an early visit to the fishing shots of the Camus.

This was a particularly pleasant May morning. The sun was rising over the quiet green banks of the river. There was nothing at all to disturb the peacefulness but the occasional flap of a salmon rising from the water to snap at a fly. With laden thoughts, Billy sat down on the sidewall of the slipway where his boat was tied, but a few yards away, looking across to the far side of the sloping structure, his eye caught sight of a man's clothing and black leather briefcase resting on the low end of the wall. Suddenly, his attention was being directed further down the riverbank by the sight of a man attired in running gear and him jogging gracefully towards him. There was no mistaking who it was, so Billy pulled off the cumbersome waders. Yes, David, the meticulous health freak had allowed himself time to take his morning run before boarding the early train that would take him away from the place for good. So even on the day of his final departure he was still in the business of tending to the well being of his body and that was how he fell into the preying hands of an infuriated Billy Mullen. He gathered speed to pass his assailant but was apprehended before gaining much distance further up the banking. "You dirty evil bastard," shouts the enraged Billy as he threw a heavy punch that missed the elusive defender.

David's agility was posing a problem for the man who relied solely on strength and hitting power. In this contest, he was finding it extremely hard to connect or catch a grip. The opponent had yet another trick, which he applied effectively against the tiring Billy. He was quite adept in a form of the martial arts and by its methods was gaining the upper hand. Several times he had the challenger on the ground and in each success lorded in the conquest. It was in the euphoria of his reveling, that he made the mistake of sniggering almost into the eyes of the ebbing Billy. That was enough to infuse a reserve of the Mullen fury and it was certainly close enough for him to catch a firm hold round the neck of the ex-monk. It was a crushing grip that brought the contest to ground level. Billy managed to get behind his foe and with both arms secured a tighter grasp around the throttle of the downed. In his furious state, Mullen was totally incapable of assessing or controlling the power of his own strength. There was no conceding of that ferocious lock.

It was the sound of the approaching train echoing down the line from further up the valley that tolled him to his senses, yet he had difficulty in loosening the hold he had on the lifeless body that lay back against him. Then, looking at what lay motionless before him, his cooling anger suffered resurgence. He placed both his feet against the dead man's back and with a forceful push-kick drove him over the edge and into the water. The train passed close to the scene that was on the hidden side of the banking. Realizing the gravity of what he had done, what if he is still alive? he thought. With that, he peeled off to the underpants. His competence in the water was enough for him to plunge in and go to the bottom. Twice he re-surfaced for air before going back down in search. Eventually he gave up and came out exhausted to the brow. The man David was definitely dead and buried in the deepest hole of the river Camus. Decisive action was now called for, so Billy re-attired and went straight to the boat to get one of the jute sacks that was used for carrying the salmon catch. Into the sack went the personal belongings of the deceased and they, like him, were never again to be seen by anyone.

With neither the will nor the energy to think about going to his place of work, the wearisome Billy trudged back to his cottage home to find that Norah had already left to begin another day at Elmwood. For that, he was greatly relieved. Her being well enough to go to work was an encouraging sign and it was best she did not see him in his ruffled state. The items he brought with him were never taken out of the dry sack that was left against the sidewall at the back of the house. As an oral stimulant the only thing available was a bowl of strong well-sugared tea that he consumed along with a slice of Norah's baked bread. Now with the place to himself, he got to thinking how best to dispose of the eerie contents of the old jute bag. There was a considerable amount of hawthorn bushes strewn along the perimeter of the half-acre cottage plot. They had been cut from the overgrown hedge the previous autumn. These were ideal fuel for the massive fire he proceeded to set at the furthermost point away from the house and with the dryness of the weather, it ignited easily. The flames surged upwards and with great intensity. The heat was overwhelming. Within one hour, every piece of hawthorn was in ashes.

So too was the incriminatory evidence.

It was the perfect crime even though the killing was unintentional. Billy Mullen had to cover his tracks and he did so with clever execution. With the dead man not reported missing, there was nothing to attract the attention of the law. What a tragic end to a life that was strangely peculiar; one that was lived in such a way that no one seemed to feel his absence; it was just as if he had never been. There would be the few whose lives he did affect and not in the most agreeable of ways. Hopefully, most of them had found a way of erasing him form their daily thoughts. As for the one who had slain him, life could never be the same. He could travel far to distant places but would never be able to hide away from what he was. He evaded the sanction of the law and retained a freedom that was a doubtful blessing to say the least. There was a life sentence to be served and it commenced over the dying embers he looked upon in solitary somberness.

Chapter Twenty-Two

America turned out to be good for Benny and Norah. Soon they became part of a very spirited Irish community with a particularly strong Donegal presence in Philadelphia. They became actively involved in the affairs of the Donegal Association that held regular social get-togethers in the city. This was their place of contact with other displaced folks trying to re-create a flavor of the old homeland. At the same time, they were enjoying a lifestyle that was agreeable and they knew it to be much better than what dear Portneill could ever afford them. The marriage that baby Annie was born into was indeed a happy one. She made her appearance two years after their arrival in the States. She was to be an only child and a blessing for all of them, not least the doting granddad, Billy Mullen, who bothered little about the social gatherings of the city life. His life was family and nothing else.

He lived and worked in the City of Penn for well over twenty years and lived long enough to see sweet Annie marry the handsome Jonny from Chestnut Hill. By that time the entire family had become totally integrated into the American way of life. They achieved relative success in all their endeavors. Their neighborhood was but a haven of friendship. Nowhere else could ever be their home. In all of his dealings and interaction with people for the previous forty and more years, never once did Benny Ryan awaken his taste buds to the tang of any form of alcoholic beverage; a fitting testimony to the love of a good wife as well as the support of family and friends. Now in the easeful days of their golden years, they had the time and means to do what was hitherto impossible; that was why Annie had so little difficulty in coaxing them towards the idea of a holiday in Donegal. She had an urge to go back to the place where her parents had grown up, and for reasons that were personally compelling, she felt the need to see it through. With the last of her three children now attending high school, they could safely be left behind with trustworthy friends of whom they had in abundance. They would gladly have brought them too, had it not been for the delicate nature of the other mission that Annie had worked tirelessly to bring to a successful conclusion. It was not a secret mission by any means. Her mum and dad were fully aware of what she was about. It was something that had the potential for great joy and all of them prayed that it would succeed in bringing just that.

It was the culmination of a venture that really began a number of years earlier when Norah had a heart-rending talk with Benny the husband she had invested herself totally in being a wife to. The story she had to tell him was a painful struggle, although she had thought deeply about it over a lengthy period and prepared for it as best she could. The final revelation was none the easier. Her disclosure was rueful and took both of them all the way back to Elmwood Estate in the glory of its heyday, to the West Household and all that had happened there over those few short years. It re-visited the turbulent days of her childhood, about her being the helpless victim of a sexual predator, which in turn took away from her the pleasure of knowing her own body. Then, in tears of demented sobbing, the truth came out.

"That was until I conceived and gave birth to my baby son, the son I have tried to forget but never could, the son I did not have the courage to tell you about for all this time. I hope you can forgive the wrong I did in not being honest with you from the start, but the truth is I was too afraid that I might lose you."

Then, resting her hand on Benny's shoulder, she asked him not to judge but rather try to understand what it was that she had to live with for all of her married life. That was about as far as she was able to go. The tiring effects of the emotional drain were beginning to weigh upon her. She asked that the remaining chapter of the story be left to another time. Benny was not her judge. In the fullness of his love, he held Norah close and thanked her for being his wife and for the love that once saved him from a state of near hopelessness.

"My dear Norah, if that is all that is bothering you I am very relieved. For a while there, I feared you were trying tell me that something serious was the matter with you. Is there now something you want to do about this?"

At last it was over. What she had dreaded for the most important years of her life was now at rest and had brought her closer to her Benny than at any other time. What had been for Norah a shameful secret, had in its airing become for the family a compelling crusade. What was set in motion on that very day would eventually bring all of them together to celebrate and play the game of being family around a dinner table in the town of Letterkenny. It was a trying ordeal for the fragile pensioner as she entered the small courtesy room that had been requested to facilitate the occasion, but she gained strength from the support of the other three that were for her. Then it actually happened. The Hotel Manager entered the room, followed closely by a brown haired man with pleasant and resembling features. The manager's stay was brief but long enough to politely address the trepidatious company.

"Mr. and Mrs. Ryan, I bring you your guest, Mr. West, Mr. Stanley West."

The man walked courtly towards the timid and gentle lady that was his natural mother and taking both her hands brought her to standing in front of him. Then, wrapping both arms around her quivering body, he hugged her warmly. It was for Norah a lot to contend with as the others watched on. It was indeed a motherly hand and arm she placed around his neck, the retrieval of the baby who had been taken away from her. For Annie, the experience was emotionally stirring. She could almost feel the melting sensation of what her precious mother was feeling within. It was a potent scene; one that words could not narrate; a setting that the genre of language could not adequately depict.

The silence was a pleasant one that Annie was loathe to break, even when she felt it was time to do just that.

"Stanley, what about your sister? Don't you want to get to know me as well? And what about these other two, one, my cute husband, the other my dad?"

That was the casual format of introduction. It was lighthearted and put everyone at ease before moving into the dining room where dinner was being served. It was a sharing in every sense of the word as they found each other to be easy in conversation. Stanley was a discrete and sensitive man who knew to stay away from the kind of questioning that might be hard for Norah to deal with in the presence of her husband. Yet there were things he wanted to know and so did she. Once again, the compassionate understanding that formed the character of Benny Ryan came swiftly into play. He needed to go into town if Annie and Jonny would be so good as to accompany him there. The time available was limited and precious. For all of this would be over by the close of the next day. At least for the present, from a practical standpoint, that was how it had to be.

He was Stanley the second; the love child and grandson of Major and Mrs. West. How he came to be was a guarded secret, orchestrated and maintained within the closed circle of the West dynasty. Norah was afraid and in a state of distress the day she went to Mrs. West with news that she was carrying the child of their paraplegic son. It was in the early weeks of her pregnancy and her endeavoring to carry on just as if this had not happened, but the stress of facing it alone had eventually become too much for her. The sheer force of desperation brought her to the living room to stand accused and to lay an unbridled confession at the feet of the lady that employed and trusted her. The initial reaction was predictable.

"This story has to be a fabrication. Our disabled son would not have been capable of the copulating act and it would be a gross betrayal on the part of the one entrusted to caring for him to engage in such a way with him." On that, Norah was not going to be drawn. The circumstances or details of this conception was not going to be shared with any other person no matter whom, of that she was determined. "I have nothing to say beyond the fact that it happened in Miss Barton's cottage during the time of my extended stay there a couple of months after Stanley's birthday party." That was the sum total of what Norah was prepared to divulge, even though her involvement with this crippled son was for her the final deliverance from the fetters of a damaged childhood.

The interview was then terminated, with Norah being sent back to kitchen duties along with a warning to maintain total silence about the sordid affair.

"The Major will have to be brought into these deliberations and that I can assure you will be happening very soon."

Norah held her composure and maintained a strength that surprised even her. "Mrs. West, I am sorry you feel that this was an act of betrayal but I tell you no lie. I am having your grandchild."

Norah kept her secret, even from the trusted father she wanted to protect against any kind of upset. So too did the Wests who moved quickly to take control of the situation and they did so with stern authority. It suited their purpose to be living in an Ireland that looked upon these things with pitiless disdain. The fallen girl had little choice but to be at the mercy of others.

"Keep your silence and we will look after you," was the proposition put to Norah the day after her reproachful encounter with Mrs. West. An ill-fettled Major, still knowing the art of control, spoke the words. There could be no dispute about what was on offer. Norah would concede as the option of choice no longer resided within her scope. The story about her going to England had to be circulated in the best possible light and in so doing the idea of her being chosen to train in a specialized field of caring seemed the most plausible. Entrusted to the care of Elizabeth Barton, Norah's gestation days were pleasant enough. At the same time she felt very much the property of them that had her there. Miss Barton treated her in a way that one could only expect from such a gentle and caring person. It was her that provided the counseling, which was undoubtedly advised by and in keeping with what the Wests had in mind. The nutritional and medical care was good in the extreme, right up to the time of parturition; so Norah was very much open to what seemed kind- natured advice.

The baby boy was born in a nearby hospital, early in the month of May. He was taken away from the distraught mother within a matter of one day, gone from her and not even given a name. Her post-natal recovery was considered enough for her to re-commence working in the care home three weeks later. She was again single and free. Totally in the dark as to what had become of her baby, Norah spent many a sleepless and weepy night self-blaming for the wrong that had befallen her. Miss Barton played the comforter good and well by assuring that Major and Mrs. West had found the perfect couple to be the adoptive parents to this fortunate child that was born into a life of privilege. He would be afforded the best of everything. As for the identity of this couple, she claimed to be as much in the dark as the poor girl she was trying to comfort. Her advice was to get on with living and that happiness would eventually come in the knowledge that what has been done was for the best.

Baby Stanley was taken to a home that was the best in most every way. He was never to see himself as anything other than the son of Steve and Stella West, who happened to have two daughters as well. It was the paternal grandparents that transported the precious bundle that would grace and bring gladness to that family home just outside Bristol. He was brought up in true West tradition, with both the Major and Mrs. West being frequent callers—a fact that taught him to know his place in the order of class. On reaching the age of mature discernment, he was given the lowdown as to who he really was. His grandfather was a man of substance a highly decorated soldier in the person of Major West. His schooling was of the highest order, being sent to a most prestigious boarding school and then to the faculty of law to fulfill what was once intended for his father. As a practicing Queen's Counsel, Stanley West was highly esteemed and moved within the upper strata of the legal profession. So, in that material sense, the life that was chosen for him yielded a better return than what would have been possible had the servant maid that gave him birth held custody of him?

The Major and Mrs. West played a decisive role in Stanley's upbringing and formation. They were in on every decision pertaining to the different stages of the boy's development. They were justly proud of him. In many ways, he was the reincarnation of the son they had lost so tragically. He gave them a renewed reason for living. Working in tandem with his adoptive parents, they made sure he was adequately briefed on the lineage of his noble ancestry. Of the mother that gave him birth, he was told nothing at all. Her name, or that of his maternal grandfather, was never spoken to him; of their existence he was unaware. As a small child he had been brought to Elmwood on a couple of occasions but always as the youngest child of cousin Steve and Stella West. That was until the decision was finally taken to abandon the estate and move permanently back to a place in the West of England, not far from the home of the worthy heir. The Major's health had again deteriorated. Following that move, the entire six hundred acres was put on the market and purchased by the Irish Land Commission for the purpose of distribution amongst local land-loving people.

That was the final winding up of the famous Elmwood Estate. The Wests were gone and so was the line of succession that emanated from the Walker Family. Major West survived for a further eight years in England. His determination to live was greatly augmented by the sense of continuity epitomized in the person of his grandson. Mrs. West progressed into old age as the ever-meddling granny but in relation to the past she maintained her silence right to the end, never once to speak the name of Norah Mullen. She had the pleasure of seeing Stanley enter into wedlock, to a bride that came highly recommended and from a sphere of class akin to her own. It was a society wedding that was lavishly celebrated, but alas social compatibility alone was not enough preserve the commitment of the nuptial requirement. She had to endure the troublesome upheaval of having to stand by him through the stress of separation and divorce. The marriage ended in agreement to share custody of their two sons. But the old lady, still resilient and resourceful, stood solidly behind this special one that she liked to call her son's child, who was born to a mother long gone from the scene. With the passage of forty and more guilt-ridden years, the fact that mother and her child were again united, was a wonderful creation; a family anew. What was to become of this new creation lay in the grip of fickle destiny, its continued existence wholly at the mercy of those who gave it life. For those whose endeavors it rightly rewarded, this had indeed been a momentous day. The melodious lilt of song from the voice of Donegal's own, Daniel, brought it to a joyful conclusion. It was a fitting way to end a day of such importance to all of them.

Still, there was yet another thing that had to be done before saying goodbye. It was go back to the place where it all began. That however had to wait until the light of morning when the parting of company took place on the mossy front door step of ruined Elmwood House. All five of them had spent an hour or more having a sentimental look around; Stanley took some pictures and wrote a few details into his notebook, these were mainly about things that Norah was at pains to relate accurately to him. The crumbling remains of the old kitchen where she and the long-deceased Madge Crawford prepared many a splendid meal for numerous people, some of who were not so splendid. Jonny was still on a high and let his intentions be known to the new English in-law. He had visions of the place in its full potential as a sedate riverside hotel that would attract the American clientele. He was very open to the idea of taking on a partner to share with him in the success of this business venture that could not go wrong, some clever venturesome kind of guy with money to invest.

Stanley was not going to be that man. His interest in the place did not go beyond the realm of family history and the circumstances of what brought him there made it all the more attention worthy. All of them regretted the fact that they had not been able to spend more time together, but the vacation was now at an end. The parting had to happen. There were no concrete arrangements made about a reunion in either England or America, just a vague promise to be in touch at a future date, Norah would have liked something better but Stanley was a busy professional man. Still, in the assurance of support from them that cared for her, she was hardly for allowing it to fizzle out to become nothing more than just a memory. The undeniable good was that it had finally happened for her. It was fulfillment in the end. After an emotional farewell, Stanley drove away leaving Norah standing with Benny at the end of the avenue where echoes of yore were incisively invasive. Then, slowly together, they commenced to walk back towards the old house where the other two were still down there assessing its potential; Jonny's dream was still in the making.

Halfway down the avenue Norah stopped and took hold of her husband's hand. "Benny, now that it's over I feel physically and mentally drained. Never did I think that this would happen for me. Now after years of pain and regret it has finally been resolved. I have been so fortunate to experience this joy and to have you and Annie with me. Even though it was a joy of short duration, the memory of it will stay with me forever. I feel so wonderfully happy about all of it, just like the day I married you, my dear husband and best friend."